Collected Poems
1931—1974

LAWRENCE DURRELL

Collected Poems
1931—1974

Edited by
James A. Brigham

THE VIKING PRESS
New York

'Solange' is reprinted by permission of E. P. Dutton from
Spirit of Place: Letters and Essays on Travel
by Lawrence Durrell, edited by Alan G. Thomas.
Copyright © 1969 by Lawrence Durrell.

Poems from *Vega and other Poems*, Overlook Press 1974,
included by permission of the publisher

Library of Congress Cataloging in Publication Data
Durrell, Lawrence.
Collected Poems of Lawrence Durrell.
I. Title.
PR6007.U76A17 1980 821'.912 80-10310
ISBN 0-670-22792-7

Printed in the United Kingdom
Set in 11pt Bembo

Contents

5

9

11

Preface

An invitation to make this edition of my Collected Poems (the third) definitive and comprehensive could not have been accepted had chance not put in my way a Canadian scholar, Dr James Brigham, who, in the pursuit of his own studies, had collected and indexed the whole of my published work. He was kind enough to let me profit from his toil, and the editing and arranging of this edition is entirely his work, which has been aided and shaped by the bibliography of Alan G. Thomas. My warm thanks go to both men for this exemplary edition which I would not have been able to assemble unaided.

LAWRENCE DURRELL

1980

To the Reader

This third collection of Lawrence Durrell's poems makes generally available for the first time all of the poems published between 1931 and 1974. The earliest items are now all quite scarce: *Quaint Fragment: Poems Written between the Ages of Sixteen and Nineteen* (1931); *Ten Poems* (1932); *Ballade of Slow Decay* (Christmas, 1932); *Transition: Poems* (1934); *Mass for the Old Year* (1935). Durrell's first real volume of verse, in terms of availability to the public, was *A Private Country* (1943), and it was followed by *Cities, Plains and People* (1946) and *On Seeming to Presume* (1948). *Deus Loci* (1950) and *Private Drafts* (1955) marked a brief return to private, limited editions, but Durrell has remained a truly public poet since *The Tree of Idleness* (also 1955). That volume was followed by *Selected Poems* (1956); the first *Collected Poems* (1960); *Selected Poems, 1935–1963* (1964); *The Ikons and Other Poems* (1966); the second *Collected Poems* (1968); *Vega and Other Poems* (1973), which included the poems published in *The Red Limbo Lingo* (1971); and *Selected Poems* (1977). All the poems published in these volumes are collected here, as are those poems which were published in little magazines but which were never collected. However, poems published as integral parts of plays or novels are not included, nor are poems which exist only in manuscript form.

My two goals in compiling this edition have been to give the reader a sense of the publishing history of Durrell's poems, and to retain the sense of intimacy which the arrangement of poems in earlier editions has given.

The poems have been arranged chronologically by year of first publication. Two dates are given beneath each poem: the date on the left is the year in which the poem was first gathered by its author as part of a volume of verse; the italicized date on the right is the year of first publication. Poems which were originally dated by the poet retain those dates, in parentheses, beneath their titles.

Over the years, and for various reasons, many of the original dedications to the poems had been removed; they have been restored in this edition. Similarly, original author's or prefatory notes which had been either pared down or completely excised have here been reinstated. Finally, epigrams from Georges Blin and Mila Repa which appeared in first edition as 'keys to a mood' but have not appeared in collected editions have been slipped into this edition in their original chronological settings.

JAMES A. BRIGHAM
Okanagan College

1980

THE GIFT

Now that I have given all that I could bring
Slit the wide, silken tassel of the purse,
Scattered its myriad bounties to the Spring.
To the rich Autumn leaves:
                            The crumbled dust
Of ancient adorations, murmurings,
And the dull story of some faded lust,
Will you remember it and, mother-wise
Thank me in these chill after-days
When I am empty-handed . . . with your eyes?

1980/*1931*

PIONEER

I built a house, far in a wilderness,
Against the arid ramparts of a sky,
Proof against occult art or wizardry:
Against my distant wanderings, comradeless.
I planted the straight, cool pine-trees all around,
And brimmed the garden with wild peony;
Here I kept silence, lived only to see
The magic in the trees, the friendly ground
Turn and put forth its tendrils of new life
Into the glowing grass: and here I dwelt,
No eloquent shadows that could break or melt
My great content;
                    Only a living strife
Calling me back from this core of desolation,
To seek an ultimate twilight in a life.

1980/*1931*

INCONSTANCY

Child, in the first few hours I lived with you,
Time beat the generous pulses of desire,
And churned the embers of a faded light to livid fever heat;
The fleeting moments laughed in mockery;
Fled with the light abruptness of a dream . . .
Time was asleep . . . Night and the stars remained
The bitter emptiness of nothing gained,
The queer half-witted stagnancy of Love
Passed like a covert whisper in the night.
And yet, they say, beneath some other skies,
Grey in the dusk there'll be another one
Another with perhaps diviner eyes.

1980/*1931*

HAPPY VAGABOND
(Amsterdam 1930)

I was a vagabond; sunset and moon
Found me a place in their hearts.
   Gladly I saw
The still, white summits of the friendly hills,
And snatched a wraith of sadness from the core
Of the deep sea, the unresisting earth:
Sang to the moon, and wove a melody
Deep in the strident archways of the sky;
Or felt the benediction of rebirth
That stirred strange anguish in this vagrant heart . . .
So there was silence in the wind that followed after,
Dim with a memory I'd left behind
Chilled into terror by the phantom of your laughter.

1980/*1931*

SONNET ASTRAY

We had a heritage that we have lost,
Ours was the whiteness and the godliness
Wings of the twilight; child-like we caress
The tawdry fragments of old dreams, embossed
With all the garishness of wandering minds,
Crazed and distraught; palsied with senile age.
The wisdom of a fool that seeks and finds
An emptiness, a gaunt penultimate stage
Before perfection! Reason fades and dies
Beneath the burden of such blasphemies;
Life is a loneliness, and heritage
A whispered mockery; yet first to go,
Killed by the fitful ravings of a sage
Was youth; youth has been dead a painted age ago ...
Sometimes the gross pendulum of time
Is swung back an aeon;
                                        And I,
Bewilderingly wonder at my great foolishness
To leave you forever alone that night by a star swept sea,
With the laughter of the dark surf in your eyes ...
Godless, and yet so very much a God.

1980/*1931*

THE BEGINNING

Oh! to blunder onto the glory of some white, majestic headland,
And to feel the clean wisdom of the curving sea,
And the dear mute calling of the wind
On the masked heels of the twilight. ...
Greying away to sundown, winding into the west;

And oh! heart of my heart to find
Dreams so oft forgotten, few fulfilled.

1980/*1931*

HIGHWAYMAN

The road is a sinister pathway paved with smoke,
A faint, white tremor; in the encircling trees
Grow the little whispers, oak to friendly oak,
Sentinels of the road.
           Darker than these
Full in the shadow of the leaning elm
A restive horse pads on the level grass,
And counts the seconds; dark, immobile sits
The masked rider, gleaming oblique slits
For eyes, watching the timid minutes pass
On stealthy feet, hurrying the approach
Of time;
          Far out upon the curving road
Glitters, an unsuspecting prey, the Midnight Coach. . . .

1980/*1931*

CRISIS

How can we find the substance of the lie;
Trace the huge source of deadlock, and complain
Of wealth denied, when we who paid the cost
Thwart our forbidden ends of destiny,
And mock our own wild laughter?
    We have lost
In the lithe whips of the soft, blinding rain,
More than a century of mingled hates . . .
More than these years of recompense forget:
Turbulence at a sleeping city's gates:
The pathos of a victim still, beset
By a reluctant Hector, finding light
In the huge heart-break of its shaken tears,
A width . . . a tenderness . . . some ultimate height
To stem the vanguard of to-day with years.

1980/*1931*

DARK GRECIAN

Down the wide shadow-streets of the city,
    By the white marble steps
Where the quiet, soft-robed people
Crowd to the glamour of the music,
Deep between the pallid shadows of the houses,
And the white fantasy of the Moonlight
    Among the columns;
Through the glazed signature of the mists
    Across the great Dome,
Sped the lithe God, the tall Grecian youth,
    Dark of limb, and fleet,
With the ebony glitter of light in his hair,
    And his full, lustrous eyes
Dim with unbidden searching.

1980/*1931*

ECHOES: I

Can you remember, oh so long ago,
How we wandered one twilight over the edge of the clouds
Over the pathway to the stars, and found
The cave . . .
The cave of the silver echoes,
And when I stood, breathless, and called your name,
It flung it back to me in little ripples
Of ecstatic, liquid sound.
Can you forget how you said mockingly,
Hand on my arm: 'If you have need of me
In some dim afterwards, when the gaunt years
Have brought no fuller harvest, greater recompense:
Or if in your poor loneliness you need my comfort,
Come one twilight under these vacant leagues,
These drowsy blue immensities of sky,
    And call my name,
And I will hear,' 'And answer me,' laughed I.

1980/*1931*

FUTILITY

Sealed with the image of man grows the fungus,
Puffed to ripe unholy promise;
A vagueness unfulfilled lies in the venom.
Illimitable design
Weighed in a madman's hand
Who swings destruction in the huge scales.
The broad vision of a Xerxes turns and cries,
Seeing his Nubian mercenaries,
    The masked furies of a night,
Wreathe and twine into the tenebrous defiles,
A living snake of blindness . . .
And to hear that old, age-weary crying,
They are such dust before the wind.

1980/*1931*

LARGESSE

The quiet murmur shakes the shadowed wood,
And stirs the larches;
Startles the timid moorhen's fluffy brood
Where the fern arches,
Pregnant with sudden, wide-eyed loneliness.
It touches the rounded nipples of the hills

With amorous fingers:
The tender crying of the wood it stills
With a touch that lingers
Silent and magic on the placid air.
It threads its dainty way to your lone bed,
And largesse throws . . .
White, wrinkled leaves on your bowed head,
White as the snows
That coldly smile on youth and life and love.

1980/*1931*

ECHOES: II

Last night I bowed before a destiny,
Deep in the night; bound with my huge grief,
Stooping beneath the desolation of my tears,
I climbed the forgotten pathway to the stars,
And knelt, half-man, half-child before our cave;
And the light fingers of the little winds
Touched my tired eyes and lips,
And the quaint fragrance of the clover . . . .
Stirred all the mournfulness of the old memories
And darkness was kind to me . . . .

When suddenly I cried in my great sorrow to the sky,
And heard your answer, growing quietly
Over the brimming silence of the deeps . . . .

So I gained comfort from one long-since dead.

1980/*1931*

CANDLE-LIGHT

So we have come to evening . . . graciously,
Through the bewildered churning of our dreams,
And found a day well spent; the candle-light
Gathers the living gloom, and wistfully
Cradles its arms about you as you sit . . .
Yet you who seek a flame, ponder and write
Bound by the hapless chatter of a quill.
While beauty grows and stirs about your chair,
Oh frail poet, under the candle-light . . .

1980/*1931*

CHRIST A MODERN

I who have lived in death, hemmed by the spears,
Born by grave victory, or by sore defeat,
Finding no vain or mercenary tears
In battle, lithe of body, fleet
To stem a wild, vainglorious afterflow,
I live that you may laugh, die that you may live;
Strew some rich largesse where the best may throw
Some broken toy, incalculably give
The widened harness of our peaceful years
Into your eager hands. I find no joy
In old wives' adoration, women's tears,
Or the reluctant praises of a boy,
. . . Being the faint shadow of a vanguard's wave,
I die
That you may live, and fear the life.

1980/*1931*

A DEDICATION
To My Mother

Pity these lame and halting parodies
Of greater, better poems; from the dawn
And from the sunset I have fashioned them
From the white wonders of the seven seas;
And from the memories of hours forlorn
When I lived goodbyes, and crushed the stem
Of conscious sadness, pillaging the sap
Of tired youth.
Strange yearning that I've had
To climb the trough of some forgotten jest
Or cry, and lay a tired head on your lap;
Sing to the moon, or yet be silent lest
In deep woods I wake some sleeping dryad....
Partly because I'm writing this to you
Perhaps because I'm only human too,
I make excuse for each strange, hopeless song:
For all this unintelligible throng
Of words inadequate. I only plead
That I have lived them all these lonely few
And made them personal ... quaint offering
Each one some little magic that belongs to you.

1980/*1931*

FINIS

There is a great heart-break in an evening sea;
Remoteness in the sudden naked shafts
Of light that die, tremulous, quivering
Into cool ripples of blue and silver ...
So it is with these songs:

                the ink has dried,
And found its own perpetual circuit here,
Cast its own net
Of little, formless mimicry around itself.
And you must turn away, smile ...

                      and forget.

1980/*1931*

TREASURE

Seal up the treasury and bar the gate.
We have enough of wonders in our store
To sit awhile at evening and relate
Wonderingly, what we did not have before.
Here in the counting-house, while daylight speeds
Nearer to us and nearer, let us tell,
Soft-voiced, with reverence, as a monk tells beads,
All the possessions that we love so well;

And fear not. In the hour before the dawn,
When cressets tremble in the icy wind
That shumbles in the parched and sleepy corn,
These will be safe for other's hands to find.

These treasures that are hoarded in our trust
Others will touch with hands, but find them dust.

1980/*1932*

DISCOVERY OF LOVE

I turned and found a new-moon at my feet:
All the long day and night made measureless:
New glamour in the traffick of the street,
And in your glance a secret holiness.
Here is a wonder that has made us wise,
Discovered all creation in a song.
We have found light and shining of the eyes,
And loyalty is with us all day long.

Most merciful, since you have turned your face,
And given this perfection to my hand,
Earth has become an autumn dancing place,
And I a traveller in enchanted land;

And all the rumour of the earth's decay
Remoter than to-morrow seems to-day.

1980/*1932*

PLEA

There must be some slow ending to this pain:
Surely some pitying god will give release,
Guerdon for service, leaving us again
The old magnificence and peace?

May we who serve such cruel apprenticeship
Find no more answer than an empty guess,
Knowing that every lip to questing lip
Must give for answer 'Yes'?

Oh turn your mind from such ungodly thought,
Let your dear, trembling mouth no longer guess:
Pleasure is greatest pain so dearly bought,
And love unfaithfulness.

1980/1932

LOST
For Nancy
'Angels desire an alms.' MASSINGER

We had endured vicissitude and change,
Laughter and lanterns, colours in the grass,
And all the foreign music of the earth:
Starlight and glamour: every subtle range
Of motion, rhythm, and power that gave us birth.

Now that the ink has dried and left its rust
On the forgotten words, the growing rhythms
Have thundered into peace; shaken to dust
Are all the restless, savage, drowsy hymns:
Vanished the echo where the music was,
Faded the lanterns: colours in the grass
Died with the laughter of the old foolish rhymes . . .

Quietly we stand aside and let them pass.

1980/1932

QUESTION

You have so dressed your eyes with love for me
That all my mind's entangled in a flame,
Crying the old despair for all to see,
The wonder of your name.
I must believe the passion of your mouth
And all its living treasure has no dearth,
But lives, exultant, through the season's drouth
In the old hiding places of the earth.

How can the anguished world remain the same;
The crowds still pass on unreturning feet
When we have cupped our hands about a flame?

1980/*1932*

LOVE'S INABILITY

In all the sad seduction of your ways
I wander as a player tries a part,
Seeking a perfect gesture all his days,
Roving the widest margins of his art.

I would drink this perfection as a wine,
Leash the wild thirst that bids me more than taste:
Hoard up the great possession that is mine,
Not squander as a drunkard makes his waste.

I will be patient if the world be wise,
And you be bountiful as you are curt,
Until a song awakes those distant eyes,
And all your weary gestures cease to hurt.

1980/*1932*

Cueillez dès Aujourd'huy les Roses de la Vie

RONSARD, *Sonnets*

You will have no more beauty in that day
When all the slow destruction of the mind,
Encompassed in a single clot of clay,
Is dust on dust, with flower-roots entwined.
No use to say 'She was both cruel and kind.
Though all her limbs have crumbled to decay,
Yet we, remembering, gather up and bind
The harvest that was all her yesterday.'

No use to shake that dear, unhappy head,
And pray for fresh beginnings, time makes one
Of all the prayers of Syria's sleeping dead,
All the choked dust of fallen Babylon.

There is no lamentation but the hours
Mourning the silent watches of the grave.
Always the gaunt reflection of the stars
Whispers 'Mad lovers, these you may not save.'

1980/*1932*

RETURN

There is some corner of a lover's brain
That holds this famous treasure, some dim room
That love has not forgotten, where the sane
Plant of this magic burgeons in the gloom,
And pushes out its roots into the mind,
Grown rich on the turned soil of days that pass.

I know there is enchantment yet to find:
April and whip-showers and the heavy grass
Leaning to the lance-points of the rain . . .

Oh we will turn someday, and find again
The pageant of the lilies as they pass
In slow procession by the lonely lake,
Down by the crying waters of the plain.
Always, to the end, these will remain,
A thirst that all our passions may not slake

April and whip-showers and the crying rain.

1980/*1932*

Je Deviens Immortel dans tes Bras

OVIDE, Les Amours

We have no more of time nor growing old,
Nor memory of lovers that are dead
While blood is on our lips; and while you hold
Those frail and tenebrous hands about my head.
Time is snuffed out as candles in a church,
And all the fume in darkness is your hair;
Licence these burning lips and let them search
For passion that lies nearest to despair.

Let us set up a gravestone in the dark,
We who are laughing sinners, let us hold
One moment as a monument to mark
The hour from which God ceased to make us old.

1980/1932

RETREAT

I would be rid of you who bind me so,
Thoughtless to the stars: I would refrain and turn
Along the unforgotten paths I used to know
Before these eyes were governed to discern
All beauty and all transcience in love.
I would return, hungry, inviolate,
To the sequestered woodland, arched above
With the unchanging skies that graciously await
My sure return from such inconstant love.

I would return ... yet would there ever be
The same clear current at the root of things?
The same resistless tides born of the sea?
The old slurred whisper of the swallow's wings?

1980/1932

BALLADE OF SLOW DECAY

This business grows more dreary year by year,
The season with its seasonable joys,
When there is so much extra now on beer,
And therefore so much less to spend on toys:
And now that Auntie Maud's had twins (both boys),
And all the family is knitting clothes—
It makes me want to stamp and make a noise:
I wish that George would pay me what he owes.

I realise that Cousin Jane is 'dear',
And that sweet Minnie has such 'grace and poise',
But why should they be planning to come here,
When Winifred my manuscript destroys,
And dearest little Bertie mis-employs
His time by crying when he sees my nose—
It makes me want to stamp and make a noise:
I wish that George would pay me what he owes.

How can a man withstand the atmosphere,
This hell compounded of such strange alloys?
Grandma's too old to do a thing but leer,
And call the home-made mince-pies 'saveloys'.
Grandpa keeps drooling on about sepoys,
The Indian situation and the snows—
It makes me want to stamp and make a noise:
I wish that George would pay me what he owes.

ENVOI

Prince, if I once disturbed your equipoise,
By sending you my old discarded hose—
Perhaps you'd help me stamp and make a noise,
And wish that George would pay me what he owes?

1980/*Christmas, 1932*

TULLIOLA

'. . . there was found the body of a young lady swimming
in a kind of bath of precious oyle or liquor, fresh and entire
as if she had been living, neither her face discolour'd, nor
her hair disorder'd: at her feete burnt a lamp which sud-
dainely expir'd at the opening of the vault; having flam'd,
as was computed, now 1,500 yeares, by the conjecture that
she was Tulliola, the daughter of Cicero whose body was
thus found, as the inscription testified.'

Only the night remains now, only the dark.
This my forever and my nevermore.
Impalpable eclipse!
Persistent as the muzzle of a dog,
Nosing me out for ever and for ever. . . .
God! that my body slips
Between smooth liquors like a floating log,
Spinning on tides of wine
So slow that not a flaw can shift
The symmetry of liquid in this basin:
Nor a chaotic wave can lift
My nostrils to the surface-fume of spice,
Bitter and odorous in gloom.

Pity me, swimming here.
Pity me, Cicero's daughter.
All the embalmer's poor artifice was this:
To strip me of the cogs and wheels of sense—
Those inner toys of motion,
Purse up my dead lips in a kiss,
And freeze the small shell of me,
Freeze me so stiff and regimental,
Then launch me in this vault's aquarium
Upon a tide of spices.
Pity me, swimming here.
Pity me, Cicero's daughter,
Partnered by inner darkness and one solemn light.

1980/*1934*

LYRIC

I am this spring,
This interlocked torment of growth.
I am leaf folding,
Leaves falling and folding,
Leaf upon leaf upon spray,
Sweet pod and sticky:
Buds that are speckled, bursting, breaking—
I am this hour.
O unbearable sliding and twining
Sinews of creeper,
Unbearable fret in the burdenous mould!
I am seed pressing,
Seeds straining and scoring
A runnel to dayshine:
All seed and all potence,
Invincible growth,
Clamped in the moist clog of soil.
I am the surge:
The shaking and loosing of strands:
Weed creaking,
Earth slipping from fingers of tendrils
And bindings of moss.
Hear me you earth-drums
Babbing and drubbing
Invincibly onward to life!
Hear me!
> *I am this spring,*
I am this forest in flux,
Urging and burgeoning.

1980/*1934*

WHEAT-FIELD
For Leslie

And all this standing butter-coloured flood
Where the vast field goes tilting to the sky,
Tilting and lifting to a red dancing sun,
A man destroys, destroys. . . .

Old arms, brown arms,
Twinkles the grinning scythe-blade in the wheat. . . .

Though the dry wind, defensive,
Break cover and descend,
Shuffling the yellow heads like cards,
Hampered and driving:
Though there is consternation and amaze,
A man destroys, destroys,
While the sun freckles the orchard
A man in a red cloak destroys.

   I have been so in dreams: rooted
And standing with the warm male sperm in me,
Hideously wary of death.
   I have been rooted wheat—
A legless stalk hanging on the ground
While a destroyer roves
Nearer and always nearer: oblivious:
Twisting the wicked sickle in my roots—
An old man
Who destroys
Under a dancing sun.

1980/*1934*

FACES
For F.A.

I

So many masks, the people that I meet,
So many coloured faces—
Carnival idols wagging in a lanterned street,
Plaster and pigment grimaces.
Not one but wears smooth porcelain for a frown,
Not one the livelong daytime,
Can I say: 'Here loveliness'? or 'Here walks guile'?
Always beneath the smile
I know the apparatus of the bone,
The structure pinned with ligament,
The sliding gristle, coil of artery:
All, all, delicate, nimble, wired, machinery,
Snugly buttoned in
A supple glove of flesh,
A snake-smooth film of skin,
Smooth, smooth, flawless and bland as rubber. . . .

II

And, if I smile
What can you see, what guess?
Your own, your little idiot uniformity
Reciprocates a perfect puppet nothingness;
A null collision of minute desires
Transliterated thus by muscle-play. . . .
Behold,
Behold your mincing jowls a-swing on wires!
No, no. My friend
We are void idols still,
Ridiculous clicking dolls,
Mumming the silly ciphers of pretence:
Always intent to end
Our awful emptiness by alphabets.
Our speech, our hapless intercourse
Seems always just removed from actual sense.

Can you deny me that the laughter-mask
Clamps back upon itself to trace
Only the raving jaw-line of the skeleton?
That in your hanging face
A smile is an expression of despairs,
With mouth a hanging flap,
A slip of skin twiddled by subcutaneous hairs,
A juggling parody of what you say?
In fine,
Your mouth's a letter-box,
A hippo's bun-trap . . .
Your mouth, my friend . . . and mine!

III

So many masks . . .
So very many faces. . . .

Will you remember, then, when next we walk
Among the lanterns and the lights,
Among the half-light of your chance desires
We are but carnival idols still—
Poor rag-dolls twitched on wincing wires
Fingered by impulse?
A couple of barking cattle
With a fool rictus gouged upon our faces!
Will you remember as we yapp and boom
How poor a condolence
The formal utterance is
For being two bloody zeros,
Mnemotechnic heroes:
Sick hack-satires on meaning by Infinity,
With not one working sense
That does not illustrate our own
And all humanity's impertinence?

1980/*1934*

LOVE POEMS

I

Lost, you may not smile upon me now:
You, nor that grey-eyed counterpart of you
Inhabiting the sunlight in still places:
Substant always in the netted moonshine.

'Remember' is a lost cry on a wind:
A hollow nothing-heard,
Most memorable, in a deaf night
That does not heed.

I have forgot even, dear pagan,
The holding of hands, the beseeching,
Intolerable darling!
No more do the loose hands of devilry
Tangle your fingers like nets in my soul.

You ... I ...
They are such very little faces—
Flowers in a stippled moonshine
Only recalled when the moon's a mad farthing,
The sky a december of steel.

II

I cannot fix the very moment or the hour,
But an inevitable sometime I shall meet
One face, your face among the faces,
Notice one step
Among the winding footfalls of a hollow street.
Perhaps at evening in smooth rain
That runs all silver-shod among the houses,
In a void gathering of men and women
Who tread their lives out on the jointed stones,
I shall be challenged by your smile again:
Your voice above the loaded gutter's monotones.

Voice among voices ...
Face among faces. ...

I cannot fix the moment, and my present clock,
The dandelion-puff, lies cruelly;
Yet, in the action of that hour's surprise
What will you do, or I?
Catch hands and laugh upon each other's eyes?
Or will some imp of the spontaneous moment
Devise some other signal than this?
Shall I, perhaps, put hands upon your elbows,
Outface your consternation with a kiss?

III

What would you have me write?
Scraps, an attentive phrase or two
To soothe your vanity's delight?
Pay down a fee of words to you,
That lesser you, who dwindle, shrink
When formal sentences of fine desire
Fix your minute reflection in a shining ink?
Would you have all of this:
A macaroni payment for a wink?
A pastiche for a kiss?

No. I'll not devise such nothings:
Not countenance dissection with my pen:
Make an essay on torment when
Ink is for fixing fables.
     O! can anything
Engendered of the mind be more than this:
A hazard flight on an imperfect wing?
The motion of the muscle in a kiss;
Features aligned for laughter; can the mind
Transliterate such metamorphosis
Evoking thence
More than a leaning pothook for a sense?

Words? They are not large enough.
The sense is never minion to the word.

IV

Absent from you, I say:
'Let there be no more songs,
Those faulty units of the heart.'
Let them defer to senses they can know,
Be pander to air's comprehended graces—
Daffodil smells and the turned earth and snow.
Let them disseminate and prove
The mere music's overture to love
Whose dear vicissitudes may never show
Upon the surface of thought's countenance.

Sure that I've tried and tried,
Leading my ink across this acreage
Of vacant pages.
I can glean nothing from the scars of heart.
Always the finer fabric of the sense protests:

'Let there be no more songs
Lest an obscuring music's overtone
Disperse the purer meaning of the words.'

V

You too will pass as other lovers pass.
    There will no more be hands to hold you by.
Love, like wet fingers dabbled on a glass,
    Traces a soon disfigured charactery.
As there is end to every narrative,
    So must the string fall silent on the air.
Dear, these poor suppliant hands may only give
    Scant loveliness to cast before despair.
To hold you will not make creation young,
    Nor all the pattern of the planets new.
Time may not grant what beauty I have sung
    More lease than sunlight to a last night's dew.

Unbearable enchantment! All and all of this
Will slip to nothingness beneath a kiss.

VI

There is no strict being in this hour,
No scent nor dust that moves:
Only this dawdling clock
Clapping a tireless knuckle at the doors
Of cogent thought:
Reviving echoes in the wasted mind.
The night-time swings resentment like a hammer—
Murderous long minutes, pendulous over me,
And all the dark divorces of the mind and body
Are cancelled quite, devoured by this hot nothing,
Night.
I am become my thought's compositor
And the laborious darkness here my devil.

I, lapt in the vacuum of this hot white bed,
What can I see beyond the triple wall?
What sense beyond soul's damage—
Your absence, white Compassionate?
The mind is windle-straws
Herded in regiments by the poignant wind:
A thimble-full of restless lava contemplating
Only the motionless elbows of these trees
Swagged hard with fruit,
Nudging the neighbour wall like a boor at table.
Marble realities!
These, only these.

Yet somewhere thoughts conspire to show you standing,
The obedient evening at your elbow,
Upon a terrace in that southern land,
Free of these dread devices of discomfort—
Silence—this hot blank silence and this bed—
My youth's warm winding-sheet—
Free of them all!
O! dear my saint, sometime I vision you,
As summer lightning winking in my brain—
All your youth's shapely arrogance!
You, limb-lusting, Pan-fleet!
Leaning upon a terrace in the south,
Forgetting and forgetting.

The wind's your only Romeo.

1980/*1934*

MASS FOR THE OLD YEAR

'*Sur le Noel, morte saison*' VILLON

Since you must pass to-night
Old year, since you must vanish and fall,
What shall we do or devise for you
To celebrate temporal death?
Will you need cakes and poor potsherds
Huddled and stale beside you—
Shall we portion you food and a leather of wine?

Since you must go and we must follow you—
Lamenting and spectral companions,
My lover's dead self and my own—
What shall we make for the three of us,
Tombstones and talismans?
Toys for our comfort in darkness,
Toys for our pillows, we three sleeping children
Now fallen and cold?

Old year, sweet year, I have laid her beside you—
Simple magnificent marble,
Parcelled in cere-cloth, oils and warm ointments:
Pure and delightful our ghostly companion,
Clenched in clean winding-cloth
Close from the mould.

Since we must go together, hand in hand,
Lead our frail steps in the darkness:
Guide our drugged limbs in the shades and the silences,
Tenebrous places—O! cherish our youth.
Old year, kind year,
Image of sunshine and nightingale-passion
Urge us so gently and smoothly away,
My lovely accomplice and I,
To the dead selves of lovers,
The voiceless, forgotten, the faded companions:
Old year, lost year, lead us away.

1980/*New Year, 1935*

THE DEATH OF GENERAL UNCEBUNKE:
A BIOGRAPHY IN LITTLE
(1938)
To Kay in Tahiti: now dead

'Not satire but an exercise in ironic compassion, celebrating
a simplicity of heart which is proof against superiority or
the tooth of the dog . . . After all, we may have had other
criteria, but they were only criteria.'

The Argument

General Uncebunke, named Konrad after his famous ancestor the
medieval schoolman (see *epistolæ obscurorum virorum*), was born in
1880, and baptised in the same year at the village church, Uncebunke,
Devon, England. On leaving Oxford he served with distinction in two
wars.
In the intervals he travelled extensively in Peru, Siberia, Tibet, and

43

Baffin Land and wrote many travel books of which *Roughing It in Tibet* is the best known to-day.

In 1925 he came home from his travels for good and settled down to country life in England, becoming Tory M.P. for Uncebunke, and increasing his literary reputation by his books of nature essays.

In 1930, owing to the death of his only daughter, he suffered from a temporary derangement of his mind and published that extraordinary volume of memoirs known as *Spernere Mundum*. He remained Tory member for Uncebunke, however, until his death on 2 April 1937.

He was laid in state for three days in the family vault; and the body was finally cremated according to his wish. His widow who survived him but three months is said to have scattered his ashes in the Channel as a tribute to a very gallant explorer and noble man.

Author's Note

You must know that this is one organic whole and must be read like a novel to be really appreciated. Also it is quite serious and should be read with the inner voice, preferably in some dialect.

FOURTEEN CAROLS

I

My uncle sleeps in the image of death.
In the greenhouse and in the potting-shed
The wrens junket: the old girl with the trowel
Is a pillar of salt, insufferably brittle.
His not to reason why, though a thinking man.
Beside his mesmeric incomprehension
The little mouse mopping and mowing,
The giraffe and the spin-turtle, these can
On my picture-book look insufferably little
But knowing, incredibly Knowing.

II

My uncle has gone beyond astronomy.
He sleeps in the music-room of the Host.
Voyage was always his entertainment
Who followed a crooked needle under Orion,
Saw the griffin, left notes on the baobab,
Charted the Yellow Coast.

He like a faultless liner, finer never took air,
But snow on the wings altered the altitude,
She paused in a hollow pocket, faltered:
The enormous lighted bird is dashed in snow.
Now in the labyrinth God will put him wise,
Correct the instruments, will alter even
The impetuous stance, the focus of the eyes.

III

Aunt Prudence, she was the eye of the needle.
Sleeping, a shepherdess of ghostly sheep.
'Thy will be done in Baden Baden.
In Ouchy, Lord, and in Vichy.'
In the garden of the vicarage sorting stamps
Was given merit of the poor in spirit
For dusting a cinquefoil, tuning the little lamps.

Well, God sends weather, the English apple,
The weeping willow.
Grum lies the consort of Prudence quite:
Mum as a long fiddle in regimentals:
This sudden IT between two tropical thumbs.
Unwrinkle him, Lord, unriddle this strange gorgon,
For tall Prudence who softens the small lamps,
Gives humble air to the organ that it hums.

IV

My uncle sleeps in the image of death.
Not a bad sport the boys will tell you,
More than a spartan in tartan.
Yet he, fearing neither God nor man,
Feared suffocation by marble,
Wrote a will in hexameters, burnt the cakes,
Came through with the cavalry, ladies from hell,
Feared neither God nor man,
Devoted to the polo-pony, mesmerized by stamps.

Now in the stable the hypnotic horse-flesh
Champ, stamp, yawn, paw in the straw,
And in the bedroom the blind warhorse
Gallops all night the dark fields of Dis.

V

My uncle has gone beyond astronomy.
His sleep is of the Babylonian deep-sea
Darker than bitumen, defter than devil's alliances.
He has seen Golgotha in carnival:
Now in the shin-bone the smart worm
Presides at the death of the sciences,
The Trinity sleeps in his knee.

Curse Orion who pins my man like moth,
Who sleeps in the monotony of his zone,
Who is a daft ankle-bone among stars,
O shame on the beggar by silent lands
Who has nothing but carbon for his own.
Uncouple the flutes! Strike with the black rod!
Our song is no more plural, the bones
Are hollow without your air, Lord God.
Give us the language of diamonds or
The speech of the little stones.

VI

Prudence shall cross also the great white barrier.
God shall fold finally up the great fan—
Benevolent wings wheeling over the rectory,
The vicar, the thatcher, the rat-catcher,
Sure in this medicine help her all they can.
O she is sure in step with the step of the Master.
Winter loosens the apple, fastens the Eskimo.
Wearing his pug-marks for slippers shall follow,
Holding to common prayer, the Great Bear;
Over the Poles, wherever his voyages go.

Shall navigate also the great circle,
Confer with the serious mammoth, the sabre-tooth,
Come to the sole goal, palace of higher things,
Where God's good silverware spills on all faces,
And hazardously the good wizard, gives wings.

VII

My uncle sleeps in the image of death.
He sleeps the steep sleep of his zone,
His downward tilting sleep beyond alarm.
Heu! he will come to harm so alone.
Who says for him the things he dare not say?
He cannot speak to angels from his rock.
This pediment of sleep is his impediment.
Grant him the speech of sleep,
Not this dank slag, the deathward sediment.
Strike with the rod, Lord God.
Here was a ruddy bareback man,
Emptied his blood upon the frozen lake,
Wheeled back the screaming mares,
Crossing the Jordan.

Excuse me, Lord God, numberer of hairs,
Sender of telegrams, the poisoned arrow,
Suffer your faithful hound, give him
At least the portion of the common sparrow.

VIII

My uncle has gone beyond astronomy.
Three, six, nine of the dead languages
Are folded under his lip.
He has crossed over into Tartary,
Burnt his boats, dragged the black ice for bodies,
Seen trees in the water, skippered God's little ship.

He is now luggage, excess baggage,
Not wanted on voyage, scaling a pass,
Or swinging a cutlass in the Caribbean,
Under Barbados chewing the frantic marsh-rice,
Seven dead men, a crooked foot, a cracked jaw,
Ten teeth like hollow dice.

My uncle is sleeping in economy.
No word is wasted for the common ghost
Speaks inwards: he lies in the status
Of death's dumb music, the dumb dead king
On an ivory coast.

IX

Prudence had no dog and but one cat,
Black of bonnet the Lord's plain precept saw
At the at-home, on Calvary, in the darkest nook
He was there; He leaned on a window smiling,
The God Shepherd crooking his ghostly crook.
Prudence did dip and delve in the Holy Book,
Alpha to omega angels told her the tale,
Feeding the parrot, pensive over a croquet-hoop:

'Once upon a time was boy and girl,
Living on cherry, berry, fisherman's silver catch.
Now the crass cock crows in the coop,
Prudence, the door dangles, lacking a latch.'

X

My uncle has gone beyond astronomy.
He sleeps the sharp sleep of the unstrung harp.
Crossed into Tartary, he lies deep
In the flora and fauna of death,
Under a black snowline sleeps the steep,
Botanical, plant-pure sleep.

The soul is folded like a little mouse.
Body is mortuary here, the clock
Foiled in its own wheels—but he may be sleeping,
Even if no toe moves no where, the sock
Be empty of all but vessels—where is he creeping?
Where is my man's address? How does he perish
Who was my relish, who was without fault?

Strike with the black rod, Lord God.
This is the marmoreal person, the rocky one.
This is the pillar of savourless salt.

XI

My uncle has gone beyond astronomy.
He sleeps in the pocket of Lapland,
Hears thunder on a Monday, has known
Bone burn to ash for the urn's hold.
He has fine nails of his finger and of his toe.
Now colder than spittle is his mettle. The hand
Is cold bone touching cold stone. So
In the sad womb he plays the trump of doom.

Lord, here is music. This fine white 'cello
Hums no more to the gust of your air.
This supercilious fellow, think what was given
To nourish his engine, salt barley and beer.
All wasted, gone over, destroyed by death's leaven,
Scent of the apple and stain of the berry.
Now only the ignorant hedgehog dare,
Smelling the fruit in him, dance and be merry.

XII

Prudence was told the tale of the chimney-corner
In the ingle beetled over the red troll's book
Ate the white lie: 'Happily ever after,
A hunchback, a thimble, a smart swan,
Ride time's tall wave, musically on and on . . .'
Was it of God to bait and wait with the hook?
Was it of him black laughter at 'happily ever after',
A grass widow, a shadow embalmed in a story-book?

Memory is morsels offered of sparrows.
First prize a jug and bowl for correcting the clock,
Sending a telegram, gathering holy campion.
Lowly Prue is glum of finger and thumb,
Toe in the ember, dismembering spools of knitting.
Patience on a monument, passion on a cushion.
God's champion darning a sock, sitting.

XIII

My uncle sleeps in the image of death.
The shadow of other worlds, deep-water penumbra
Covers his marble: he is past sighing,
Body a great slug there, a fine white
Pike in a green pond lying.
My uncle was a red man. The dead man
Knew to shoe horses: the habits of the owl,
Time of tillage, foison, cutting of lumber,
Like Saint Columba,
Could coax the squirrels into his cowl.

Heu! for the tombeau, the sombre flambeau,
Immanent with God he lies in Limbo.
Break punic rock. Weather-man of the tomb,
We are left among little mice and insects,
Time's clock-work womb.

XIV

Prudence sweetly sang both crotchet and quaver,
Death riped an eyeball, the dog-days
Proffered salt without savour, the cards were cut.
She heard a primordial music, the Host's tune
For the guest's swoon—God going the gamut.
Honour a toast for the regimental mascot,
The thin girl, the boys of the blue fourteenth,
Driving to Ascot: a wedding under the sabres,
Tinker and tailorman, soldier or sailor,
Lads of the village entering harbour,
O respect also those windowless features,
The stainless face of the provincial barber.

Prudence plays monumental patience by candles:
The puffins sit in a book: the muffins are molten:
The crass clock chimes,
Timely the hour and deserved.
Presently will come the two welcome angels
Noise in the hall, the last supper be served.

1943/*1938*

FIVE SOLILOQUIES UPON THE TOMB OF UNCEBUNKE

I

My uncle has entered his soliloquy.
He keeps vigil under the black sigil.
To be or not to be at God's suggestion.
That is the question, to know or not to know.

Smoke powder-blue and soft brass handles,
The puma swoons among the silken candles,
O Elsinore, my son, my son,
Tiger of the zenith, heifer of the red herd,
His fugue of flesh and ours in counterpoint,
Which moves, or seems to move.

It is only God's breath in the nave,
Moving the cinquefoils, only the footwork
Of mongols, cretins, and mutes smelling of beer.
(The candles breathe in their pollen)

He that hath ears to hear, let him hear,
Let him bear false witness,
Cough out the candles, covet his neighbour.
Let him crack the ten tablets, burn the puma,
Set up as father, son and ghost,

This, my black humour.

World without end means voyage beyond feeling.
Trek without turning spells voyage without meaning.
Being, seeing, is voyage at morning.
Dying and praying are travel by kneeling.

II

Friends, Romans, countrymen,
Conduct his entry to soliloquy
With this marginal ritual.
We come to bury Caesar, not to praise him.
God will raise up his bachelor, this widow's mite
A foothold for the scientific worm.

(Deliver us from evil.
Deliver us from the trauma of death's pupil,
From the forked tongue of devil,
Deliver us from the vicar's bubonic purple,
From the canine hysteria, the lethal smile,
O deliver us from botanical sleep,
The canonical sugar, the rabbinical pose,
Deliver us from death's terrific pinnacle,
Biological silence, a clinical sleep.)

This man, my friends,
The lion and the lizard keep,
Mourned by the cottagers on windy porches,
By the cracked hearth-stone, the calendar,
Mourned at the vicarage among the larches:
The shoe full of nails, the ploughboy
Whetting his axe on a bush remembers,
Recalls and regrets: Whom the Gods love
Is death's superlative decoy.

Numen inest. Only the stone puma,
Fluminous under the butter of candles,
Shares this fierce humour.

Little man's food is brief barley.
His patron is black malt.
Afterwards death is his matron.
Bringing musical bread:
God with his footwork
Bringing musical bread.
Dipped in the heart's dark salt.

III

Friends, Humans, Englishmen!
Officer at the bar and gentleman in bed,
Kings in your counting-houses, clerks at cricket,
All you who play in this desperate game,
Hopes of the side, the tenth wicket,
Who will be certainly raised to the rank of aunt
In the new millennium: permit
The bromoid encomium of the harmonium,
Wear the heart at half-mast and signal
A feudal death of an old order,
The dissolving warrior in his iron hat.
Observe the soul's decorum: stand, my son,
Hymn number one.

ANTHEM

Poor Tom, whose hope was sterile dust
Now perches on an angel's thumb.
While cherubims with silky limbs
Around him hymn and hum.

IV

My uncle has entered his soliloquy;
Under the black sigil the old white one
Kneels in the Lamb's blood,
Hymned by portentous crotchets,
Keeps his smart vigil.

Puma of powder-blue whose stony lip
Reflects the candles, with a mineral eye
Covets the blood, but does not dare to sip.

This man, my Romans, was a Roman,
A breaker of skyline, took first prize
In the regatta for men past menopause,
Passed through the eye of the needle, broke
The hug of the Great Bear, the hug
Of a glacier's hairy back and oxygen claws.
Spat on Orion, left his shoes in a church,
Hung a harp on every weeping willow,
Took tiffin by the Indian bulrushes, saw
The last deranged crater, swallowed the Word.
Shot his bolt in the Gobi.
Was left in the lurch,
Then like a Roman, fell upon his sword.

This prince, this bug, this human,
Who sleeps under the great cat sleeping,
Shares with the smiling paranoiac,
Shares with the baby in the creeping-suit,
An amniotic balance, the diver's grief.
Has followed a Roman nose past Mandalay,
Ladybird on a leaf.

ANTHEM

Simple addition, simple subtraction.
One is left and the other is taken:
Simple condition but multiple fraction.
One is a doll: the other will waken.
Simple reflection, simple refraction.
Plus or minus, but never just ONE.
Simple equation but multiple action
Ten little nigger boys: now there are none.

V

My uncle has entered his soliloquy.
The candles shed their fur.
O world be nobler for her sake.
The boys hang in the vestry, the days
Are drawing in. Blow out the flesh,
The three-score ten of candles,
This squalid birthday-cake.
Give us to God with slim and shining handles.

All this Peter and Paul knew,
Talked over in the nazarene evenings,
Walked over Galilee arm in arm,
Moved by no wires, by pure imagination.
The prophet who sat under the tall rock
Wrote in a small pure hand this canon
For stockbrokers to read at Cannon Street,
At the Metropole, around the Maypole,
Or smiling in the Ritz: perhaps to endow
An evening conversation at the Plough.

Cousin Judas, let us admit
It is the hour for affirmations,
Let us affirm the no-claim bonus,
The wages of sin, let us admit
Chaos itself as a form of order,
Bear the sinner's pretty onus,
Rediscover the taste of ashes,
Crucify the choirboys: and above all
Preserve the senseless trajectory,
The doom of the bobbin in the loom,
From the rectory to the priory,
From bed to refectory,
From little womb eke to little tomb.

In the name of the Great Whale, then,
Be hale and whole! Amen.

1943/*1938*

EGYPTIAN POEM[1]

And to-day death comes to the house.
To-day upon the waters, the sunset sail,
Death enters and the swallow's eye
Under the roof is no larger and darker
Than this scent of death.

A disciple crossed over by water.
The acorn was planted.
In the Ionian villa among the marble
The fountain plays the sea's piano,
And by the clock the geometric philosopher
Walks in white linen while death
Squats in the swallow's eye.

The dogs are muzzled. Lord,
See to the outer gate, our protection.
I rest between the born and the unborn.
The father, the mother, the baby unicorn
Intercede for me, attended the christening.
Exempt me.
I have friends in the underworld.

1943/*1938*

[1] Originally published as 'Egyptian Pastiche'.

CAROL ON CORFU
(1937)

I, per se I, I sing on.
Let flesh falter, or let bone break
Break, yet the salt of a poem holds on,
Even in empty weather
When beak and feather have done.

I am such fiddle-glib strokes,
As play on the nerves, glance the bare bone
With the madman's verve I quicken,
Leaven and liven body's prime carbon,
I, per se I, alone.

This is my medicine: trees speak and doves
Talk, woods walk: in the pith of the planet
Is undertone, overtone, status of music: God
Opens each fent, scent, memory, aftermath
In the sky and the sod.

O per se O, I sing on.
Never tongue falters or love lessens,
Lessens. The salt of the poem lives on
Like this carol of empty weather
Now feather and beak have gone.

1943/*1938*

LINES TO MUSIC

Ride out at midnight,
You will meet your sun.
Into what arsenal now seem fallen
The germs of the plum and the peppercorn?
The born and the unborn will report
What poison licks the wheat,
Or in the melon's gold retort
Repeat what melody fattens the leopard
From his mother's dusky teat.

Ride out at midnight
And number the sparrows.
Who put great wings to the Ark?
Who gave the unicorn spurs?
Only the women with thighs like mackerel,
Nourish the germ of the man of sorrows,
Are true to their monsters.
Be you to yours.

1960/*1938*

THEMES HERALDIC

I

If I say what I honestly mean
It's only because
I honestly mean what I say.

Shall I renounce you for a new theme
Who are a warm green stone, green girl,
Warm in a white bone bed?

It is no victory to write you,
But to become you. Gnosis
By osmosis. Knowing in becoming.

Desire is quite heraldic yet—
A lion or griffin on a playing-card,
Or Fiat Voluntas, and a page of uncials.

What do we care, though? I imagine always
Someone much later to read us here.
Open this garish album of the flesh
Kept to horrify children,
Silence the late traveller,
Pore on us. Point. Stop eating. There!

An Ice Age you and me!

1980/*1938*

II

You have been surely as a great moon.
There have been utterly drawn up
Frantic and magnetic liners, voyagers,
Ships in a doldrum, destroyers
Prowling a trade-route, gulls.
Even the amputated earth herself
Pours suicidal tidal water,
Ebbs upwards, up along homeward elastic
On the long tug wombward. Tides
Shine between your ribs, my moon's
White suicidal tides.

Everything is drawn in. Often
The known world will melt magnetic.
The glacier thaw and soften.
Then Man, Monkey, Microscope
Litter the long water lunatic.

No. The pale face offers no comment
On an uprooted cosmos. Only now
I can sniff gongs in the blood,
Drums in the water. Masks.
Rivers of seed flowing.

Moon of my blood
So suicidal a watch must be
As for the tidal world, for me,
Absolute ebb and flood.

1980/*1938*

Delicate desire,
She moves in belly's soft pocket,
At the wrist, like worm turning,
Apprehending morning, meaning
In all things. Rivers.
As tongue to mouth
Or eye to socket.

The swan, the candid unicorn
Fear nothing, caged in myth:
Have all green history's page
To frolic on.

Delicate desire,
As knife-thrust upward from beneath,
Grant two deep
Having, holding, folding,
Fading and inclining,
Dance into sleep
As tongue to tongue,
As knife to sheath.

1980/*1937*

[1] First published as 'A Lyric for Nikh'.

IV

Unblade the brighter passions one by one.
See, like swords shaken, angels' heels,
The bright things crowd upon us unawares.
Terrific toys the limbs like children cherish,
You in the night, I in the night—O falling.
Straws join on a collapsing flood and we
Pouring, forever pouring as we perish.

The night. Orion's black proscenium
Invites: and, mortal here, we perish
Whose face I shall not see nor thaw whose sperm.
Only I tell a mouth as cold as coin
Breast finger chilly as the loin I cherish.

Now what pale allegory hangs between the stars?
What mouth sips out the candles of the body?
See, here is war and yet I bring no weapon,
My theme is simply visionary paper.
Darling no message but the eventual
Limbs junction, sockets of pleasure turning.
No pomp but the visitor at the window, Orion.

O I carry no sword but the inevitable
Statuary dagger, the reaping sword alive,
Against my belly, under the belt of stars.

1980/1938

V

A girl has four partners in heraldry,
Elbow, wrist, ankle, knee.
Four bone gates the body uses
In its delicate abuses.

Ink become wine! Wine be blood!
O spirit, the leopard, eat body's food!

Girl, girl, girl, you have become
A valley of dead saints' bones,
A volley of hollow words, words, words.

Lie still. Watch the great heavy,
The flashing coloured boxer, Night,
Gong back the paleface, Day.
Opal and extravagant as a cat.

Lastly the moon will wake in him, too,
The stiff victorious grin o' the skull.

1980/*1938*

VI

Call back the stars. They are too many, Lord.
Death takes us man by man. Old wars
Covet us with the trumpet, cover us. April
Gives in deceit her stammering flowers.

Desire like a doom, the boom boom of the surf
Tells us. The slow-motion dive of the pole star
To the rim of the morning, the meaning of things,
Builds your tent where we are.

How shall it be? Caught in the sun's red loom,
Be woven to rock, to water, a new manufacture.
By the moon drawn, a green dolphin,
Up into death sans fracture?

Answer. At wedding, at tea-time, in snow?
Or in the dog-days, surprised at an oar,
In a drawn breath
Shall see save me too near the fatal,
Your absolute and ghostly impact, Lord,
The white yacht—death?

1980/*1938*

VII¹
(1937)

At last the serious days of summer
When from the red forge dancing,
The blacksmith sunshine hammers
New beaks for the flesh.
From the black mint
Steel for new flint.

State me no theme for misery. The season
Like a woman lies open, is folding,
Secret, growth upon growth. The black fig,
Desire, is torn again from the belly of Reason.
Our summer is gravid at last, is big.

All you, who know desire in these seas,
Have souls or equipment for loneliness, loneliness,
Lean now like fruitage. The Hesperides
Open. This is the limbo, the doldrum.
Seal down the eye of your cyclops,
Silence time's drum.

1943/*1938*

1 Also published as 'Summer in Corfu'.

VIII[1]

The paladin of the body is rock,
Dark rock, the anonymous
Stark stone, the prime ingot.

This crystal of darkness is flesh.
Call on Him and the rock
Becomes flesh and the flesh
God. Rock is His pseudonym.

This black rock does not feel
The kiss of the rivet, man's iron
So the body's armature seems
Bone: but is really stone.
God in the marrow
Borrows the belly's zone,
Shatters the mind's great lock,
And there visible is the Sphinx,
Whatever one thinks. God
Prime in the black rock.

1980/*1938*

1 Also published as 'The Sermon of One'.

The father is in death.
Let him now enter into the sun's attic,
Enter the floating chambers of the sea.
Who will bear witness how foreign,
How musical with the silence
And alphabets we three be?

The father is in death.
The shadow lobs at the western wall.
The wheel has a broken spoke.
O conjure, my brothers, the pelican
That its monstrous egg is not laid here
Lest dogs snap the poisoned yolk.

The father is strangled in his vine.
We will go sideways out of the house
Leaving only by the oven to nestle
A small rabbit on her perch-grass:
She is too soft a thing, too abhorred
A morsel for the twelve angers,
The pestle and mortar of the Lord.

1980/1938

¹ Also published as 'Poem to Gerald' and 'The Three Sons'.

LOGOS

Thy kingdom come. They say the prophet
In private house lies with his myth:
Sees strange particularities in flesh
That poison his beatitude.

Onlie begetter, shining one
We travel a same rare latitude
To fringe the Arctic Circle of the Word:
Carry no compass, flag to plant, but bone.
The ageless humour of the skeleton.

His myth is grace: no less our absolute,
Locust and honey, scrip and wallet. Woman
Can be a wilderness enough for body
To wander in: is a true human
Genesis and exodus. A serious fate.

She the last crucifixion on the Word.
We press on her as Roman on his sword.

1960/*1939*

THE HANGED MAN

From this glass gallows in famous entertainment,
Upside down and by the dust yellowed,
The hanged man considers a green county,
Hallowed by gallows on a high hill.

The rooks of his two blue eyes eating
A mineral diet, that smile not while
The invaders move: on the dark down there
Owls with soft scissors cherish him.

Yellower than plantains by the dust touched
These hands in their chamber-music turning,
As viol or cello, these might easily be
The sullen fingers of a fallen Charles.

So will the horseman speculate in his cloak,
The felloes of the wagon cease their screech,
While one widens the eye of the farm-girl
Telling how rope ripens on a high hill.

1943/*1939*

FATHER NICHOLAS HIS DEATH: CORFU
(1939)

Hush the old bones their vegetable sleep,
For the islands will never grow old.
Nor like Atlantis on a Monday tumble,
Struck like soft gongs in the amazing blue.

Dip the skull's chinks in lichens and sleep,
Old man, beside the water-gentry.
The hero standing knee-deep in his dreams
Will find and bind the name upon his atlas,
And put beside it only an X marked spot.

Leave memory to the two tall sons and lie
Calmed in smiles by the elegiac blue.
A man's address to God is the skeleton's humour,
A music sipped by the flowers.

Consider please the continuous nature of Love:
How one man dying and another smiling
Conserve for the maggot only a seed of pity,
As in winter's taciturn womb we see already
A small and woollen lamb on a hilltop hopping.

The dying and the becoming are one thing,
So wherever you go the musical always is;
Now what are your pains to the Great Danube's pains,
Your pyramids of despair against Ithaca
Or the underground rivers of Dis?

Your innocence shall be as the clear cistern
Where the lone animal in these odourless waters
Quaffs at his own reflection a shining ink.
Here at your green pasture the old psalms
Shall kneel like humble brutes and drink.

Hush then the finger bones their mineral doze
For the islands will never be old or cold
Nor ever the less blue: for the egg of beauty
Blossoms in new migrations, the whale's grey acres,
For men of the labyrinth of the dream of death.
So sleep.
All these warm when the flesh is cold.
And the blue will keep.

1943/*1939*

ADAM

I have nibbled the mystical fruit. Cover me.
Lest the prophetic fish follow and swallow me.
I dare not tread among the lilies
Though lambswool cover my footfall,
Though the adder call, the Word walk,
In the orchard voices follow, hands hallow me.

Thy will be done as it was in Eden.
We were a long time—I am afraid—
Naked among silver fish and shadows,
A long time and in silence naked. Only
The fountains falling, the hornet's drum
Calling, sunny and drunk with dew.

I am Adam, of singular manufacture,
A little clay, water, and prophetic breath;
On the waters of chaos a lamp of red clay.
The Word owns me. I have no armament
Only my fear of the walking Thing.

The rib follows me everywhere: and everywhere
A shadow follows the rib. Eve,
I am afraid. The Host walks and talks
In the baobab shade: the unknowable Thing
Is crossing the paths: the breath, woman,
Is on us: a white light: O cover me
From the unthinkable razor of thought
Whose whisper hangs over me.

Eve, we are in this thing to the very end,
You, your shadow, and shadowless Adam, I.
O rib and morsel of anguish, bone of contention,
After the thing has shone and gone,
After it enters the terrible wood,
We will win through, perhaps: cover us deep
Beyond clue with the leaves of the wood:
Be silent until it passes: and kiss me, kiss me.
Ah! but the apple, the apple was good!

1960/*1939*

PARIS JOURNAL
For David Gascoyne
(1939)

Monday escapes destruction.
Record a vernal afternoon,
Tea on the lawn with mother,
A parochial interest in love, etc.
By the deviation of a hair,
Is death so far, so far, no further.

Tuesday: visibility good: and Wednesday.
A little thunder, some light showers.
A library book about the universe.
The absence of a definite self.
O and already by Friday hazardous,
To Saturday begins the slow reverse.
A Saturday without form. By midnight
The equinox seems forever gone:
Yet the motionless voice repeating:
'Bless the hills in paradigms of smoke,
Manhair, Maidenhair meeting.'

But today Sunday. The pit.
The axe and the knot. Cannot write.
The monster in its booth.
At a quarter to one the mask repeating:
'Truth is what is
Truth is what is Truth?'

1943/*1939*

THE POET

Time marched against my egg,
But Saturn hatched it:
Furnished two rusty claws,
The antelope's logic:
While by the turtle's coma in summer
The new moon watched it.

Four seasons conspired
To poison my water: with scissors
A late spring lanced the bud,
Tightened the caul on my skull,
Lulled me in dragon's blood.

Sun withered this crucible head,
Wove me by a tragical loom.
Nine moons heard of my coming,
The drumming of mythical horses
On the walls of the womb.

Winter buried the eyes like talents.
Tightened the temple's bony ring,
And now the pie is opened,
Feathered the head of the owlet—
What shall the monster sing?

1960/*1939*

THE EGG[1]
(1939)

Who first wrapped love in a green leaf,
And spread warm wings on the egg of death,
That my heart was hatched like a smooth stone,
And love in a green leaf locked?

Pity was naked: who dried her feathers
By the ancient pillow with cold ankles?
(Pity, my friend, fell in with the scorpion:
Murder with his bottle took my sweet.)

Who found passion without a leg,
Shrieked like the canticle of a ghost?
A bat spat his blood in the nursery:
A vessel in darkness but without a compass.

Anger first opened the book of the egg,
A bible of broken boys and natural women.
The choir sang like a bee in a bush,
And hunger, the dog, hummed in his paws.

Now time is wrapped in a green bay-leaf,
And a Roman summer covers the underworld,
O remember the heart hatched like cold stone,
And love in a green leaf locked.

1943/*1939*

[1] Originally published as 'The Ego's Own Egg'.

A SMALL SCRIPTURE
To Nancy
(1939)

Now when the angler by Bethlehem's water
Like a sad tree threw down his trance
What good was the needle of resurrection,
A bat-like soul for the father Adam,
But to bury in haystacks of common argument
The Fish's living ordinance?

A bleeding egg was the pain of testament,
Murder of self within murder to reach the Self:
The grapnel of fury like a husband's razor
Turned on his daughter in a weird enchantment
To cut out the iron mask from the iron man,
His double, the troubled elf.

Now one eye was the cyclop's monstrous ration,
But this face looked forward to Heliopolis,
Rehearsed its charm in other exilic lovers
God-bound near Eden on the crutches of guilt;
Aimed like a pistol through the yellow eyes—
Your heart and mine know the truth of this.

This we make to the double Jesus, the nonpareil,
Whose thought snapped Jordan like a dam.
Darling and bully with the bloody taws,
Both walked in this tall queen by the green lake.
Both married when the aching nail sank home.
Weep for the lion, kneel to the lamb.

1943/*1939*

71

'A SOLILOQUY OF HAMLET'
Dedicated to Anne Ridler and the Lady in the Painting
Ophelia

I

Here on the curve of the embalming winter,
Son of the three-legged stool and the Bible,

By the trimmed lamp I cobble this sonnet
For father, son, and the marble woman.

Sire, we have found no pardonable city
Though women harder than the kneeling nuns,

Softer than clouds upon the stones of pain,
Have breathed their blessings on a candle-end.

Some who converted the English oak-trees:
The harmless druids singing in green places.

Some who broke their claws upon islands:
The singing fathers in the boats of glory.

Some who made an atlas of their hunger:
The enchanted skulls lie under the lion's paw.

II

One innocent observer in a foreign cell
Died when my father lay beside his ghost.

Dumb poison in the hairy ear of kings
Can map the nerves and halt the tick of hearts.

The phoenix burning at his window-sill
Put peace around him like a great basin.

So whether the ocean curved beneath his dreams
On floors full of the sea-shell's music,

His privacy aims like a pointed finger:
Death grows like poison-ivy on a stick.

Truly his unruly going grows like a green wand
Between the broken pavements of the heart,

And all whose blood ticks fast at funerals
Must dread the tapping of the vellum drum.

III

Guilt can lie heavier than house of tortoise.
Winter and love, O desperate medicines,

Under the turf we bless the wishing spring,
The seed from the index-finger of the saint.

To the snow I sing out this hoarse prescription:
'Sweet love, from the enduring geometric egg,

An embryo grinning in its coloured cap,
O I walk under a house of horn, seeking a door.'

The charming groans of ladies come to me
From the nursery sills of an invented climate:

My outlawed mother patient at the loom,
Behind her, oaks, their nude machinery,

The dark ones shining on their snowy tuffets.
I take this image on a screaming nib.

IV

Here in the hollow curvature of the world,
Now time turns through her angles on a dial,

The unspeaking surgeon cuts beneath the fur,
And pain forever green winds her pale horn.

Make in the beautiful harbours of the heart,
For scholars sitting at their fire-lit puzzles,

The three-fold climate and the anchorage.
Make in the dormitory of the self

For sleepless murders combing out the blood
A blessing and an armistice to fear.

Though bankers pile debentures to the worm,
And death like Sunday only brings the owls

Though some must founder trying for the rock,
Bless mice and women in their secret places.

V

To you in high heaven the unattainable,
The surnamed Virgin, I lift a small scripture,

Brushed by the quill of a black boy's madness;
Pour one sweet drop of mercy on the mind!

You three, being holy and great linguists,
The oval singers of the Cretan eikon,

Give to the ghost your charity's ghostly shirt,
Defence by pity and a green captivity.

Consider: here the thorn crawled in the heart,
Here traitors laid an axe upon the root.

Grant like a bruise his sweetest homecoming,
Find laughing Hamlet sitting in a tree,

The silken duchess frowning at her baubles,
And swart Ophelia crooning at her lauds.

VI

Winter and love are Euclid's properties.
The charm of candles smoking on a coffin

Like nursery years upon a birthday cake,
Teach, like the soft declensions of the term,

How dust being sifted from the sheet of nuns,
Returns beneath the swollen veil once more,

So women bend like trees and utter figs,
And children from their pillows prophesy.

The unnumbered garrison still holds the womb.
O suffer the mirages of the dazed ladies,

Give love with all its tributary patience
That when the case of bones is broken open,

The heart can bless, or the sad skin of saints
Be beaten into drum-heads for the truth.

VII

Walk upon dreams, and pass behind the book.
Hamlet is nailed between the thieves of love.

Wear the black waistcoat, boy, for death is king,
His margin is a waxen candle-dip at night:

By day a grace-note in the mid of silence,
The gambler smiling in his royal sheet.

For this I put the obol in the lips.
For this I wear my sex beneath a towel.

I take the round skull of the nunnery girl
To bless until the tears break in the brain;

75

As those who by the Babylonian fable
Hung up their piercing harps beside the waters,

I hang my heart, being choked, upon a noun.
I hang her name upon this frantic pothook.

VIII

I close an hinge on the memorial days.
I perch my pity on an alp of silence.

Cold water took my pretty by the beard,
Flatter than glass she blew to the tongueless zone.

I learn now from nightingale on the spit
The science of the cowl and killing-bottle.

I hum now the harsh tune of the too finite swan,
Piping behind the ambush of my guilt.

My comfort smiled on me and gave me flowers:
Freckles, as on a sparrow's egg, and quiet faces.

The water strips her humour like a bean.
Barbarian ladies with their fingernails,

Strip off her simple reason like a wedding-dress.
She turns upon the pedals of her prison.

IX

Pain hangs more bloody than the mystic's taws.
Down corridors of pain I follow patience,

Make notes behind the nerve-ends of the brain.
Lean, lean on the iron elbow of the armoured man,

Button the nipples on his coat of mercy,
The widow walking in a rubber mask!

Your murderer's napkin hangs upon a bush,
And the king who stiffens in a shirt of blood,

Too good, too grave to number with the crumbs,
Can leave an incubus to this winter castle.

Shoot back the lips like bolts upon your grace.
Make thimble of the mouth to suck your fly.

I cool my spittle on the smoking hook.
I take these midnight thoughts between a tong.

X

As husband is laid down beside the lute,
Widow and minstrel in a single cerement,

So I on the plinth of passing, shall I marry
The lunatic image in the raven frock?

The curved meridian of hazard like a bow
Paints on the air the dark tree of my death

Gums without ivory for the skeletal smile:
A natal joker squeaking in his crib.

Here birth and death are knitted by a vowel.
A mariner must sail his crew of furies

Beyond the hook of hazard to the oceanic lands.
His prayers will bubble up before the throne.

I, now, go, where the soliloquy of the sad bee
O numbs the nettles and the hieroglyphic stone.

XI

On the stone sill of the embalming winter
I tell my malady by the wheel and the berry,

The hunters making their necklace on the hills.
The escaping dead hang frozen down like flags,

A breathing frost upon the eyeball lens
Blooms like still poison in a dish of quinces.

Spawn of the soft, the unwrinkled womb of queens,
I add my number to the world's defeated,

I learn the carrion's scientific torpor,
The five-day baby swollen with its gases,

The nun who fell from the ladder of Jacob.
My love hangs longer than the tongue of hound.

I kneel at the keyhole of death's private room
To meet His eye, enormous in the keyhole.

XII

This pain goes deeper than the fish's fathom.
Peel me an olive-branch and hold it shining:

You have Ophelia smiling at her chess,
The suit of love gored by the courtier's fang.

You have my mother folded like a rag,
Whiter than piano-keys the canine smile.

The marble statues bleed if she walks by,
Pacing the margins of the chequerboard

Where the soft rabbit and her man in black
Play move for move, the pawn against the prince.

O men have made cradles of their loving fingers
To rock my youth, and I have slipped between,

Led like the magi to the child's foul crib,
To hear my hands nailed up between two thieves.

XIII

Then walk where roses like disciples can
Aim at the heart their innocent attention.

Where the apostle-spring beneath the cover
Of throstle and dove, loves in his green asylum.

Time shall bestow a pupil to the nipple,
A red and popular baby born for the urn.

For him I make a book by the moving finger-bone,
A rattle, cap and comedy of queens.

Then suckle the weather if the winter will not,
Seal down a message in a dream of spring,

More than this painful meditation of feet,
The frigid autist pacing out his rope.

The candle and the lexicon have picked your bones.
The tallow spills upon my endless bible.

XIV

To you by whom the sweet spherical music
Makes in heaven a tree-stringed oracle,

I bend a sonnet like a begging-bowl,
And hang my tabor from the greenest willow-wand.

Give to the rufus sons of Pudding Island
The stainless sheet of a European justice,

That death's pure canon smiling in the trees
Can lure the fabulous lion from his walks.

My ash I dress to dance upon the void,
My mercy in a wallet like a berry bright,

And when hemp sings of murder bless your boy,
The double fellow in the labyrinth,

Whose maps were stifled with him in the maze,
Whose mother dropped him like the seedless pod.

1943/1939

THE SERMON
From A Verse Play

[Now the Prompter will come before the curtain and speak
the following lines. He must not recite this address, but
deliver it in the manner of one making an intimate speech
to friends.]

Ladies and gentlemen: or better still,
Men and women: or best, perhaps, of all,
My children: for we speak to the child under the title
Of players acting a play which is not the less life
For being enacted: not the less a play for being lived
On both sides of the lamp, under ordinary coats.

Understanding is a neuter gift which lies between
The mind and the heart, to neither absolute.
To understand is to become wholly aware, to become holy,
To stand between the causal and the casual
As Darwin stands grinning, between two types of ape,
As the angel stood with the knife of sex and division,
As Hamlet for all time in the helmet of the prince.

So many shadows lie between all of us here:
Between I, an actor, and the live men on the stage:
Between I, the actor, and you who are playing at life.
I would be glad to reach out among your imaginations
And touch the walker on water, your inmost saints,
But thought, like sex, is only the rubbing of two
Sticks, making only a fire by which to consume itself.

Do you understand what has gone before? Well then,
You will guess more easily what we have to follow.
Death and sex are symbols of division in chaos.
Life lies on the Whole, along a circumference pure.
Duality is distress, like the image of pins in mirrors.
The first law of optics is the eye: and the first law
Of Life is Time, the endless tepid all-consuming ray.

Consider the magic of your wife or your daughter's
Love, so partial a gift, defenceless against iron.
Why is this? Because the receiver is partial not whole.
Imperfect of reception, you are a ventriloquist's idiot,
Acting and speaking by inherited voices and vices.
Now what is dumber than the voice of the dummy?
What more deadly than the voice of Esau in Jacob?

I will provide a text for your refreshment here:
Let it come like a foreign grace between the food
And the tongue, between the lip and the next glass.
It is: nothing can save you, because salvation
Is in what is lost, not saved: what is spent unmeasured.
Think, even as you sit here blessing you are cursed.
As you turn in your minds to escape you are damned.

The detention is ended, Ladies
And gentlemen: or what is worse perhaps,
Men and women: or what is worst of all
Children: for we speak to children under the title of Man.
Farewell.

1980/*1940*

THE PRAYER-WHEEL[1]
(1939)

Only to affirm in time
That sequence dwells in consequence,
The River's quietly flowing muscle
Turning in the hollow cup
Will teach the human compromise.
Sword and pen win nothing here
Underneath the human floor:
Loved and loving move between
The counterpoint of universes,
Neither less and neither more.

The sage upon his snowy wheel
Secure among the flight of circles
By the calculus of prayer
Underneath the human floor
Founds a commune in the heart.
Time in love's diurnal motion,
Suffering untold migrations,
Islanded and garlanded,
Deep as the ministry of fishes
Lives by a perpetual patience.

Teach us the already known,
Turning in the invisible saucer
By a perfect recreation
Air and water mix and part.
Reaffirm the lover's process,
Faith and love in flesh alloyed,
Spring the cisterns of the heart:
Build the house of entertainment
On the cold circumference
Candle-pointed in the Void.

Cross the threshold of the circle
Turning in its mesmerism
On the fulcrum of the Breath:
Learn the lovely mannerism
Of a perfect art-in-death.
Think: two amateurs in Eden,
Spaces in the voiceless garden,
Ancestors whose haunted faces
Met upon the apple's bruises,
Broke the lovely spell of pardon.

Flower, with your pure assertion,
Mythical and sea-born olive,
Share the indivisible air,
Teach the human compromise:
From a zero, plus or minus,
Born into the great Appearance,
Building cities deep in gardens,
Deeply still the law divines us
In its timeless incoherence.

What is known is never written.
By the equal distribution
He and She and It are genders,
Sparks of carbon on the circle
Meeting in the porch of sex.
Faces mix and numbers mingle
Many aspects of the One
Teach the human compromise.
Speech will never stain the blue,
Nor the lover's occult kisses
Hold the curves of Paradise.

The voices have their dying fall.
The fingers resting on the heart,
The dumb petitions in the churchyard
Under the European sword
Spell out our tribal suicide.
Grass is green but goes to smoke:
You, my friend, and you, and you,
Breathe on the divining crystal,
Cut down History, the oak:
Prepare us for the sword and pistol.

1948/*1940*

¹ Originally published as 'Poem in Space and Time'.

GREEN MAN

Four small nouns I put to pasture,
Lambs of cloud on a green paper.
My love leans like a beadle at her book,
Her smile washes the seven cities.

I am the spring's greenest publicity,
And my poem is all wrist and elbow.
O I am not daedal and need wings,
My oracle kisses a black wand.

One great verb I dip in ink
For the tortoise who carries the earth:
A grammar of fate like the map of China,
Or as wrinkles sit in the palm of a girl.

I enter my poem like a son's house.
The ancient thought is: nothing will change.
But the nouns are back in the bottle,
I ache and she is warm, was warm, is warm.

1960/*1940*

IN CRISIS
For Nancy
(1939)

My love on Wednesday letting fall her body
From upright walking won by weariness,
As on a bed of flesh by ounces counted out,
Softer than snuff or snow came where my body was.

So in the aboriginal waterways of the mind,
No word being spoken by a familiar girl,
One may have a clear apprehension of ghostly matters,
Audible, as perhaps in the sea-shell's helix

The Gulf Stream can rub soft music from a pebble
Like quiet rehearsal of the words 'Kneel down':
And cool on the inner corridors of the ear
Can blow on memory and conscience like a sin.

The inner man is surely a native of God
And his wife a brilliant novice of nature.
The woman walks in the dark like a lantern swung,
A white spark blown between points of pain.

We do not speak, embracing with the blood,
The tolling heart marking its measures in darkness
Like the scratch of a match or the fire-stone
Struck to a spark in the dark by a colder one.

So, lying close, the enchanted boy may hear
Soon from Tokio the crass drum sounding,
From the hero's hearth the merry crotchet of war.
Flame shall swallow the lady.

Tall men shall come to cool the royal bush,
Over the grey waters the bugler's octaves
Publish aloud a new resurrection of terror.
Many will give suck at the bomb's cold nipple.

Empty your hearts: or fill from a purer source.
That what is in men can weep, having eyes:
That what is in Truth can speak from the responsible dust
And O the rose grow in the middle of the great world.

1943/1940

AT CORINTH
For V.
(1940)

At Corinth one has forgiven
The recording travellers in the same past
Who first entered this land of doors,
Hunting a precise emotion by clues,
Haunting a river, or a place in a book.
Here the continuous evocations are washed
Harder than tears and brighter,
But less penetrating than the touch of flesh,
(Our fingers pressed upon eyelids of stone),
Yet more patient, surely, watching
To dissolve the statues and retire
Night after night with a dissolving moon.

The valley mist ennobles
Lovers disarmed by negligence or weather,
And before night the calm
Discovers them, breathing upon the nerves,
The scent of the exhausted lamps.
Here stars come soft to pasture,
And all doors lead to sleep.
What lies beneath the turf forbids
A footstep on the augustan stair,
The intrusion of a style less pure,
Seen through the camera's lens,
Or the quotations of visitors.

My skill is in words only:
To tell you, writing this letter home,
That we, whose blood was sweetened once
By Byron or his elders in the magic,
Entered the circle safely, found
No messenger for us except the smiles.
Owls sip the wind here. Well,
This place also was somebody's home,
Whipped by the gulf to thorns,
A house for proverbs by a broken well.
Winter was never native here: nor is.
Men, women, and the nightingales
Are forms of Spring.

1943/*1940*

NEMEA
(1940)

A song in the valley of Nemea:
Sing quiet, quite quiet here.

Song for the brides of Argos
Combing the swarms of golden hair:
Quite quiet, quiet there.

Under the rolling comb of grass,
The sword outrusts the golden helm.

Agamemnon under tumulus serene
Outsmiles the jury of skeletons:
Cool under cumulus the lion queen:

Only the drum can celebrate,
Only the adjective outlive them.

A song in the valley of Nemea:
Sing quiet, quiet, quiet here.

Tone of the frog in the empty well,
Drone of the bald bee on the cold skull,

Quiet, Quiet, Quiet.

1943/*1940*

IN ARCADIA
(1940)

By divination came the Dorians,
Under a punishment composed an arch.
They invented this valley, they taught
The rock to flow with odourless water.

Fire and a brute art came among them.

Rain fell, tasting of the sky.
Trees grew, composing a grammar.
The river, the river you see was brought down
By force of prayer upon this fertile floor.

Now small skills: the fingers laid upon
The nostrils of flutes, the speech of women
Whose tutors were the birds; who singing
Now civilized their children with the kiss.

Lastly, the tripod sentenced them.

Ash closed on the surviving sons.
The brown bee memorized here, rehearsed
Migration from an inherited habit.
All travellers recorded an empty zone.

Between rocks 'O death', the survivors.
O world of bushes eaten like a moon,
Kissed by the awkward patience of the ant.
Within a concave blue and void of space.

Something died out by this river: but it seems
Less than a nightingale ago.

1943/1940

A NOCTUARY IN ATHENS

I

I have tasted my quantum of misfortune,
Have prayed before the left-handed woman;

Now as the rain of heaven downfalling tastes of space,
So the swimmer in the ocean of self, alone,

Utters his journey like a manual welcome,
Sculptures his element in search of grace.

II

I have sipped from the flask of resurrection,
Have eaten the oaten cake of redemption,

And love, sweet love, who weeps by the water-clock
Can bring if she will the sexton and the box,

For I wear my age as wood wears voluble leaves,
The temporal hunger and the carnal locks.

III

I have buried my wife under a dolmen,
Where others sleep as naked as the clouds,

Where others lie and weigh their dreams by ounces,
Where tamarisk, lentisk lean to utter sweets,

And angels in their shining moods retire:
Where from the wells the voice of truth pronounces.

IV

I have tasted my quantum of misfortune.
In the desert, the cities of ash and feathers,

In front of others I have spoken the vowel,
Knelt to the curly wool, the uncut horns;

Have carried my tribulation in a basket of wattle,
Solitary in my penitence as the owl.

V

I have set my wife's lip under the bandage,
O pound the roses, bind the eye of the soul,

Recite the charm of the deep and heal soon,
For the mountains accuse, and the sky's walls.

Let the book of sickness be put in the embers.
I have tasted my quantum of misfortune.

1943/1940

DAPHNIS AND CHLOE
(1937)

This boy is the good shepherd.
He paces the impartial horizons,
Forty days in the land of tombs,
Waterless wilderness, seeking waterholes:
Knows the sound of the golden eagle, knows
The algebraic flute blue under Jupiter:
Supine in myrtle, lamb between his knees,
Has been a musical lion upon the midnight.

This was the good shepherd, Daphnis,
Time's ante-room by the Aegean tooth,
Curled like an umber snake above the spray,
Mumbling arbutus among the chalk-snags,
The Grecian molars where the green sea spins,
Suffered a pastoral decay.

This girl was the milk and the honey.
Under the eaves the dark figs ripen,
The leaves' nine medicines, a climbing wine.
Under the tongue the bee-sting,
Under the breast the adder at the lung,
Like feathered child at wing.

Life's honey is distilled simplicity:
The icy crystal pendant from the rock,
The turtle's scorching ambush for the egg,
The cypress and the cicada,
And wine-dark, blue, and curious, then,
The metaphoric sea.

This was Chloe, the milk and honey,
Carved in the clear geography of Time,
The skeleton clean chiselled out in chalk,
For our Nigerian brown to study on.
From the disease of life, took the pure way,
Declined into the cliffs, the European waters,
Suffered a pastoral decay.

1943/1941

FANGBRAND

A BIOGRAPHY
For Stephan Syriotis
(Mykonos, 1940)

Fangbrand was here once,
A missionary man,
Borne down by the Oxus,
Pursued by the lilies,
Inhabited by the old voice of sorrows,
In a black hat and sanitary boots.

The island recognised him,
Giving no welcome, lying
Trembling among her craters:
The blue circlets of stone,
On a sea blotted with fictions.
He came to the wharf with long oars.

The Ocean's peculiar spelling
Haunts here, cuddled by syllables
In caves perpendicular, a blue recitation
Of water washing the dead,
On the pediments of the statues,
Came the strange man, the solitary man,

Fangbrand the unsuspecting,
Missionary one in thick soles,
Measuring penance by the pipkin,
Step-brother to the gannet,
Travelling the blue bowl of the world,
His virtues in him rough as towels.

His brows that bent like forests
Over the crystal-gazing eyes;
His brows that bent like forests,
A silver hair played on his neck.
He saw this rock and the seal asleep,
With the same mineral stare.

This place he made pastance
For the platonic ass; in this
Cottage by the water supported
The duellers, the twins,
Of argument and confusion,
Alone in a melancholy hat.

Those who come to this pass,
Ask themselves always how
A rock can become a parish,
Pulpits whitened by the sea-birds,
Mean more than just house, rock,
A tree, a table and a chair.

His window was Orion;
At night standing upon the deep,
His eyes smaller than commas
Watched without regret the ships
Passing, one light in a void,
One pure point on the wave's floor.

Measured in the heart's small flask
The spirit's disturbance: the one voice
Saying 'Renounce', the other
Answering 'Be'; the division
Of the darkness into faces
Crying 'Too late' 'Too late'.

At night the immediate
Rubbing of the ocean on stones,
The headlands dim in her smoke
And always the awareness
Of self like a point, the quiver
As of a foetal heart asleep in him.

Continuous memory, continual evocations.
An old man in a colony of stones,
Frowning, exilic, upon a thorn,
Learning nothing of time:
Sometimes in a windy night asleep
His lips brushed the forbidden apples.

Everything reproached him, the cypress
Revising her reflection in pools,
The olive's stubborn silver in wind,
The nude and statuary hills all
Saying 'Turn back. Turn back.
Peace lies another way, old man'.

It seemed to him here at last
His age, his time, his sex even
Were struck and past; life
In a flood carrying all idols
Into the darkness, struck
Like floating tubs, and were gone.

The pathfinder rested now,
The sick man found silence
Like the curved ear of a shell;
A roar of silence even
Diminishing the foolish cool
Haunting note of the dove.

By day he broke his fruit
Humbly from the tree: his water
From wells as deep as Truth:
Living on snails and waterberries,
Marvelling for the first time
At the luminous island, the light.

His body he left in pools
Now dazed by fortune, like an old
White cloth discarded where
Only the fish were visitors.
Their soft perverted kisses
Melted the water on his side.

The rich shadow of the vine's tent
Like a cold cloth on his skull;
Spring water blown through sand,
Bubbled on mineral floors,
Ripened in smooth cisterns
Dripped from a hairy lintel on his tongue.

Truth's metaphor is the needle,
The magnetic north of purpose
Striving against the true north
Of self: Fangbrand found it out,
The final dualism in very self,
An old man holding an asphodel.

Everywhere night lay spilled,
Like coolness from spoons,
And his to drink, the human
Surface of the sky, the planes
And concaves of the eye reflecting
A travelling mirror, the earth.

He regarded himself in water,
The torrid brow's beetle,
The grammarian's cranium-bone.
He regarded himself in water
Saying 'X marks the spot,
Self, you are still alive!'

From now the famous ten-year
Silence fell on him; disciples
Invented the legend; now
They search the white island
For a book perhaps, a small
Paper of revelation left behind.

Comb out the populous waters,
Study the mud: what kept,
Held, fed, fattened him?
The hefts of stone are the only
Blossoms here: nothing grows,
But the ocean expunges.

Time's chemicals mock the hunter
For crumbs of doctrine; Fangbrand
Died with his art like a vase.
The grave in the rock,
Sweetened by saffron, bubbles water
Like a smile, an animal truth.

Death interrupted nothing.
Like guarded towns against alarms,
Our sentries in the nerves
Never sleep; but his one night
Slept on their arms, Hesperus shining,
And the unknowns entered.

So the riders of the darkness pass
On their circuit: the luminous island
Of the self trembles and waits,
Waits for us all, my friends,
Where the sea's big brush recolours
The dying lives, and the unborn smiles.

1943/1941

AT EPIDAURUS

The islands which whisper to the ambitious,
Washed all winter by the surviving stars
Are here hardly recalled: or only as
Stone choirs for the sea-bird,
Stone chairs for the statues of fishermen.
This civilized valley was dedicated to
The cult of the circle, the contemplation
And correction of famous maladies
Which the repeating flesh has bred in us also
By a continuous babyhood, like the worm in meat.

The only disorder is in what we bring here:
Cars drifting like leaves over the glades,
The penetration of clocks striking in London.
The composure of dolls and fanatics,
Financed migrations to the oldest sources:
A theatre where redemption was enacted,
Repentance won, the stones heavy with dew.
The olive signs the hill, signifying revival,
And the swallow's cot in the ruin seems how
Small yet defiant an exaggeration of love!

Here we can carry our own small deaths
With the resignation of place and identity;
A temple set severely like a dice
In the vale's Vergilian shade; once apparently
Ruled from the whitest light of the summer:
A formula for marble when the clouds
Troubled the architect, and the hill spoke
Volumes of thunder, the sibyllic god wept.
Here we are safe from everything but ourselves,
The dying leaves and the reports of love.

The land's lie, held safe from the sea,
Encourages the austerity of the grass chambers,
Provides a context understandably natural
For men who could divulge the forms of gods.
Here the mathematician entered his own problem,
A house built round his identity,
Round the fond yet mysterious seasons
Of green grass, the teaching of summer-astronomy.
Here the lover made his calculations by ferns,
And the hum of the chorus enchanted.
We, like the winter, are only visitors,
To prosper here the breathing grass,

Encouraging petals on a terrace, disturbing
Nothing, enduring the sun like girls
In a town window. The earth's flowers
Blow here original with every spring,
Shines in the rising of a man's age
Into cold texts and precedents for time.
Everything is a slave to the ancestor, the order
Of old captains who sleep in the hill.

Then smile, my dear, above the holy wands,
Make the indefinite gesture of the hands,
Unlocking this world which is not our world.
The somnambulists walk again in the north
With the long black rifles, to bring us answers.
Useless a morality for slaves: useless
The shouting at echoes to silence them.
Most useless inhabitants of the kind blue air,
Four ragged travellers in Homer.
All causes end within the great Because.

1943/1941

LETTER TO SEFERIS THE GREEK
'Ego dormio sed cor meum vigilat'
(1941)

No milestones marked the invaders,
But ragged harps like mountains here:
A text for Proserpine in tears: worlds
With no doors for heroes and no walls with ears:
Yet snow, the anniversary of death.

How did they get here? How enact
This clear severe repentance on a rock,
Where only death converts and the hills
Into a pastoral silence by a lake,
By the blue Fact of the sky forever?

'Enter the dark crystal if you dare
And gaze on Greece.' They came
Smiling, like long reflections of themselves
Upon a sky of fancy. The red shoes
Waited among the thickets and the springs,
In fields of unexploded asphodels,
Neither patient nor impatient, merely
Waited, the born hunter on his ground,
The magnificent and funny Greek.

We will never record it: the black
Choirs of water flowing on moss,
The black sun's kisses opening,
Upon their blindness, like two eyes
Enormous, open in bed against one's own.

Something sang in the firmament.
The past, my friend compelled you,
The charge of habit and love.
The olive in the blood awoke,
The stones of Athens in their pride
Will remember, regret and often bless.

Kisses in letters from home:
Crosses in the snow: now surely
Lover and loved exist again
By a strange communion of darkness.
Those who went in all innocence,
Whom the wheel disfigured: whom
Charity will not revisit or repair,
The innocent who fell like apples.

Consider how love betrays us:
In the conversation of the prophets
Who daily repaired the world
By profit and loss, with no text
On the unknown quantity
By whose possession all problems
Are only ink and air made words:
I mean friends everywhere who smile
And reach out their hands.

Anger inherits where love
Betrays: iron only can clean:
And praises only crucify the loved
In their matchless errand, death.
Remember the earth will roll
Down her old grooves and spring
Utter swallows again, utter swallows.

Others will inherit the sea-shell,
Murmuring to the foolish its omens,
Uncurving on the drum of the ear,
The vowels of an ocean beyond us,
The history, the inventions of the sea:
Upon all parallels of the salt wave,
To lovers lying like sculptures
In islands of smoke and marble,
Will enter the reflections of poets
By the green wave, the chemical water.

I have no fear for the land
Of the dark heads with aimed noses,
The hair of night and the voices
Which mimic a traditional laughter:
Nor for a new language where
A mole upon a dark throat
Of a girl is called 'an olive':
All these things are simply Greece.

Her blue boundaries are
Upon a curving sky of time,
In a dark menstruum of water:
The names of islands like doors
Open upon it: the rotting walls
Of the European myth are here
For us, the industrious singers,
In the service of this blue, this enormous blue.

Soon it will be spring. Out of
This huge magazine of flowers, the earth,
We will enchant the house with roses,
The girls with flowers in their teeth,
The olives full of charm: and all of it
Given: can one say that
Any response is enough for those
Who have a woman, an island and a tree?

I only know that this time
More than ever, we must bless
And pity the darling dead: the women
Winding up their hair into sea-shells,
The faces of meek men like dials,
The great overture of the dead playing,
Calling all lovers everywhere in all stations
Who lie on the circumference of ungiven kisses.

Exhausted rivers ending in the sand;
Windmills of the old world winding
And unwinding in musical valleys your arms.
The contemptible vessel of the body lies
Lightly in its muscles like a vine;
Covered the nerves: and like an oil expressed
From the black olive between rocks,
Memory lulls and bathes in its dear reflections.

Now the blue lantern of the night
Moves on the dark in its context of stars.
O my friend, history with all her compromises
Cannot disturb the circuit made by this,
Alone in the house, a single candle burning
Upon a table in the whole of Greece.

Your letter of the 4th was no surprise.
So Tonio had gone? He will have need of us.
The sails are going out over the old world.
Our happiness, here on a promontory,
Marked by a star, is small but perfect.
The calculations of the astronomers, the legends
The past believed in could not happen here.
Nothing remains but Joy, the infant Joy
(So quiet the mountain in its shield of snow,
So unconcerned the faces of the birds),
With the unsuspected world somewhere awake,
Born of this darkness, our imperfect sight,
The stirring seed of Nostradamus' rose.

1943/1941

FOR A NURSERY MIRROR

Image, Image, Image answer
Whether son or whether daughter,
The persuader or the dancer:
A bird's beak poking out of the flesh,
A bird's beak singing between the eyes.

'The earth is a loaf,
Image, Image, Image,
The wet part is joined to the dry,
Like the joints of Adam.'

It is dark now. Rise.
Between the Nonself and the Self
Cover the little wound
With soft red clay,
From the hit of the wind of Death,
From the chink of the pin of Day.

The heart's cold singing part,
Image of the Dancer in water,
Close up with the soft red clay
The wound in the mystical bud:
For the dancers walking in the water
This is the body, this the blood.

1946/1942

TO PING-KÛ, ASLEEP

You sleeping child asleep, away
Between the confusing world of forms,
The lamplight and the day; you lie
And the pause flows through you like glass,
Asleep in the body of the nautilus.

Between comparison and sleep,
Lips that move in quotation;
The turning of a small blind mind
Like a plant everywhere ascending.
Now our love has become a beanstalk.

Invent a language where the terms
Are smiles; someone in the house now
Only understands warmth and cherish,
Still twig-bound, learning to fly.

This hand exploring the world makes
The diver's deep-sea fingers on the sills
Of underwater windows; all the wrecks
Of our world where the sad blood leads back
Through memory and sense like divers working.

Sleep, my dear, we won't disturb
You, lying in the zones of sleep.
The four walls symbolise love put about
To hold in silence which so soon brims
Over into sadness: it's still dark.

Sleep and rise a lady with a flower
Between your teeth and a cypress
Between your thighs: surely you won't ever
Be puzzled by a poem or disturbed by a poem
Made like fire by the rubbing of two sticks?

1943/1942

TO ARGOS

The roads lead southward, blue
Along a circumference of snow,
Identified now by the scholars
As a home for the cyclops, a habitation
For nymphs and ancient appearances.
Only the shepherd in his cowl
Who walks upon them really knows
The natural history in a sacred place;
Takes like a text of stone
A familiar cloud-shape or fortress,
Pointing at what is mutually seen,
His dark eyes wearing the crowsfoot.

Our idols have been betrayed
Not by the measurement of the dead ones
Who are lying under these mountains,
As under England our own fastidious
Heroes lie awake but do not judge.
Winter rubs at the ice like a hair,
Dividing time; and a single tree
Reflects here a mythical river.
Water limps on ice, or scribbles
On doors of sand its syllables,
All alone, in an empty land, alone.
This is what breaks the heart.

We say that the blood of Virgil
Grew again in the scarlet pompion,
Ever afterwards reserving the old poet
Memorials in his air, his water: so
In this land one encounters always
Agamemnon, Agamemnon; the voice
Of water falling on hair in caves,
The stonebreaker's hammer on walls,
A name held closer in the circles
Of bald granite than even these cyclamen,
Like children's ears attentive here,
Blown like glass from the floors of snow.

Truly, we the endowed who pass here
With the assurance of visitors in rugs
Can raise from the menhir no ghost
By the cold sound of English idioms.
Our true parenthood rests with the eagle,
We recognize him turning over his vaults.
Bones have no mouths to smile with
From the beds of companionable rivers dry.
The modern girls pose on a tomb smiling;
Night watches us on the western horn;
The hyssop and the vinegar have lost their meaning,
And this is what breaks the heart.

1943/1942

'Je est un Autre'

RIMBAUD

He is the man who makes notes,
The observer in the tall black hat,
Face hidden in the brim:
In three European cities
He has watched me watching him.

The street-corner in Buda and after
By the post-office a glimpse
Of the disappearing tails of his coat,
Gave the same illumination, spied upon,
The tightness in the throat.

Once too meeting by the Seine
The waters a moving floor of stars,
He had vanished when I reached the door,
But there on the pavement burning
Lay one of his familiar black cigars.

The meeting on the dark stairway
Where the tide ran clean as a loom:
The betrayal of her, her kisses
He has witnessed them all: often
I hear him laughing in the other room.

He watches me now, working late,
Bringing a poem to life, his eyes
Reflect the malady of De Nerval:
O useless in this old house to question
The mirrors, his impenetrable disguise.

1943/1942

CONON IN EXILE

Author's Note

Conon is an imaginary Greek philosopher who visited me
twice in my dreams, and with whom I occasionally identify
myself; he is one of my masks, Melissa is another; I want
my total poetic work to add up as a kind of tapestry of
people, some real, some imaginary. Conon is real.

I

Three women have slept with my books,
Penelope among admirers of the ballads,
Let down her hair over my exercises
But was hardly aware of me; an author
Of tunes which made men like performing dogs;
She did not die but left me for a singer in a wig.

II

Later Ariadne read of *The Universe*,
Made a journey under the islands from her own
Green home, husband, house with olive trees.
She lay with my words and let me breathe
Upon her face; later fell like a gull from the
Great ledge in Scio. Relations touched her body
Warm and rosy from the oil like a scented loaf,
Not human any more—but not divine as they had hoped.

III

You who pass the islands will perhaps remember
The lovely Ion, harmless, patient and in love.
Our quarrels disturbed the swallows in the eaves,
The wild bees could not work in the vine;
Shaken and ill, one of true love's experiments,
It was she who lay in the stone bath dry-eyed,
Having the impression that her body had become
A huge tear about to drop from the eye of the world.
We never learned that marriage is a kind of architecture,
The nursery virtues were missing, all of them,
So nobody could tell us why we suffered.

IV

It would be untrue to say that *The Art of Marriage*
And the others: *Of Peace in the Self* and *Of Love*
Brought me no women; I remember bodies, arms, faces,
But I have forgotten their names.

V

Finally I am here. Conon in exile on Andros
Like a spider in a bottle writing the immortal
Of Love and Death, through the bodies of those
Who slept with my words but did not know me.
An old man with a skinful of wine
Living from pillow to poke under a vine.

At night the sea roars under the cliffs.
The past harms no one who lies close to the Gods.
Even in these notes upon myself I see
I have put down women's names like some
Philosophical proposition. At last I understand
They were only forms for my own ideas,
With names and mouths and different voices.
In them I lay with myself, my style of life,
Knowing only coitus with the shadows,
By our blue Aegean which forever
Washes and pardons and brings us home.

1943/1942

ON FIRST LOOKING INTO LOEB'S HORACE

I found your Horace with the writing in it;
Out of time and context came upon
This lover of vines and slave to quietness,
Walking like a figure of smoke here, musing
Among his high and lovely Tuscan pines.

All the small-holder's ambitions, the yield
Of wine-bearing grape, pruning and drainage
Laid out by laws, almost like the austere
Shell of his verses—a pattern of Latin thrift;
Waiting so patiently in a library for
Autumn and the drying of the apples;
The betraying hour-glass and its deathward drift.

Surely the hard blue winterset
Must have conveyed a message to him—
The premonitions that the garden heard
Shrunk in its shirt of hair beneath the stars,
How rude and feeble a tenant was the self,
An Empire, the body with its members dying—
And unwhistling now the vanished Roman bird?

The fruit-trees dropping apples; he counted them;
The soft bounding fruit on leafy terraces,
And turned to the consoling winter rooms
Where, facing south, began the great prayer,
With his reed laid upon the margins
Of the dead, his stainless authors,
Upright, severe on an uncomfortable chair.

Here, where your clear hand marked up
'The hated cypress' I added 'Because it grew
On tombs, revealed his fear of autumn and the urns',
Depicting a solitary at an upper window
Revising metaphors for the winter sea: 'O
Dark head of storm-tossed curls'; or silently
Watching the North Star which like a fever burns

Away the envy and neglect of the common,
Shining on this terrace, lifting up in recreation
The sad heart of Horace who must have seen it only
As a metaphor for the self and its perfection—
A burning heart quite constant in its station.

Easy to be patient in the summer,
The light running like fishes among the leaves,
Easy in August with its cones of blue
Sky uninvaded from the north; but winter
With its bareness pared his words to points
Like stars, leaving them pure but very few.

He will not know how we discerned him, disregarding
The pose of sufficiency, the landed man,
Found a suffering limb on the great Latin tree
Whose roots live in the barbarian grammar we
Use, yet based in him, his mason's tongue;
Describing clearly a bachelor, sedentary,
With a fond weakness for bronze-age conversation,
Disguising a sense of failure in a hatred for the young,

Who built in the Sabine hills this forgery
Of completeness, an orchard with a view of Rome;
Who studiously developed his sense of death
Till it was all around him, walking at the circus,
At the baths, playing dominoes in a shop—
The escape from self-knowledge with its tragic
Imperatives: *Seek, suffer, endure*. The Roman
In him feared the Law and told him where to stop.

So perfect a disguise for one who had
Exhausted death in art—yet who could guess
You would discern the liar by a line,
The suffering hidden under gentleness
And add upon the flyleaf in your tall
Clear hand: 'Fat, human and unloved,
And held from loving by a sort of wall,
Laid down his books and lovers one by one,
Indifference and success had crowned them all.'

1946/1943

ON ITHACA STANDING
(1937)

Tread softly, for here you stand
On miracle ground, boy.
A breath would cloud this water of glass,
Honey, bush, berry and swallow.
This rock, then, is more pastoral, than
Arcadia is, Illyria was.

Here the cold spring lilts on sand.
The temperature of the toad
Swallowing under a stone whispers: 'Diamonds,
Boy, diamonds, and juice of minerals!'
Be a saint here, dig for foxes, and water,
Mere water springs in the bones of the hands.

Turn from the hearth of the hero. Think:
Other men have their emblems, I this:
The heart's dark anvil and the crucifix
Are one, have hammered and shall hammer
A nail of flesh, me to an island cross,
Where the kestrel's arrow falls only,
The green sea licks.

1943/1943

EXILE IN ATHENS
(1940)

To be a king of islands,
Share a boundary with eagles,
Be a subject of sails.

Here, on these white rocks,
In cold palaces all winter,
Under the salt blanket,

Forget not yet the tried intent,
Pale hands before the face: face
Before the sea's blue negative,

Washing against the night,
Pushing against the doors,
Earth's dark metaphors.

Here alone in a stone city
I sing the rock, the sea-squill,
Over Greece the one punctual star.

To be king of the clock—
I know, I know—to share
Boundaries with the bird,

With the ant her lodge:
But they betray, betray.
To be the owner of stones,

To be a king of islands,
Share a bed with a star,
Be a subject of sails.

1943/*1943*

A BALLAD OF THE GOOD LORD NELSON

The Good Lord Nelson had a swollen gland,
Little of the scripture did he understand
Till a woman led him to the promised land
    Aboard the Victory, Victory O.

Adam and Evil and a bushel of figs
Meant nothing to Nelson who was keeping pigs,
Till a woman showed him the various rigs
    Aboard the Victory, Victory O.

His heart was softer than a new laid egg,
Too poor for loving and ashamed to beg,
Till Nelson was taken by the Dancing Leg
    Aboard the Victory, Victory O.

Now he up and did up his little tin trunk
And he took to the ocean on his English junk,
Turning like the hour-glass in his lonely bunk
    Aboard the Victory, Victory O.

The Frenchman saw him a-coming there
With the one-piece eye and the valentine hair,
With the safety-pin sleeve and occupied air
    Aboard the Victory, Victory O.

Now you all remember the message he sent
As an answer to Hamilton's discontent—
There were questions asked about it in Parliament
    Aboard the Victory, Victory O.

Now the blacker the berry, the thicker comes the juice.
Think of Good Lord Nelson and avoid self-abuse,
For the empty sleeve was no mere excuse
    Aboard the Victory, Victory O.

'England Expects' was the motto he gave
When he thought of little Emma out on Biscay's wave,
And remembered working on her like a galley-slave
    Aboard the Victory, Victory O.

The first Great Lord in our English land
To honour the Freudian command,
For a cast in the bush is worth two in the hand
    Aboard the Victory, Victory O.

Now the Frenchman shot him there as he stood
In the rage of battle in a silk-lined hood
And he heard the whistle of his own hot blood
    Aboard the Victory, Victory O.

Now stiff on a pillar with a phallic air
Nelson stylites in Trafalgar Square
Reminds the British what once they were
    Aboard the Victory, Victory O.

If they'd treat their women in the Nelson way
There'd be fewer frigid husbands every day
And many more heroes on the Bay of Biscay
    Aboard the Victory, Victory O.

1943/1943

COPTIC POEM[1]

A Coptic deputation, going to Ethiopia,
Disappeared up one morning like the ghost in Aubrey

'With a Sweet Odour and a Melodious Twang'.
Who saw them go with their Melodious Odour?

I, said the arrow, the aboriginal arrow,
I saw them go, Coptic and Mellifluous,

Fuzzy-wig, kink-haired, with cocoa-butter shining,
With stoles on poles, sackbuts and silver salvers

Walking the desert ways howling and shining:
A Coptic congregation, red blue and yellow,

With Saints on parchment and stove-pipe hats,
All disappeared up like the ghost in Aubrey

Leaving only a smell of cooking and singing,
Rancid goat-butter and the piss of cats.

1946/1943

¹ Originally published as 'Mythology'.

MYTHOLOGY

All my favourite characters have been
Out of all pattern and proportion:
Some living in villas by railways,
Some like Katsimbalis heard but seldom seen,
And others in banks whose sunless hands
Moved like great rats on ledgers.

Tibble, Gondril, Purvis, the Duke of Puke,
Shatterblossom and Dude Bowdler
Who swelled up in Jaffa and became a tree:
Hollis who had wives killed under him like horses
And that man of destiny,

Ramon de Something who gave lectures
From an elephant, founded a society
To protect the inanimate against cruelty.
He gave asylum to aged chairs in his home,
Lampposts and crockery, everything that
Seemed to him suffering he took in
Without mockery.

The poetry was in the pity. No judgement
Disturbs people like these in their frames
O men of the Marmion class, sons of the free.

1946/1943

MATAPAN

Unrevisited perhaps forever
Southward from the capes of smoke
Where past and present to the waters are one
And the peninsula's end points out
Three fingers down the night:
On a corridor of darkness a beam
To where the islands, at last, the islands . . .

Abstract and more lovely
Andros Delos and Santorin,
Transpontine headlands in crisp weather,
Cries amputated by the gulls,
Formless, yet made in marble
Whose calm insoluble statues wear
Stone vines for hair, forever sharing
A sea-penumbra, the darkened arc
Where mythology walks in a wave
And the islands are.

Leaving you, hills, we were unaware
Or only as sleepwalkers are aware
Of a key turned in the heart, a letter
Posted under the door of an empty house;
Now Matapan and her forebodings
Became an identity, a trial of conduct,
Rolled and unrolled by the surges
Like a chart, mapped by a star,
With thistle and trefoil blowing,
An end of everything known
A beginning of water.

> Here sorrow and beauty shared
> Like time and place an eternal relation,
> Matapan . . .

> Here we learned that the lover
> Is contained by love, not containing,
> Matapan, Matapan:

Here the lucky in summer
Tied up their boats; a mile from land
The cicada's small machine came like a breath;
Touching bottom saw their feet become
Webbed and monstrous on the sandy floors.
Here wind emptied the snowy caves: the brown

Hands about the tiller unbuckled.
Day lay like a mirror in the sun's eye.
Olives sleeping, rocks hanging, sea shining
And under Arbutus the scriptural music
Of a pipe beside a boy beside a bay
Soliloquised in seven liquid quibbles.

Here the lucky in summer
Made fast like islanders
And saw upon the waters, leaning down
The haunted eyes in faces torn from books:
So painted the two dark-blue Aegean eyes
And θεὸς δίκαιος 'God the Just'
Under them upon the rotting prows.

Inhabitants of reflection going:
We saw the dog-rose abloom in bowls,
Faces of wishing children in the wells
Under the Acropolis the timeless urchin
Carrying the wooden swallow,
Teller of the spring; on the hills of hair
Over Athens saw the night exhaling.

Later in islands, awaiting passage,
By waters like skin and promontories,
Were blessed by the rotation
Of peach-wind, melon-wind,
Fig-wind and wind of lemons;
Every fruit in the rotation of its breath.
And in the hills encountered
Sagacious and venerable faces
Like horn spoons: forms of address:
Christian names, politeness to strangers.

Heard the ant's pastoral reflections:
'Here I go in Arcadia, one two
Saffron, sage, bergamot, rue,
A root, a hair, a bead—all warm.
A human finger swarming
With little currents: a ring:
A married man.'

In a late winter of mist and pelicans
Saw the thread run out at last; the man
Kiss his wife and child good-bye
Under the olive-press, turning on a heel.
To enter April like swimmer,
And memory opened in him like a vein,
Pushed clear on the tides a pathless keel.

Standing alone on the hills
Saw all Greece, the human
Body of this sky suspending a world
Within a crystal turning,
Guarded by the green wicks of cypresses.

Far out on the blue
Like notes of music on a page
The two heads: the man and his wife.
They are always there.

It is too far to hear the singing.

1943/1943

ECHO

To Nancy
And
To Ping-Kû
for her second birthday out of Greece

Nothing is lost, sweet self,
Nothing is ever lost.
The unspoken word
Is not exhausted but can be heard.
Music that stains
The silence remains
O echo is everywhere, the unbeckonable bird!

1956/1943

THIS UNIMPORTANT MORNING

This unimportant morning
Something goes singing where
The capes turn over on their sides
And the warm Adriatic rides
Her blue and sun washing
At the edge of the world and its brilliant cliffs.

Day rings in the higher airs
Pure with cicadas, and slowing
Like a pulse to smoke from farms,
Extinguished in the exhausted earth,
Unclenching like a fist and going.

Trees fume, cool, pour—and overflowing
Unstretch the feathers of birds and shake
Carpets from windows, brush with dew
The up-and-doing: and young lovers now
Their little resurrections make.

And now lightly to kiss all whom sleep
Stitched up—and wake, my darling, wake.
The impatient Boatman has been waiting
Under the house, his long oars folded up
Like wings in waiting on the darkling lake.

1946/1944

BYRON

The trees have been rapping
At these empty casements for a year,
Have been rapping and tapping and
Repeating to us here
Omens of the defeating wind,
Omens of the defeating mind.

Headquarters of a war
House in a fever-swamp
Headquarters of a mind at odds.

Before me now lies Byron and behind,
Belonging to the Gods,
Another Byron of the feeling
Shown in this barbered hairless man,
Splashed by the candle-stems
In his expensive cloak and wig
And boots upon the dirty ceiling.

Hobbled by this shadow,
My own invention of myself, I go
In wind, rain, stars, climbing
This ladder of compromises into Greece
Which like the Notself looms before
My politics, my invention and my war.
None of it but belongs
To this farded character
Whose Grecian credits are his old excuse
By freedom holding Byron in abuse.

Strange for one who was happier
Tuned to women, to seek and sift
In the heart's simple mesh,
To know so certainly
Under the perfume and the politics
What undertow of odours haunts the flesh:
Could once resume them all
In lines that gave me rest,
And watch the fat fly Death
Hunting the skeleton down in each,
Like hairs in plaster growing,
Promising under the living red the yellow—
I helped these pretty children by their sex
Discountenance the horrid fellow.

I have been a secretary (I sing)
A secretary to love . . .

In this bad opera landscape
Trees, fevers and quarrels
Spread like sores: while the gilded
Abstractions like our pride and honour
On this brute age close like doors
Which pushing does not budge.

Outside them, I speak for the great average.
My disobedience became
A disguise for a style in a new dress.
Item: a lock of hair.
Item: a miniature, myself aged three,
The innocent and the deformed
Pinned up in ribbons for posterity.

And now here comes
The famous disposition to weep,
To renounce. Picture to yourself
A lord who encircled his life
With women's arms; or another
Who rode through the wide world howling
And searching for his mother.

Picture to yourself a third: a cynic.
This weeping published rock—
The biscuits and the glass of soda-water:
Under Sunium's white cliffs
Where I laboured with my knife
To cut a 'Byron' there—
I was thinking softly of my daughter.

A cock to Aesculapius no less . . .

You will suggest we found only
In idleness and indignation here,
Plucked by the offshore dancers, brigs
Like girls, and ports of call
In our commerce with liberty, the Whore,
Through these unbarbered priests
And garlic-eating captains:
Fame like the only porch in a wall
To squeeze our shelter from
By profit and by circumstance
Assist this rocky nation's funeral.

The humane and the lawful in whom
Art and manners mix, who sent us here,
This sort of figures from a drawing-room
Should be paused themselves once
Under these legendary islands.
A landscape hurled into the air
And fallen on itself: we should see
Where the frail spines of rivers
Soft on the backbone intersect and scribble
These unbarbered gangs of freedom dribble
Like music down a page and come
Into the valleys with their small
Ordnance which barks and jumps.
I, Byron: the soft head of my heart bumps
Inside me as on a vellum drum.

Other enemies intervene here,
Not less where the valet serves
In a muddle of papers and consequences;
Not less in places where I walk alone
With Conscience, the defective: my defences
Against a past which lies behind,
Writing and rewriting to the bone
Those famous letters in my mind.

Time grows short. Now the trees
Are rapping at the empty casements.
Fevers are closing in on us at last—
So long desired an end of service
To the flesh and its competitions of endurance.
There is so little time. Fletcher
Tidies the bed at dusk and brings me coffee.

You, the speaking and the feeling who come after:
I sent you something once—it must be
Somewhere in *Juan*—it has not reached you yet.

O watch for this remote
But very self of Byron and of me,
Blown empty on the white cliffs of the mind,
A dispossessed His Lordship writing you
A message in a bottle dropped at sea.

1946/1944

LA ROCHEFOUCAULD
'*Nous arrivons tout nouveaux aux divers âges de la vie*'

'A penny for your thoughts. I wasn't joking.'
Most of it I learned from serving-girls,
Looking into eyes mindless as birds, taking
The pure for subject or the unaware.
When empty mouths so soon betray their fear
Kisses can be probes. Mine always were.

Yes, everywhere I sorted the betraying
Motive, point by point designed
This first detective-story of the heart,
Judge, jury, victim, all were in my aspect,
Pinned on the clear notation of the mind—
I primed them like an actor in a part.

I was my own motive—I see you smile:
The one part of me I *never* used or wrote,
Every comma paused there, hungry
To confess me, to reveal the famished note.

Yet in reason I mastered appetite,
And taught myself at last the tragic sense;
Then through appetite and its many ambushes
I uncovered the politics of feeling, dense
Groves for the flocks of sin to feed in.
Yet in the end the portrait always seemed
Somehow faked, or somehow still in need
Of gender, form and present tense.

I could not get beyond this wall.

No. The bait of feeling was left untasted:
Deep inside like ruins lay the desires
To give, to trust, to be my subjects' equal,
All wasted, wasted.
Though love is not the word I want
Yet it will have to do. There is no other.

So the great Lack grew and grew.
Of the Real Darkness not one grain I lifted.
Yet the whole story is here like the part
Of some great man's body,
Veins, organs, nerves,
Unhappily illustrating neither death nor art.

1946/1944

PEARLS

Now mark, the Lady one fine day
To refresh her pearls she comes
And buries them in the sand here,
Letting the sea feed on them,
To lick back by salt
The lustre of them and the prize.

Ten summers, lazy as fishes follow.
Ten winters, nude as thimbles
Bear on their gradual curves
The drinkers of the darkness.

The pearls drink and recover
But their lovely Neck
Becomes one day the target for an Axe,
Bows swan-like down
Its unrepenting lovely stump.

Something is incomplete here,
Something in the story is unfinished,
A tale with no beginning,
The fragment of a voice that interrupts,
Like this unbroken coast,
Like this half-drawn landscape,
Like this broken torso of a poem.

1946/1945

HELOISE AND ABELARD

Heloise and Abelard
Nature's great hermaphrodites,
Arists in the human way,
Turned their sad endearing eyes,
Passionate and tiger-bright,
Closed the animal.
Yet in deprivation found
By a guess
Love unseal its loveliness.

Patents of their time and sex,
Body's rude containers
With their humours up like wicks,
Passionate and tiger-bright,
Made them foreigners
To themselves while still awake.
Yet with this he lights the stake
Feeds like faggots tied
Innocence and pride,
Bits of what had died.

Tombs may lie by two and two
On the Jordan's bends;
Death's unshrinking little noun
Marks them for his own,
The passionate and tiger-bright
Couples in their shadows lie
Till the action ends.
Death by lovelessness for these
Was unsealed in mysteries
By the enduring Friend.

Lucky who can sort out
The barren and the sown,
Whose punishments are given joy,
Who their own bodies own.
Who can discriminate,
Under reason's cruel rod
Between the friend in them
And enemy of God.

1946/1945

CONON IN ALEXANDRIA

Ash-heap of four cultures,
Bounded by Mareotis, a salt lake,
On which the winter rain rings and whitens,
In the waters, stiffens like eyes.

I have been four years bound here:
A time for sentences by the tripod:
Prophecies by those who were born dead,
Or who lost their character but kept their taste.

A solitary presumed quite happy,
Writing those interminable whining letters,
On the long beaches dimpled by the rain,
Tasting the island wind

Blown against wet lips and shutters out of Rhodes.
I say 'presumed', but would not have it otherwise.

* * *

Steps go down to the port
Beyond the Pharos. O my friends,
Surely these nightly visitations
Of islands in one's sleep must soon be over?

I have watched beside the others,
But always the more attentive, the more exacting:
The familiar papers on a table by the bed,
The plate of olives and the glass of wine.

You would think that thoughts so long rehearsed
Like the dry friction of ropes in the mind
Would cease to lead me where in Greece
The almond-candles and the statues burn.

The moon's cold seething fires over this white city,
Through four Februaries have not forgotten.

*　*　*

Tonight the stars press idly on the nerves
As in a cobweb, heavy with dispersal:
Points of dew in a universe too large
Too formal to be more than terrible.

'There are sides of the self
One can seldom show. They live on and on
In an emergency of anguish always,
Waiting for parents in another.'

Would you say that later, reading
Such simple propositions, the historian
Might be found to say: 'The critic
In him made a humour of this passion.

The equations of a mind too conscious of ideas,
Fictions, not kisses, crossed the water between them'?

*　*　*

And later, Spring, which compels these separations
Will but define you further as she dies
In flowers downless and pure as Portia's cheek,
Interrupting perhaps the conversations of friends

On terraces where the fountains plane at time,
To leave this small acid precipitate to memory,
Of something small, screwed-up, and thrown aside.
'Partings like these are lucky. At least they wound.'

And later by the hearthstone of a philosophy
You might have added: 'The desert, yes, for exiles.
But its immensity only confines one further.
Its end seems always in oneself.'

A gown stained at the arm-pits by a woman's body.
A letter unfinished because the ink gave out.

*   *   *

The lovers you describe as *'separating each other
Further with every kiss'*: and your portrait
Of a man *'engaged in bitterly waiting
For the day when art should become unnecessary'*,

Were in the style and order, as when you say
'Freedom alone confines'; but do they show a love,
Fragmented everywhere by conscience and deceit,
Ending on this coast of torn-out lighthouses?

Or that neglected and unmerited Habit,
The structure that so long informed our growth?
Questions for a nursery wall! But are they true to these?

I have passed all this day in what they would call patience.
Not writing, alone in my window, with my flute,
Having read in a letter that last immortal February
That *'Music is only love, looking for words'*.

1946/1945

MAREOTIS

For Diana Gould

Now everywhere Spring opens
Like an eyelid still unfocused,
Unsharpened in expression yet or depth,
But smiling and entire, stirring from sleep.

Birds begin, swindlers of the morning.
Flowers and the wild ways begin:
And the body's navigation in its love
Through wings, messages, telegrams
Loose and unbodied roam the world.

Only we are held here on the
Rationed love—a landscape like an eye,
Where the wind gnashes by Mareotis,
Stiffens the reeds and glistening salt,
And in the ancient roads the wind,
Not subtle, not confiding, touches once again
The melancholy elbow cheek and paper.

1946/1945

CONON THE CRITIC ON THE SIX LANDSCAPE PAINTERS OF GREECE

ON PETER OF THEBES

'This landscape is not original in its own mode. First smells were born—
of resin and pine. Then someone got drunk on arbutus berries. Finally
as an explanatory text someone added this red staunch clay and roots.
You cannot smell one without tasting the other—as with fish and red
sauce.'

ON MANOLI OF CRETE

'After a lifetime of writing acrostics he took up a brush and everything
became twice as attentive. Trees had been trees before. Distinctions
had been in ideas. Now the old man went mad, for everything undres-
sed and ran laughing into his arms.'

On Julian of Arcadia

'Arcadia is original in a particular sense. There is no feeling of "Therefore" in it. Origin, reason, meaning it has none in the sense of recognizable past. In this, both Arcadia and all good poems are original.'

On Spiridon of Epirus

'You look at this landscape for five years. You see little but something attentive watching you. Another five and you remark a shape that is barely a shape; a shadow like the moon's penumbra. Look a lifetime and you will see that the mountains lie like the covers of a bed; and you discern the form lying under them.'

On Hero of Corinth

'Style is the cut of the mind. Hero was not much interested in his landscape, but by a perpetual self-confession in art removed both himself and his subject out of the reach of the people. Thus one day there remained only a picture-frame, an empty studio, and an idea of Hero the painter.'

On Alexander of Athens

'Alexander was in love with Athens. He was a glutton and exhausted both himself and his subject in his art. Thus when he had smelt a flower it was quite used up, and when he painted a mountain it felt that living on could only be a useless competition against Alexander's painting of it. Thus with him Athens ceased to exist, and we have been walking about inside his canvases ever since looking for a way back from art into life.'

1946/1945

WATER MUSIC

Wrap your sulky beauty up,
From sea-fever, from winterfall
Out of the swing of the
Swing of the sea.

Keep safe from noonfall,
Starlight and smokefall where
Waves roll, waves toll but feel
None of our roving fever.

From dayfever and nightsadness
Keep, bless, hold: from cold
Wrap your sulky beauty into sleep
Out of the swing of the
Swing of sea.

1946/1945

DELOS
For Diana Gould

On charts they fall like lace,
Islands consuming in a sea
Born dense with its own blue:
And like repairing mirrors holding up
Small towns and trees and rivers
To the still air, the lovely air:
From the clear side of springing Time,
In clement places where the windmills ride,
Turning over grey springs in Mykonos,
In shadows with a gesture of content.

The statues of the dead here
Embark on sunlight, sealed
Each in her model with the sightless eyes:
The modest stones of Greeks,
Who gravely interrupted death by pleasure.

And in harbours softly fallen
The liver-coloured sails—
Sharp-featured brigantines with eyes—
Ride in reception so like women:
The pathetic faculty of girls
To register and utter a desire
In the arms of men upon the new-mown waters,
Follow the wind, with their long shining keels
Aimed across Delos at a star.

1946/1945

THE PILOT
To Dudley Honor

Sure a lovely day and all weather
Leading westward to Ireland and our childhood.
On the quarters of heaven, held by stars,
The Hunter and Arcturus getting ready—
The elect of heaven all burning on the wheel.

This lovely morning must the pilot leaning
In the eye of heaven feel the island
Turning beneath him, burning soft and blue—
And all this mortal globe like a great lamp
With spines of rivers, families of cities
Seeming to the solitary boy so
Local and queer yet so much part of him.

The enemies of silence have come nearer.
Turn, turn to the morning on wild elbows:
Look down through the five senses like stars
To where our lives lie small and equal like two grains
Before Chance—the hawk's eye or the pilot's
Round and shining on the open sky,
Reflecting back the innocent world in it.

1946/1945

THE PARTHENON
For T. S. Eliot

Στεριὲς καὶ νησιὰ

Put it more simply: say the city
Swam up here swan-like to the shallows,
Or whiteness from an overflowing jar
Settled into this grassy violet space,
Theorem for three hills,

Went soft with brickdust, clay and whitewash,
On a plastered porch one morning wrote
Human names, think of it, men became the roads.

The academy was given over
To the investigation of shade an idle boy
Invented, tearing out the heart
Of a new loaf, put up these slender columns.

Later the Parthenon's small catafalque
Simple and congruent as a wish grew up,
Snow-blind, the marbles built upon a pause
Made smoke seem less surprising, being white.

Now syntax settled round the orderless,
Joining action and reflection in the arch,
Then adding desire and will: four walls:
Four walls, a house. 'How simple' people said.

Man entered it and woman was the roof.

A vexing history, Geros, that becomes
More and more simple as it ends, not less;
And nothing has redeemed it: art
Moved back from pleasure-giver to a humour

As with us ... I see you smile ...

Footloose on the inclining earth
The long ships moved through cities
Made of loaf-sugar, tamed by gardens,
Lying hanging by the hair within the waters

And quickened by self-knowledge
Men of linen sat on marble chairs
In self-indulgence murmuring 'I am, I am'.

Chapters of clay and whitewash. Others here
Find only a jar of red clay, a Pan
The superstitious whipped and overturned.
Yet nothing of ourselves can equal it

Though grown from causes we still share,
The natural lovely order, as where water
Touches earth, a tree grows up,
A needle touching wax, a human voice.

But for us the brush, the cone, the candle,
The spinning-wheel and clay are only
Amendments to an original joy.

Lost even the flawless finishing strokes,
White bones among the almonds prophesying
A death itself that seemed a coming-of-age.

Lastly the capes and islands hold us,
Tame as a handclasp,
Causes locked within effects, the land—
This vexed clitoris of the continental body,
Pumice and clay and whitewash
Only the darkness ever compromises

Or an eagle softly mowing on the blue . . .

And yet, Geros, who knows? Within the space
Of our own seed might some day rise,
Shriek truth, punish the blue with statues.

1948/1945/6

IN EUROPE
Recitative for a Radio Play
To Elie

Three Voices to the accompaniment of a drum and bells,
and the faint grunt and thud of a dancing bear.

MAN

The frontiers at last, I am feeling so tired.
We are getting the refugee habit,

WOMAN

Moving from island to island,
Where the boundaries are clouds,
Where the frontiers of the land are water.

OLD MAN

We are getting the refugee habit,

WOMAN

We are only anonymous feet moving,
Without friends any more, without books
Or companionship any more. We are getting—

MAN

The refugee habit. There's no end
To the forest and no end to the moors:
Between the just and the unjust
There is little distinction.

OLD MAN

Bodies like houses, without windows and doors:

WOMAN

The children have become so brown,
Their skins have become dark with sunlight,

MAN

They have learned to eat standing.

OLD MAN

When we come upon men crucified,
Or women hanging downward from the trees,
They no longer understand.

WOMAN

How merciful is memory with its fantasies.
They are getting the refugee habit . . .

OLD MAN

How weary are the roads of the blood.
Walking forwards towards death in my mind
I am walking backwards again into my youth;
A mother, a father, and a house.
One street, a certain town, a particular place:
And the feeling of belonging somewhere,
Of being appropriate to certain fields and trees.

WOMAN

Now our address is the world. Walls
Constrain us. O do you remember
The peninsula where we so nearly died,
And the way the trees looked owned,
Human and domestic like a group of horses?
They said it was Greece.

MAN

Through Prussia into Russia,
Through Holland to Poland,
Through Rumania into Albania.

WOMAN

Following the rotation of the seasons.

OLD MAN

We are getting the refugee habit:
The past and the future are not enough,
Are two walls only between which to die:
Who can live in a house with two walls?

MAN

The present is an eternal journey;
In one country winter, in another spring.

OLD MAN

I am sick of the general deaths:
We have seen them impersonally dying:
Everything I had hoped for, fireside and hearth,
And death by compromise some summer evening.

MAN

You are getting the refugee habit:
You are carrying the past in you
Like a precious vessel, remembering
Its essence, ownership and ordinary loving.

WOMAN

We are too young to remember.

OLD MAN

Nothing disturbed such life as I remember
But telephone or telegram,
Such death-bringers to the man among the roses
In the garden of his house, smoking a pipe.

WOMAN

We are the dispossessed, sharing
With gulls and flowers our lives of accident:
No time for love, no room for love:
If only the children—

MAN

Were less wild and unkept, belonged
To the human family, not speechless,

OLD MAN

And shy as the squirrels in the trees:

WOMAN

If only the children

138

OLD MAN

Recognized their father, smiled once more.

OLD MAN + WOMAN

They have got the refugee habit,
Walking about in the rain hunting for food,
Looking at their faces in the bottom of wells:

OLD MAN

They are living the popular life.
All Europe is moving out of winter
Into spring with all boundaries being
Broken down, dissolving, vanishing.
Migrations are beginning, a new habit
From where the icebergs rise in the sky
To valleys where corn is spread like butter . . .

WOMAN

So many men and women: each one a soul.

MAN

So many souls crossing the world,

OLD MAN

So many bridges to the end of the world.
Frontiers mean nothing any more . . .

WOMAN

Peoples and possessions,
Lands, rights,
Titles, holdings,
Trusts, Bonds . . .

OLD MAN

Mean nothing any more, nothing.
A whistle, a box, a shawl, a cup,
A broken sword wrapped in newspaper.

WOMAN

All we have left us, out of context,

OLD MAN

A jar, a mousetrap, a broken umbrella,
A coin, a pipe, a pressed flower

WOMAN

To make an alphabet for our children.

OLD MAN

A chain, a whip, a lock,
A drum and a dancing bear . . .

WOMAN

We have got the refugee habit.
Beyond tears at last, into some sort of safety
From fear of wanting, fear of hoping,
Fear of everything but dying.
We can die now.

OLD MAN

Frontiers mean nothing any more. Dear Greece!

MAN

Yes. We can die now.

1946/1946

PRESSMARKED URGENT

'*Mens sana in corpore sano*' Motto for Press Corps

DESPATCH ADGENERAL PUBLICS EXTHE WEST
PERPETUAL MOTION QUITE UNFINDING REST
ADVANCES ETRETREATS UPON ILLUSION
PREPARES NEW METAPHYSICS PERCONFUSION

PARA PERDISPOSITION ADNEW EVIL
ETREFUSAL ADCONCEDE OUR ACTS ADDEVIL
NEITHER PROFIT SHOWS NOR LOSS
SEDSOME MORE PROPHETS NAILED ADCROSS

ATTACK IN FORCE SURMEANS NONENDS
BY MULTIPLYING CONFUSION TENDS
ADCLOUD THE ISSUES WHICH ARE PLAIN
COLON DISTINGUISH PROFIT EXGAIN

ETBY SMALL CONCEPTS LONG NEGLECTED
FIND VIRTUE SUBACTION CLEAR REFLECTED
ETWEIGHING THE QUANTUM OF THE SIN
BEGIN TO BE REPEAT BEGIN.

1946/1946

TWO POEMS IN BASIC ENGLISH

I

SHIPS. ISLANDS. TREES

These ships, these islands, these simple trees
Are our rewards in substance, being poor.
This earth a dictionary is
To the root and growth of seeing,
And to the servant heart a door.
Some on the green surface of the land
With all their canvas up in leaf and flower,
And some empty of influence
But from the water-winds,
Free as love's green attractions are.

Smoke bitter and blue from farms.
And points of feeble light in houses
Come after them in the scale
Of the material and the beautiful;
Are not less complex but less delicate
And less important than these living
Instruments of space,
Whose quiet communication is
With older trees in ships on the grey waves:
An order and a music
Like a writing on the skies
Too private for the reason or the pen;
Too simple even for the heart's surprise.

II

NEAR EL ALAMEIN

This rough field of sudden war—
This sand going down to the sea, going down,
Was made without the approval of love,
By a general death in the desire for living.
Time got the range of impulse here:
On old houses with no thought of armies,
Burnt guns, maps and firing:
All the apparatus of man's behaviour
Put by in memories for books on history:
A growth like these bitter
Green bulbs in the hollow sand here.
But ideas and language do not go.
The rate of the simple things—
Men walking here, thinking of houses,
Gardens, or green mountains or beliefs:
Units of the dead in these living armies,
Making comparison of this bitter heat,
And the living sea, giving up its bodies,
Level and dirty in the mist,
Heavy with sponges and the common error.

1946/1946

LEVANT

Gum, oats and syrup
The Arabians bore.
Evoking nothing from the sea but more
And more employ to christen them
With whips of salt and glittering spray,
Their wooden homes rocked on the chastening salt.

Lamps on altars, breath of children;
So coming and going with their talk of bales,
Lading and enterprises marked out
And fell on this rusty harbour
Where tills grew fat with cash
And the quills of Jews invented credit,
And in margins folded up
Bales, gum-arabic, and syrup;
Syrian barley in biffed coracles
Hugging the burking gulf or blown
As cargoes from the viny breath
Of mariners, the English or the Dutch.
In manners taught them nothing much
Beyond the endurance in the vile.
Left in history words like
Portuguese or Greek
Whose bastards can still speak and smile.

After this, lamps
Confused the foreigners;
Boys, women and drugs
Built this ant-hill for grammarians
Who fed upon the fathers fat with cash,
Turned oats and syrup here
To ribbons and wands and rash
Patents for sex and feathers,
Sweets for festivals and deaths.

Nothing changes. The indifferent
Or the merely good died off, but fixed
Here once the human type 'Levant'.
Something fine of tooth and with the soft
Hanging lashes to the eye,
Given once by Spain and kept
In a mad friendship here and sadness
By the promiscuous sea upon this spit of sand.

Something money or promises can buy.

1946/1946

GREEK CHURCH: ALEXANDRIA

The evil and the good seem undistinguished,
Indeed all half asleep; their coming was
No eloquent proposition of natures
Too dense for material ends, quartered in pain.
But a propitiation by dreams of belief
A relief from the chafing ropes of thought.

Piled high in Byzance like a treasure-ship
The church heels over, sinking in sound
And yellow lamplight while the arks and trolleys
And blazing crockery of the orthodox God
Make it a fearful pomp for peasants,
A sorcery to the black-coated rational,
To the town-girl an adventure, an adventure.

Now however all hums and softly spins
Like a great top, the many-headed black
Majority merged in a single sea-shell.

Idle thoughts press in, amazing one—
How the theologians with beards of fire
Divided us upon the boiling grid of thought,
Or with dividers spun for us a fine
Conniving cobweb—traps for the soul.

144

Three sailors stand like brooms.
The altar has opened like a honeycomb;
An erect and flashing deacon like a despot howls.
Surely we might ourselves exhale
Our faults like rainbows on this incense?

If souls did fire the old Greek barber
Who cut my hair this morning would go flying,
Not stand, a hopeless, window-bound and awkward
Child at this sill of pomp,
Moved by a hunger money could not sate,
Smelling the miracle and softly sighing.

1946/1946

NOTEBOOK[1]
For Eve

Mothers and sculptors work
By small rehearsed caresses in the block
Each to redeeming ends,
By shame or kisses print
Good citizens, good lovers and good friends.

Your impatient hero so admired
In all his epic scenery
Was such a vessel once, unfired,
A chaos on the wheel and rocked
In a muse on the womb's dark Galilee.

And the lovers, those two characters,
Who have their exits and their entrances,
A certain native style may give
As predetermined in the bone,
Speak through the crude gags of the grave.

Their luck and hazard rests, my dear,
So lightly on us in our dreams
As voices rich with tears,
Whom no poetic justice gave
A friendship mad as ours.

1946/1946

¹ Originally published as 'For Gipsy Cohen'.

EIGHT ASPECTS OF MELISSA

I

BY THE LAKE

If seen by many minds at once your image
As in a prism falling breaks itself,
Or looking upwards from a gleaming spoon
Defies: a smile squeezed up and vanishing
In roundels of diversion like the moon.

Yet here you are confirmed by the smallest
Wish or kiss upon the rising darkness
But rootless as a wick afloat in water,
Fatherless as shoes walking over dead leaves;
A patient whom no envy stirs but joy
And what the harsh chords of your experience leave—

This dark soft eye, so liquid now and hoarse
With pleasure: or your arms in mirrors
Combing out softly hair
As lovely as a planet's and remote.

How many several small forevers
Whispered in the rind of the ear
Melissa, by this Mediterranean sea-edge,
Captured and told?
How many additions to the total silence?

Surely we increased you by very little,
But as with a net or gun to make your victims men?

II

CAIRO[1]

Cut from the joints of this immense
Darkness upon the face of Egypt lying,
We move in the possession of our acts
Alone, the dread apostles of our weakness.

For look. The mauve street is swallowed
And the bats have begun to stitch slowly.
At the stable-door the carpenter's three sons
Bend over a bucket of burning shavings,
Warming their inwardness and quite unearthly
As the candle-marking time begins.

Three little magi under vast Capella,
Beloved of all as shy as the astronomer,
She troubles heaven with her golden tears,
Tears flowing down upon us at this window,
The children rapt, the mauve street swallowed,
The harps of flame among the shadows
In Egypt now and far from Nazareth.

[1] Also published as 'The Night'.

III

THE ADEPTS

Some, the great Adepts, found it
A lesser part of them—ashes and thorns—
Where this sea-sickness on a bed
Proved nothing calm and virginal,
But animal, unstable, heavy as lead.

Some wearied for a sex
Like a science of known relations:
A God proved through the flesh—or else a mother.
They dipped in this huge pond and found it
An ocean of shipwrecked mariners instead,
Cried out and foundered, losing one another.

But some sailed into this haven
Laughing, and completely undecided,
Expecting nothing more
Than the mad friendship of bodies,
And farewells undisguised by pride:

They wrote those poems—the diminutives of madness
While at a window someone stood and cried.

IV

THE ENCOUNTER

At this the last yet second meeting,
Almost the autumn was postponed for us—
Season when the fermenting lovers lie
Among the gathered bunches quietly.

So formal was it, so incurious:
The chime of glasses, the explorer,
The soldier and the secret agent
With a smile inviting like a target.

Six of a summer evening, you remember.
The painful rehearsal of the smile
And the words: 'I am going into a decline,
Promised by summer but by winter disappointed.'

The face was turned as sadly as a hare's,
Provoked by prudence and discretion to repeat:
'Some of them die, you know, or go away.
Our denials are only gestures—can we help it?'

Turn to another aspect of the thing.
The cool muslin dress shaken with flowers—
It was not the thought that was unworthy
Knowing all you knew, it was the feeling.

Idly turning from the offered tea I saw
As swimmers see their past, in the lamplight
Burning, particular, fastidious and lost
Your figure forever in the same place,
Same town and country, sorting letters
On a green table from many foreign cities,
The long hare's features, the remarkable sad face.

V

Petron, the Desert Father

Waterbirds sailing upon the darkness
Of Mareotis, this was the beginning:
Dry reeds touched by the shallow beaks he heard
On the sand trash of an estuary near Libya,
This dense yellow lake, ringing now
With the insupportable accents of the Word.

Common among the commoners of promise
He illustrated to the ordinary those
Who found no meaning in the flesh's weakness—
The elegant psychotics on their couches
In Alexandria, hardly tempted him,
With talk of business, war and lovely clothes.

The lemon-skinned, the gold, the half-aware
Were counters for equations he examined,
Grave as their statues fashioned from the life;
A pioneer in pleasure on the long
Linen-shaded colonnades he often heard
Girls' lips puff in the nostrils of the fife.

Now dense as clouded urine moved the lake
Whose waters were to be his ark and fort
By the harsh creed of water-fowl and snake,
To the wave-polished stone he laid his ear
And said: 'I dare not ask for what I hope,
And yet I may not speak of what I fear.'

VI

THE RISING SUN

Now the sun again, like a bloody convict,
Comes up on us, the wheels of everything
Hack and catch the luckless rising;
The newly married, the despairing,
The pious ant and groom,
Open like roses in the darkened bed-room.
The bonds are out and the debentures
Shape the coming day's adventures,
The revising of money by strategy or tears—

And here we lie like riders on a cloud
Whom kisses only can inform
In breath exhaling twenty thousand years
Of curses on the sun—but not too loud.

While the days of judgement keep,
Lucky ladies sleek with sleep,
Lucky ladies sleek with sleep.

VII

VISITATIONS

Left like an unknown's breath on mirrors,
The enchanters, the persuaders
Whom the seasons swallow up,
Only leave us ash in saucers,
Or to mice the last invaders
Open cupboard-doors or else
Lipstick-marks upon a cup.

Fingerprint the crook of time,
Ask him what he means by it,
Eyes and thoughts and lovely bodies,
David's singing, Daphne's wit
Like Eve's apple undigested
Rot within us bit by bit.

Experience in a humour ends,
Wrapped in its own dark metaphor,
And divining winter breaks:
Now one by one the Hungers creep
Up from the orchards of the mind
Here to trouble and confuse
Old men's after-dinner sleep.

VIII

A PROSPECT OF CHILDREN

All summer watch the children in the public garden,
The tribe of children wishing you were like them—
These gruesome little artists of the impulse
For whom the perfect anarchy sustains
A brilliant apprehension of the present,
In games of joy, of love or even murder
On this green springing grass will empty soon
A duller opiate, Loving, to the drains.

Cast down like asterisks among their toys,
Divided by the lines of daylight only
From adventure, crawl among the rocking-horses,
And the totems, dolls and animals and rings
To the tame suffix of a nursery sleep
Where all but few of them
The restless inventories of feeling keep.

Sleep has no walls. Sleep admits
The great Imago with its terror, yet they lie
Like something baking, candid cheek on finger,
With folded lip and eye
Each at the centre of the cobweb seeking
His boy or girl, begotten and confined
In terror like the edges of a table
Begot by passion and confirmed in error.

What can they tell the watcher at the window,
Writing letters, smoking up there alone,
Trapped in the same limitation of his growth
And yet not envying them their childhood
Since he endured his own?

1946/1946

POSSIBLE WORLDS

Suppose one died
Or ended this
This love like a long consumption,
Unlighted by a common kiss,
In desperation
To cut away, cut down,
This faithless hand
Like ivy clinging to your own,
Made solitariness not passion
The wild soul's iron ration . . .

Stars have winked out
A thousand year
But the numb star of death
The widow's mite and portion
Must never catch you here;
Only cut down and heal
Beneath the thorns of sense
And in this darkness dense
O feel again and find
The limb that will not bind.

Listen to them now,
The inner voices pleading:
'Death would not be
Like separation is or changing,
But a deep luxurious bleeding:
Last of the malaises, like
The muzzle of a dog that drops
In the darkness to your lap:
Softly you could take the cue.
No one would be watching you.'

So one recalls
As if deep underground
The fortune-teller's promises;
Your body idle now as sound,
Green as the hanging-tree,
And your sad mouth
Whose leaves are printed here
Where sky and landscape meet
Like virgins lame of touch,
Smiles, but says nothing much.

And so the long long
Parting wears us both away
To winterfall and the return;
Softly every night
The great horned branch of heaven rises
With its blossoms white;
And time bleeds in us like a wound
While the forest of the future
Separating stands,
Reaching out its hands.

1946/1946

ALEXANDRIA

To the lucky now who have lovers or friends,
Who move to their sweet undiscovered ends,
Or whom the great conspiracy deceives,
I wish these whirling autumn leaves:
Promontories splashed by the salty sea,
Groaned on in darkness by the tram
To horizons of love or good luck or more love—
As for me I now move
Through many negatives to what I am.

Here at the last cold Pharos between Greece
And all I love, the lights confide
A deeper darkness to the rubbing tide;
Doors shut, and we the living are locked inside
Between the shadows and the thoughts of peace:
And so in furnished rooms revise
The index of our lovers and our friends
From gestures possibly forgotten, but the ends
Of longings like unconnected nerves,
And in this quiet rehearsal of their acts
We dream of them and cherish them as Facts.

Now when the sea grows restless as a conscript,
Excited by fresh wind, climbs the sea-wall,
I walk by it and think about you all:
B. with his respect for the Object, and D.
Searching in sex like a great pantry for jars
Marked 'Plum and apple'; and the small, fell
Figure of Dorian ringing like a muffin-bell—
All indeed whom war or time threw up
On this littoral and tides could not move
Were objects for my study and my love.

And then turning where the last pale
Lighthouse, like a Samson blinded, stands
And turns its huge charred orbit on the sands
I think of you—indeed mostly of you,
In whom a writer would only name and lose
The dented boy's lip and the close
Archer's shoulders; but here to rediscover
By tides and faults of weather, by the rain
Which washes everything, the critic and the lover.

At the doors of Africa so many towns founded
Upon a parting could become Alexandria, like
The wife of Lot—a metaphor for tears;
And the queer student in his poky hot
Tenth floor room above the harbour hears
The sirens shaking the tree of his heart,
And shuts his books, while the most
Inexpressible longings like wounds unstitched
Stir in him some girl's unquiet ghost.

So we, learning to suffer and not condemn
Can only wish you this great pure wind
Condemned by Greece, and turning like a helm
Inland where it smokes the fires of men,
Spins weathercocks on farms or catches
The lovers at their quarrel in the sheets;
Or like a walker in the darkness might,
Knocks and disturbs the artist at his papers
Up there alone, upon the alps of night.

1946/1946

POGGIO

The rubber penis, the wig, the false breasts . . .
The talent for entering rooms backwards
Upon a roar of laughter, with his dumb
Pained expression, wheeling there before him
That mythological great hippo's bum:

'Who should it be but Poggio?' The white face,
Comical, flat, and hairless as a cheese.
Nose like a member: something worn:
A Tuscan fig, a leather can, or else,
A phallus made of putty and slapped on.

How should you know that behind
All this the old buffoon concealed a fear—
And reasonable enough—that he might be
An artist after all? Always after this kind
Of side-splitting evening, sitting there
On a three-legged stool and writing, he

Hoped poems might form upon the paper.
But no. Dirty stories. The actress and the bishop.
The ape and the eunuch. This crapula clung
To him for many years between his dinners . . .
He sweated at them like a ham unhung.

And like the rest of us hoped for
The transfigured story or the mantic line
Of poetry free from this mortuary smell.
For years slept badly—who does not?
Took bribes, and drugs, ate far too much and dreamed.
Married unwisely, yes, but died quite well.

1946/1946

BLIND HOMER

A winter night again, and the moon
Loosely inks in the marbles and retires.

The six pines whistle and stretch and there,
Eastward the loaded brush of morning pauses

Where the few Grecian stars sink and revive
Each night in glittering baths of sound.

Now to the winter each has given up
Deciduous stuff, the snakeskin and the antler,

Cast skin of poetry and the grape.

Blind Homer, the lizards still sup the heat
From the rocks, and still the spring,

Noiseless as coins on hair repeats
Her diphthong after diphthong endlessly.

Exchange a glance with one whose art
Conspires with introspection against loneliness

This February 1946, pulse normal, nerves at rest:
Heir to a like disorder, only lately grown

Much more uncertain of his gift with words,
By this plate of olives, this dry inkwell.

1948/1946

FABRE

The ants that passed
Over the back of his hand,
The cries of welcome, the tribes, the tribes!

Happier men would have studied
Children, more baffling than pupae,
Their conversation when alone, their voices,

The dream at the tea-table or at geography:
The sense of intimacy when moving in lines
Like caterpillars entering a cathedral.

He refused to examine the world except
Through the stoutest glasses;
A finger of ground covered with pioneers.

A continent on a bay-leaf moving.
If real women were like moths he didn't notice.
There was not a looking-glass in the whole house.

Ah! but one day he might dress
In this black discarded business suit,
Fly heavily out on to the lawn at Arles.

What friendships lay among the flowers!
If he could be a commuter among the bees,
This pollen-hunter of the exact observation!

1946/1946

CITIES, PLAINS AND PEOPLE
(Beirut 1943)

I

Once in idleness was my beginning,

Night was to the mortal boy
Innocent of surface like a new mind
Upon whose edges once he walked
In idleness, in perfect idleness.

O world of little mirrors in the light.
The sun's rough wick for everybody's day:
Saw the Himalayas like lambs there
Stir their huge joints and lay
Against his innocent thigh a stony thigh.

Combs of wind drew through this grass
To bushes and pure lakes
On this tasteless wind
Went leopards, feathers fell or flew:
Yet all went north with the prayer-wheel,
By the road, the quotation of nightingales.

Quick of sympathy with springs
Where the stone gushed water
Women made their water like thieves.

Caravans paused here to drink Tibet.
On draughty corridors to Lhasa
Was my first school
In faces lifted from saddles to the snows:
Words caught by the soft klaxons crying
Down to the plains and settled cities.

So once in idleness was my beginning.
Little known of better then or worse
But in the lens of this great patience
Sex was small,
Death was small,
Were qualities held in a deathless essence,
Yet subjects of the wheel, burned clear
And immortal to my seventh year.

To all who turn and start descending
The long sad river of their growth:
The tidebound, tepid, causeless
Continuum of terrors in the spirit,
I give you here unending
In idleness an innocent beginning

Until your pain become a literature.

II

Nine marches to Lhasa.

Kùrseong:
India
The Nepalese
ayah
Kasim

Those who went forward
Into this honeycomb of silence often
Gained the whole world: but often lost each other.
In the complexion of this country tears
Found no harbour in the breast of rock.
Death marched beside the living as a friend
With no sad punctuation by the clock.

159

But he for whom steel and running water
Were roads, went westward only
To the prudish cliffs and the sad green home
Of Pudding Island o'er the Victorian foam.

Here all as poets were pariahs.
Some sharpened little follies into hooks
To pick upon the language and survive.
Some in search could only found
Pulpits of smoke like Blake's *Jerusalem.*

For this person it was never landfall,
With so many representative young men
And all the old being obvious in feeling,
But like good crafty men

He saw the business witches in their bowlers,
The blackened Samsons of the green estate,
The earls from their cockney-boxes calling,
And knew before it was too late, London
Could only be a promise-giving kingdom.

Yet here was a window
Into the great sick-room, Europe,
With its dull set-books,
The Cartesian imperatives, Dante and Homer,
To impress the lame and awkward newcomer.

Here he saw Bede who softly
Blew out desire and went to bed,
So much greater than so many less
Who made their unconquered guilt in atrophy
A passport to the dead.
Here St. Augustine took the holy cue
Of bells in an English valley; and mad Jerome
Made of his longing half a home from home.

*'In Rimbaud
the sense of
guilt was
atrophied,
not con-
quered'
Henry
Miller*

Scythes here faithfully mark
In their supple practice paths
For the lucky and unambitious owners.
But not a world as yet. Not a world.

Death like autumn falls
On the lakes its sudden forms, on walls
Where everything is made more marginal
By the ruling planes of the snow;
Reflect how Prospero was born to a green cell
While those who noted the weather-vane
In Beatrice's shadow sang
With the dying Emily: 'We shall never
Return, never be young again'.

The defeat of purpose in days and lichens.
Some here unexpectedly put on the citizen,
Go walking to a church
By landscape rubbed in rain to grey
As wool on glass,
Thinking of spring which never comes to stay.

(The potential passion hidden, Wordsworth
In the desiccated bodies of postmistresses.
The scarlet splash of campion, Keats.
Ignorant suffering that closes like a lock.)

So here at last we did outgrow ourselves.
As the green stalk is taken from the earth,
With a great juicy sob, I turned him from a Man
To Mandrake, in Whose awful hand I am.

III

Prospero upon his island
Cast in a romantic form,
When his love was fully grown
He laid his magic down.

Truth within the tribal wells,
Innocent inviting creature
Does not rise to human spells
But by paradox

Teaches all who seek for her
That no saint or seer unlocks
The wells of truth unless he first
Conquer for the truth his thirst.

IV

So one fine year to where the roads
Dividing Europe meet in Paris.

The gnome was here and the small
Unacted temptations. Tessa was here whose dark
Quickened hair had brushed back rivers,
Trembling with stars by Buda,
In whose inconstant arms he waited   *Paris*
For black-hearted Descartes to seek him out   *H.V.M.*
With all his sterile apparatus.   *Anaïs*
Now man for him became a thinking lobe,   *Nancy*
Through endless permutations sought repose.   *Teresa*
By frigid latinisms he mated now
To the hard frame of prose the cogent verb.

To many luck may give for merit
More profitable teachers. To the heart
A critic and a nymph:
And an unflinching doctor to the spirit.

All these he confined in metaphors,
She sleeping in his awkward mind
Taught of the pace of women or birds
Through the leafy body of man
Enduring like the mammoth, like speech
From the dry clicking of the greater apes
To these hot moments in a reference of stars
Beauty and death, how sex became
A lesser sort of speech, and the members doors.

V

Faces may settle sadly
Each into its private death
By business travel or fortune,
Like the fat congealing on a plate
Or the fogged negative of labour
Whose dumb fastidious rectitude
Brings death in living as a sort of mate.

*'All bearings
are true'*.
The
Admiralty
Pilot

Here however man might botch his way
To God via Valéry, Gide or Rabelais.
All rules obtain upon the pilot's plan
So long as man, not manners, makyth man.
Some like the great Victorians of the past
Through old Moll Flanders sailed before the mast,
While savage Chatterleys of the new romance
Get carried off in Sex, the ambulance.
All rules obtain upon the pilot's chart
If governed by the scripture of the heart.

VI

Now November visiting with rain
Surprises and humbles with its taste of elsewhere,
Licks in the draughty galleries there,
Like a country member quickened by a province,
Turning over books and leaves in haste,
Takes at last her slow stains of waste
Down the stone stairs into the rivers.

163

And in the personal heart, weary
Of the piercing innocents in parks
Who sail the rapt subconscious there like swans,
Disturbs and brightens with her tears, thinking:

'Perhaps after all it is we who are blind,
While the unconscious eaters of the apple
Are whole as ingots of a process
Punched in matter by the promiscuous Mind.'

VII

By the waters of Buda
We surrendered arms, hearts, hands,
Lips for counting of kisses,
Fingers for money or touch,
Eyes for the hourglass sands.

Uncut and unloosened
Swift hair by the waters of Buda
In the shabby balcony rooms
Where the pulses waken and wonder
The churches bluff one as heart-beats
On the river their dull boom booms.

By the waters of Buda
Uncomb and unlock then,
Abandon and nevermore cherish
Queer lips, queer heart, hands.
There to futurity leave
The luckier lover who's waiting,
As, like a spring coiled up,
In the bones of Adam, lay Eve.

So Time, the lovely and mysterious
With promises and blessings moves
Through her swift degrees,
So gladly does he bear
Towards the sad perfect wife,
The rocky island and the cypress-trees.

Taken in the pattern of all solitaries,
An only child, of introspection got,
Her only playmates, lovers, in herself.
Nets were too coarse to hold her
Where the nymph broke through
And only the encircling arms of pleasure held.

Here for the five lean dogs of sense
Greece moved in calm memorial
Through her own unruffled blue,
Bearing in rivers upside down
The myrtle and the olive, in ruins
The faces of the innocents in wells.

Salt and garlic, water and dry bread,
Greek bread from the comb they knew
Like an element in sculpture:
By these red aerial cherries,
Or flawed grapes painted green
But pouted into breasts: as well
By those great quarries of the blood—
The beating crimson hearts of the grenades:
All far beyond the cupidity of verses
Or the lechery of images to tell.

Here worlds were confirmed in him.

Differences that matched like cloth
Between the darkness and the inner light,
Moved on the undivided breath of blue.
Formed moving, trees asserted here
Nothing but simple comparisons to
The artist's endearing eye.

Sleep. Napkins folded after grace.

Veins of stealing water
By the unplumbed ruins, never finding peace.
A watershed, a valley of tombs,
Never finding peace.

'Look' she might say 'Press here
With your fingers at the temples.
Are they not the blunt uncut horns
Of the small naked Ionian fauns?'

Much later, moving in a dark,
Snow-lit landscape softly
In her small frock walked his daughter
And a simile came into his mind
Of lovers, like swimmers lost at sea,
Exhausted in each other's arms,
Urgent for land, but treading water.

IX

Red Polish mouth,
Lips that as for the flute unform,
Gone round on nouns or vowels,
To utter the accepting, calm
'Yes', or make terrible verbs
Like 'I adore, adore'.

Persuader, so long hunted
By your wild pack of selves,
Past peace of mind or even sleep,
So longed for and so sought,
May the divider always keep
Like unshed tears in lashes
Love, the undeclarèd thought.

X

Athens.
Katsimbalis,
Wallace and
Anna
Southam.
Seferiades
Stephanides

Now earth turns her cold shoulders to us,
Autumn with her wild packs
Comes down to the robbing of the flowers.
On this unstained sky, printless
Snow moves crisp as dreamers' fingers,
And the rate of passion or tenderness
In this island house is absolute.

Within a time of reading
Here is all my growth
Through the bodies of other selves,
In books, by promise or perversity
My mutinous crew of furies—their pleading
Threw up at last the naked sprite
Whose flesh and noise I am,
Who is my jailor and my inward night.

'Anya, my
angel, my
darling. This
is an act of
folly I'm com-
mitting, a
feebleness, a
crime, I know
it, but . . .'
Dostoevsky's
Letters to his
wife

In Europe, bound by Europe,
I saw them moving, the possessed
Fëdor and Anna, the last
Two vain explorers of our guilt,
Turn by turn holding the taws,
Made addicts of each other lacking love,
Friendless embittered and alone.
The lesser pities held them back
Like mice in secrecies,
Yet through introspection and disease,
Held on to the unflinching bone,
The sad worn ring of Anna,
Loyal to filth and weakness,
Hammered out on this slender bond,
Fëdor's raw cartoons and episodes.
By marriage with this ring,
Companioned each their darkness.
In cracked voices we can hear
These hideous mommets now
Like westering angels over Europe sing.

XI

So knowledge has an end,
And virtue at the last an end,
In the dark field of sensibility
The unchanging and unbending;
As in aquariums gloomy
On the negative's dark screen
Grow the shapes of other selves,
So groaned for by the heart,
So seldom grasped if seen.

Love bears you. Time stirs you.
Music at midnight makes a ground,
Or words on silence so perplex
In hidden meanings there like bogies
Waiting the expected sound.

Art has limits and life limits
Within the nerves that support them.

So better with the happy
Discover than with the wise
Who teach the sad valour
Of endurance through the seasons,
In change the unchanging
Death by compromise.

XII

Now darkness comes to Europe
Dedicated by a soft unearthly jazz.
The greater hearts contract their joys
By silence to the very gem,
While the impertinent reformers,
Barbarians with secretaries move,
Whom old Cavafy pictured,
Whom no war can remove.

Alexandria
'The mythical
Yellow Em-
peror, first
exponent of
the Tao'.
Classical
Chinese
Philosophy

Through the ambuscades of sex,
The follies of the will, the tears,
Turning, a personal world I go
To where the yellow emperor once
Sat out the summer and the snow,
And searching in himself struck oil,
Published the first great Tao
Which all confession can only gloze
And in the Consciousness can only spoil.

Apparent opposition of the two
Where unlocked numbers show their fabric,
He laid his finger to the map,
And where the signs confuse,
Defined the Many and the None
As base reflections of the One.

What bifid Hamlet in the maze
Wept to find; the *döppelgänger*
Goethe saw one morning go
Over the hill ahead; the man
So gnawed by promises who shared
The magnificent responses of Rimbaud.
All that we have sought in us,
The artist by his greater cowardice
In sudden brush-strokes gave us clues—
Hamlet and Faust as front-page news.
The yellow emperor first confirmed
By one Unknown the human calculus,
Where feeling and idea,
Must fall within this space,
This personal landscape built
Within the Chinese circle's calm embrace.

Dark Spirit, sum of all
That has remained unloved,
Gone crying through the world:
Source of all manufacture and repair,
Quicken the giving-spring
In ferns and birds and ordinary people
That all deeds done may share,
By this our temporal sun,
The part of living that is loving,
Your dancing, a beautiful behaviour.

Darkness, who contain
The source of all this corporal music,
On the great table of the Breath
Our opposites in pity bear,
Our measure of perfection or of pain,
Both trespassers in you, that then
Our Here and Now become your Everywhere.

*'Duality,
the great
European
art-subject,
which is re-
solved by the
Taoist
formulas'.
Anaïs Nin*

*'The Con-
tinuous I be-
hind dis-
continuous
Me's'.
E. Graham
Howe*

XIII

The old yellow Emperor
With defective sight and matted hair
His palace fell to ruins
But his heart was in repair.

Veins like imperfect plumbing
On his flesh described a leaf.
His palms were mapped with cunning
Like geodesies of grief.

His soul became a vapour
And his limbs became a stake
But his ancient heart still visits us
In Lawrence or in Blake.

XIV

All cities plains and people
Reach upwards to the affirming sun,
All that's vertical and shining,
Lives well lived,
Deeds perfectly done,
Reach upwards to the royal pure
Affirming sun.

Accident or error conquered
By the gods of luck or grace,
Form and face,
Tribe or caste or habit,
All are aspects of the one
Affirming race.

Ego, my dear, and id
Lie so profoundly hid
In space-time void, though feeling,
While contemporary, slow,
We conventional lovers cheek to cheek
Inhaling and exhaling go.

The rose that Nostradamus
In his divining saw
Break open as the world;
The city that Augustine
Founded in moral law,
By our anguish were compelled
To urge, to beckon and implore.

Dear Spirit, should I reach,
By touch or speech corrupt,
The inner suffering word,
By weakness or idea,
Though you might suffer
Feel and know,
Pretend you do not hear.

XV

Bombers bursting like pods go down
And the seed of Man stars
This landscape, ancient but no longer known.
Only the critic perseveres
Within his ant-like formalism
By deduction and destruction steers;
Only the trite reformer holds his own.

See looking down motionless
How clear Athens or Bremen seem
A mass of rotten vegetables
Firm on the diagram of earth can lie;
And here you may reflect how *genus epileptoid*
Knows his stuff; and where rivers
Have thrown their switches and enlarged
Our mercy or our knowledge of each other
Wonder who walks beside them now and why,
And what they talk about.

There is nothing to hope for, my Brother.
We have tried hoping for a future in the past.
Nothing came out of that past
But the reflected distortion and some
Enduring, and understanding, and some brave.
Into their cool embrace the awkward and the sinful
Must be put for they alone
Know who and what to save.

XVI

Small temptations now—to slumber and to sleep,
Where the lime-green, odourless
And pathless island waters
Crossing and uncrossing, partnerless
By hills alone and quite incurious
Their pastures of reflection keep.

For Prospero remains the evergreen
Cell by the margin of the sea and land,
Who many cities, plains, and people saw
Yet by his open door
In sunlight fell asleep
One summer with the Apple in his hand.

1946/1946

RODINI

Windless plane-trees above Rodini
To the pencil or the eye are tempters

Where of late trees have become ears in leaf
Curved for the cicada's first monotony.

Hollow the comb, mellow the sweetness
Amber the honey-spoil, drink, drink.

In these windless unechoing valleys
The mind slips like a chisel-hand

Touching the surface of this clement blue
Yet must not damage the solitary Turk

Gathering his team and singing, in whose brain
The same disorder and the loneliness—

The what-we-have-in-common of us all.
Is there enough perhaps to found a world?

Then of what you said once, the passing
Of something on the road beyond the tombstones

Reflecting on dark hair with its sudden theft
Of blue from the darkness of violets

And below the nape of the neck a mole
All mixed in this odourless water-clock of hours.

So one is grateful, yes, to the ancient Greeks
For the invention of time, lustration of penitents,

Not so much for what they were
But for where we lie under the windless planes.

1948/1946

IN THE GARDEN: VILLA CLEOBOLUS

The mixtures of this garden
Conduct at night the pine and oleander,
Perhaps married to dust's thin edge
Or lime where the cork-tree rubs
The quiet house, bruising the wall:

And dense the block of thrush's notes
Press like a bulb and keeping time
In this exposure to the leaves,
And as we wait the servant comes,

174

A candle shielded in the warm
Coarse coral of her hand, she weaves
A pathway for her in the golden leaves,
Gathers the books and ashtrays in her arm
Walking towards the lighted house,

Brings with her from the uninhabited
Frontiers of the darkness to the known
Table and tree and chair
Some half-remembered passage from a fugue
Played from some neighbour's garden
On an old horn-gramophone,

And you think: if given once
Authority over the word,
Then how to capture, praise or measure
The full round of this simple garden,
All its nonchalance at being,
How to adopt and raise its pleasure?

Press as on a palate this observed
And simple shape, like wine?
And from the many undeserved
Tastes of the mouth select the crude
Flavour of fruit in pottery
Coloured among this lovely neighbourhood?

Beyond, I mean, this treasure hunt
Of selves, the pains we sort to be
Confined within the loving chamber of a form,
Within a poem locked and launched
Along the hairline of the normal mind?

Perhaps not this: but somehow, yes,
To outflank the personal neurasthenia
That lies beyond in each expiring kiss:
Bring joy, as lustrous on this dish
The painted dancers motionless in play
Spin for eternity, describing for us all
The natural history of the human wish.

1948/*1947*

ETERNAL CONTEMPORARIES:
SIX PORTRAITS

I

MANOLI OF COS

Down there below the temple
Where the penitents scattered
Ashes of dead birds, Manoli goes
In his leaky boat, a rose tied to the rudder.

This is not the rose of all the world,
Nor the rose of Nostradamus or of Malory:
Nor is it Eliot's clear northern rose of the mind,
But precisely and unequivocally
The red rose Manoli picked himself
From the vocabulary of roses on the hill by Cefalù.

1948/*1947*

II

MARK OF PATMOS

Mark has crossed over to Mount Olivet,
Putting aside the banneret and the drum.
He inhabits now that part of himself
Which lay formerly desolate and uncolonized.
He works that what is to pass may come
And the birth of the common heart be realized.

What passed with him? A flower dropped
In the boat by a friend, the cakes
His sister brought with the unposted letter.
Yet all the island loafers watched, disturbed,
The red sails melt into the sky, distended,
And each turned angrily to his lighted house
Feeling, not that something momentous
Had begun, but that their common childhood
Had foundered in the Syrian seas and ended.

1948/1947

III

BASIL THE HERMIT

Banished from the old roof-tree Patmos
Where the dynasts gathered honey,
Like dancing bears, with smoking rituals,
Or skimmed the fat of towns with levy-money,
Uncaring whether God or Paradise exist,
Laid up themselves estates in providence
While greed crouched in each hairy fist,

Basil, the troubled flower of scepticism,
Chose him a pelt, and a cairn of chilly stone,
Became the author of a famous schism:
A wick for oil, a knife, a broken stool
Were all, this side of hell, he dared to own.
For twenty years in Jesus went to school.

Often, looking up, he saw them there
As from some prism-stained pool:
Dark dots like birds along the battlements,
Old rooks swayed in a rotten tree.
They waved: he did not answer, although he
Felt kindly to them all, for they could do
What he could not: he did not dare to pray.
His inner prohibitions were a sea
On which he floated spellbound day by day.

World and its fevers howled outside: within
The Omen and the Fret that hemmed him in,
The sense of his complete unworthiness
Pressed each year slowly tighter like a tourniquet.

1948/1947

IV

DMITRI OF CARPATHOS

Four card-players: an ikon of the saint
On a pitted table among eight hands
That cough and spit or close like manacles
On fortunate court-cards or on the bottle
Which on the pitted paintwork stands.
Among them one whose soft transpontine nose
Fuller of dirty pores pricked on a chart
Has stood akimbo on the turning world,
From Cimbalu to Smyrna shaken hands,
Tasted the depths of every hidden sound:
In wine or poppy a drunkard with a drunkard's heart
Who never yet was known to pay his round.

Meanwhile below in harbour his rotten boat,
Beard green from winter quarters turns
Her scraggy throat to nudge the northern star,
And like a gipsy burns and burns; goes wild
Till something climbs the hill
And stands beside him at the tavern table
To pluck his drunken elbow like a child.

1948/1947

PANAGIOTIS OF LINDOS

Dark birds in nature redevise
Their linings every year: are not
The less like these weaving fishermen
Bent so exactly at their tattered seines
On a rotten wharf, their molten catch
Now sold and loaded: though they feather only
For fathoms of sea and the fishes within it,
Needles passing in a surf of lights.

Panagiotis has resigned it all
For an enamel can and olive shade:
His concern a tavern prospect,
Miles of sweet chestnut and borage.

This armament of wine he shares now
With the greatest philosopher, the least
Inventor, the meanest doctrine of rest,
Mixing leisure and repose like wine and water,
Tutor and pupil in the crater.

His dark sleep is bruised by each
Sink of the sun below the castle
Where the Sporades have opened
Their spokes, and the whole Aegean
In brilliant soda turns the darkening bays.

1948/1948

VI

A RHODIAN CAPTAIN

Ten speechless knuckles lie along a knee
Among their veins, gone crooked over voyages,
Made by this ancient captain. Life has now
Contracted like the pupil of an eye
To a slit in space and time for images—

All he has seen of sage and arbutus:
Touched berries where the golden eagle crashes
From its chariot of air and dumb trap:
Islands fortunate as Atlantis was . . .
Yet while we thought him voyaging through life
He was really here, in truth, outside the doorpost,
In the shade of the eternal vine, his wife,
With the same tin plate of olives on his lap.

1948/1947

ELEGY ON THE CLOSING OF THE FRENCH BROTHELS
For Henry Miller and George Katsimbalis

I

Last of the great autumnal capitals
Disengaging daily like a sword
The civil codes, behaviour, friendship, love,
In houses of shining glass,
On tablecloths stained with pools of light,
By the rambling river's evening scents
Carried our freight of pain so lightly:
And towards evening when the inkwells overturn
And at last the figure which has sat
Motionless for hours, pours himself out
One glass of moonlight, drinks it, and retires.

By the railway arches a stone plinth.
Under the shadows of the lamps the figures.
So many ways of dividing up the self:
Correspondences moving outwards along a line
Of nerves, the memory of letters
Smelling like apples in an empty cupboard,
And at midnight the pall of clocks,
At odds among themselves, the shuffling
Of innumerable packs of cards where each shall see
One day his face instead of fortune's be.

II

Bound here to the great axis of the sex,
Black source that feeds your manners, gives
Information and vivacity to food and linen,
Determined as the penetration into self-abuse—
For each separation by kisses forges new bonds:
Three or four words on the back of a letter,
Tessa waiting on a corner with all she feels,
Rain glittering in that peacock's eye,
As heavy with sense as a king's letter with seals.

Here the professional observer met you,
The amateur in melancholy,
To the swish of an invisible fountain,
Drinking from a glass under a man on horseback,
Talking to a lady with a poisoned finger.

Women turned over by the mind and each
A proper noun, an act of trespass,
Improper for its aberration but accepted
As in a mirror one is twice but accepts.
So in these magazines of love they moved,
Experience misbegotten in each face like rings
In wood, were commentators on our weakness,
Through cycles of repentance in the blood,
Exhausted the body's ugly contents in a sigh,
Left, hard as ash, the object's shape: an art
Eros began, self-murder carries on.

III

Of all the sicknesses, autumnal Paris,
This self-infection was the best, where friends
Like self-possession could be learned
Through the mystery of a slit
Like a tear in an old fur coat,
A hole in a paper lantern where the seeing I
Looked out and measured one:
The ferocious knuckle of a sex
Standing to acknowledge like a hambone
Our membership in the body of a tribe
Holy and ridiculous at once:
Symbol of unrecognised desire, pain, pain.

You might have seen silence flower in eyes,
The tobacco eyes of every human critic,
Or a mouth laid along the meniscus
Of a lighted glass blazing like a diamond.

All the great brothels closed save Sacré Coeur!
Windows boarded up from the inheritors,
The nameless donors inhabiting marble fanes
On peninsulas with cocks of gold in sunlight,
Under the oleanders, printed in warm moss,
The bare ankles playing on a flute,
Selecting the bodies of boys, the temporary
Refuge for a kiss on the silver backs of mirrors:
Powder of statues in a grove born old,
Born sightless, wingless, never to be loved.

IV

Crude man in his coat of nerves and hair
Whose kisses like apostles go about
On translated business never quite his own,
Derives from the obscure medium of the body,
As through some glass coffin, a retrievéd sprite,
Himself holding the holy bottle, fast asleep.

All these rotten galleries were symbols
Of us, where the girls like squirrels
Leaned in the tarnished mirrors sadly sighing:
The wind in empty clothing, while the destroyer
Sorted the bottles for just the right medicine.

Below us, far below on the stairway somewhere
Tessa had already combed the dark disorder
Of curls, the flash of pectorals in a mirror,
Invented already this darker niece of Egypt,
Who leaves the small hashish-pipe by the pillow,
Uneasy in red slippers like the dust in urns,
The smashed columns, wells full of leaves,
The faces white as burns.

V

We suffer according to the terms we make
With time in cities: allowing to be rooted from us
Like useless teeth the few great healers
Who understand the penalties of confession,
And cannot fear these half-invented Gods,
Inhabiting our own cities of unconquered pain.

Now the capitals settle slowly in the sea
Of their failures. All the common brute has done
Building like a rat the rotten shanties
Of his self-esteem beside the water's edge,
His fear and prejudice into a dead index.
It is not enough. We have still to outgrow
The prohibitions in us with the fears they grow from:
For the beloved will be no happier
Nor the unloved less hungry when the miracle begins:
Yet both will be ineffably disclosed
In their own natures by simplicity
Like roses in a giving off of grace.

1948/1947

Puisqu'il lui est interdit d'éluder la contradiction aussi bien par le divertissement que par le suicide ou par le 'saut' mystique, quelle forme de vie adoptera L'Homme Absurde pour rester fidèle à sa vocation de lucidité?

Il s'attache à dégager non seulement l'opacité d'un corps de pierre ou d'une 'chose de beauté', mais aussi l'objectivité angoissante du Moi à l'égard du Je.

C'est ainsi que le Séducteur, le Comédien, le Conquérant et L'Artiste présentent ces traits communs de vivre dans L'Immédiat, de tendre à un renouvellement indéfini de leurs expériences, de sauvegarder à chaque moment leur lucidité dérisoire et leur libre disponibilité, d'accepter, enfin, le risque d'être damnés ou condamnés pour n'avoir prétendu recevoir leur bonheur que de leurs propres mains.

Le Sens de L'Absurde
GEORGES BLIN

POMONA DE MAILLOL
For Eve

An old man tamed his garden with wet clay
Until Pomona rose, a bubble in his arms.

The time and place grow ripe when the idea
Marries its proper image in volition,
When desire and intention kiss and bruise.

A cord passed round the body of the mermaid
Drew her sleeping from the underworld,
As when the breath of resin like a code
Rises from some unguarded still, Pomona
Breathing, surely a little out of breath
The image disengaging from the block,
A little out of breath, and wondering

If art is self-reflection, *who* he was
She woke within the side of, *what* old man
In his smock and dirty cap of cloth,
Drinking through trembling fingers now
A ten year siege of her, the joy in touching
The moistened flanks of her idea with all
An old man's impatience of the carnal wish?

1948/1948

ANNIVERSARY
For T. S. Eliot

Poetry, science of intimacies,
In you his early roots drove through
The barbarian compost of our English
To sound new veins and marbled all his verses
Through and through like old black ledgers,
Hedging in pain by form, and giving
Quotations from the daily treaty poets make
With men, possessions or a private demon:
Became at last this famous solitary
Sitting at one bleak uncurtained window
Over wintry London patiently repeating
That art is determined by its ends
In conscience and in morals. This was startling.
Yet marriages might be arranged between
Old fashions and contemporary disorders.
Sole student of balance in a falling world
He helped us mend the little greenstick fractures
Of our verse, taught polish in austerity.

Others who know him will add private humours,
And photographs to albums; taken near Paris,
Say, drinking among some foreign dons all night
From leather bubbles in a tavern: a remark
That silenced a fussy duke: yet these
Alluding and delimiting can only mystify
The singer and his mystery more, they do not chain.
Neither may we ever explain but pointing
To a new star one needs new vision for
Like some late hornbeam risen over England,
Relate it to a single sitting man,
In a high window there, beside a lamp,
Some crumpled paper, a disordered bed.

1980/1948

THE CRITICS

They never credit us
With being bad enough
The boys that come to edit us:
Of simply not caring when a prize,
Something for nothing, comes our way,
A wife, a mistress, or a holiday
From People living neckfast in their lies.

No: Shakespear's household bills
Could never be responsible, they say,
For all the heartbreak and the 1,000 ills
His work is heir to, poem, sonnet, play . . .
Emended readings give the real reason:
The times were out of joint, the loves, the season.

Man With A Message—how could you forget
To read your proofs, the heartache and the fret?
The copier or the printer
Must take the blame for it in all
The variants they will publish by the winter.

'By elision we quarter suffering.' Too true.
'From images and scansion can be learned.' . . .
Yet under it perhaps may be discerned
A something else afoot—a Thing
Lacking both precedent and name and gender:
An uncreated Weight which left its clue,
Making him run up bills,
Making him violent or distrait or tender:
Leaving for Stratford might have heard It say:
'Tell them I won't be back on Saturday.
My wife will understand I'm on a bender.'

And to himself muttering, muttering: 'Words
Added to words multiply the space
Between this feeling and my expressing It.
The wires get far too hot. Time smoulders
Like a burning rug. I *will* be free.' . . .

And all the time from the donkey's head
The lover is whispering: 'This is not
What I imagined as Reality.
If truth were needles surely eyes would see?'

1948/1948

PHILEREMO

A philosopher in search of human values
Might have seen something in the coarse
Black boots the guide wore when he led us:
Boots with cracked eyes and introspective
Laces, rich in historical error as this
Old wall we picked the moss from, reading
Into it invasions by the Dorians or Medes.

But the bearded arboreal historian
Saw nothing of it all, was nothing then.
His education had derailed the man
Until he moved, a literary reminiscence,
Through quotations only, fine as hair.

The stones spoke to him. Reflected there
In a cistern I heard you thinking: Europe
Also, the whole of our egopetal culture
Is done for and must vanish soon.

And still we have not undergone the poet's truth.

Could he comfort us in more than this
Blue sea and air cohering blandly
Across that haze of flats,
The smoking middens of our history—
Aware perhaps only of the two children
Asleep in the car beside a bear in cotton gloves?

1948/1948

SONG FOR ZARATHUSTRA

Le saltimbanque is coming with
His heels behind his head.
His smile is mortuary and
His whole expression dead.

The acrobat, the acrobat,
Demanding since the Fall
Little enough but hempen stuff
To climb and hang us all.

Mysterious inventions like
The trousers and the hat
Bewitched our real intentions:
We sewed the fig-leaves flat.

Man sewed his seven pockets
Upon his hairy clothes
But woman in her own white flesh
Has one she seldom shows.

An aperture on anguish,
A keyhole on disgrace:
The features stay grimacing
Upon the mossy face.

A cup without a handle
A staff without a crook,
The sawdust in the golly's head,
The teapot with the nook.

The Rib is slowly waking
Within the side of Man
And *le guignol* is making
Its faces while it can.

Compose us in the finder
Our organs upside down,
The parson in his widow's weeds,
The doctor in his gown.

What Yang and Yin divided
In one disastrous blunder
Must one day be united and
Let no man put asunder.

1948/1948

POLITICS
To George Seferis

Chemists might compare their properties:
The Englishman with his Apologising Bag,
The Ainu with interesting stone-age cuffs,
Or whoever invented stars as a witness:
Nations which through excess of sensibility
Repose in opium under a great leaf:
The French with their elastic manual code:
And so comparing, find the three common desires,
Of hunger, smiling, and of being loved.

Outside, I mean, the penumbra of the real
Mystery, the whole world as a Why.
Living purely in the naked How, so join
As the writer unites dissimilars
Or the doctor with his womb-bag joins
The cumbersome ends of broken bones in
A simple perishable function,
To exhale like a smoke ring the O: Joy.

1948/1948

THE DAILY MIRROR

Writing this stuff should not have been like
Suicide over some ordinary misapprehension:

A man going into his own house, say,
Turning out all the lights before undressing,

At the bedside of some lovely ignoramus
Whispering: 'Tomorrow I swear is the last time.'

Or: 'Believe, and I swear you will never die.'
This nib dragged out like the late train

Racing on iron bars for the north.
Target: another world, not necessarily better,

Of course, but different, completely different.
The hour-glass shifting its trash of seconds.

If it does not end this way perhaps some other.
Gossip lying in a furnished room, blinds drawn.

A poem with its throat cut from ear to ear.

1948/1948

SONG

Proffer the loaves of pain
Forward and back again,
By time's inflexible quantum
They shall not meet this autumn.

Stone islets, stars in stations,
Crab up their false equations,
Whether they run or saunter
They shall not meet this winter.

Boredom of breathless swan
Whiteness they gazed upon,
At skylight a roamer.
They shall not meet in summer.

Fast on these capes of green
Silence falls in between
Finger and wedding-ring.
They shall not meet in spring.

1948/1948

PENELOPE

Look, on that hill we met
On this shoreline parted.

The experts sailed off northwards
With their spears, with the connivance
Of oracles to back them. I remained.

Tears weigh little upon the hands,
Tears weigh less in the eye than seeds
Shaken from the feverish totals
Blossoming on time's pronouncing tree.

The seasons file their summaries
Overheard by the echoes in the wells,
Overlooked by the mirrors shod in horn,
Copied by spies, interpreters or witnesses.

The augurs in the delta have not *once*
Foreseen this dust upon an ageing eyeball,
Vitreous as sea-spun glass, this black
Sperm of winter sea we walk beside,
The marble onanism of these nymphs.

1948/*1948*

SWANS

Fraudulent perhaps in that they gave
No sense of muscle but a swollen languor
Though moved by webs: yet idly, idly
As soap-bubbles drift from a clay-pipe
They mowed the lake in tapestry,

Passing in regal exhaustion by us,
King, queen and cygnets, one by one.
Did one dare to remember other swans
In anecdotes of Gauguin or of Rabelais?
Some became bolsters for the Greeks,
Some rubber Lohengrins provided comedy.
The flapping of the wings excited Leda.
The procession is over and what is now
Alarming is more the mirror split
From end to end by the harsh clap
Of the wooden beaks, than the empty space
Which follows them about,
Stained by their whiteness when they pass.

We sit like drunkards and inhale the swans.

1948/1948

BERE REGIS

The colonial, the expatriate walking here
Awkwardly enclosing the commonwealth of his love
Stoops to this lovely expurgated prose-land
Where winter with its holly locks the schools
And spring with nature improvises
With the thrush on ploughland, with the scarecrow.

Moss walls, woollen forests, Shakespear, desuetude:
Roots of his language as familiar as salt
Inhaling cattle lick in this mnemonic valley
Where the gnats assort, the thrush familiarises,
And over his cottage a colloquial moon.

1948/1948

ON SEEMING TO PRESUME

On seeming to presume
Where earth and water plan
No place for him, no home
Outside the confining womb,
Mistake him if you can.
The rubber forceps do their job
And here at least stands man.

Refined by no technique
Beyond the great 'I will',
They pour the poison in,
Confuse the middle ear
Of his tormented dust,
Before the brute can speak
'I will' becomes 'I must'.

Excluded from the true
Participating love
His conscience takes its due
From this excluding sense
His condemnation brought.
From past to future tense
He mutters on 'I ought'.

He mutters on 'I ought'.

Yet daring to presume
He follows to the stews
His sense of loathsomeness,
Frustration, daily news.
A scholarship in hate
Endows him limb by limb.
'My mother pushed me from behind,
And so I learned to swim.'

The bunsen's head of hair,
All fancy free and passion,
Till iron circumstance
Confirms him in his lies,
To walk the Hamlet fashion.
He wrings his hands and cries
'I want to live', but dies.

He wants to live but dies.

Return, return and find
Beneath what bed or table
The lovers first in mind
Composed this poor unstable
Derivative of clay,
By passion or by play,
That bears the human label.

What king or saint could guide
This caliban of gloom
So swaddled in despair
To breathe the factory's air,
Or locked in furnished room
Weep out his threescore there
For daring to presume,

For daring to presume?

1948/1948

SELF TO NOT-SELF

Darkness, divulge my share in light
As man in name though not in nature.
Lay down truth's black hermetic wings
For less substantial things
To call my weight my own
By love's nomenclature:
Matriculate by harmlessness
From this tuistic zone,
Possessing what I almost own.

And where each heap of music falls
Burns like a star below the sea
To light the ocean's cracked saloons
And mirror its plurality
Through nature's tideless nights and noons
Teach me the mastery of the curse,
The bending circumstance to free,
And mix my better with my worse.

1960/*1948*

PATMOS

Early one morning unremarked
She walked abroad to see
Black bitumen and roses
Upon the island shelf
To hear those inexperienced
Thrushes repeat their clauses
From some corruptible tree
All copied in herself.

When from the Grecian meadows
Responsive rose the larks,
Stiffly as if on strings,
Ebbing, drew thin as tops
While each in rising squeezed
His spire of singing drops
On that renewed landscape
Like semen from the grape.

1948/1948

THE LOST CITIES
For Paddy and Xan

One she floats as Venice might,
Bloated among her ambiguities:
What hebetude or carelessness shored up
Goths were not smart enough to capture.
The city, yes: the water: not the style.

Her dispossession now may seem to us
Idle and ridiculous, quivering
In the swollen woodwork of these
Floating carcases of the doges,
Dissolving into spires and cages of water:
Venice blown up, and turning green.

Another wears out humbly like a craft:
Red wells where the potter's thumb
Sealed his jars of guaranteed oil.
That fluent thumb which presses
On history's vibrating string,
Pressing here, there, in a wounded place.

Some have left names only: Carthage:
Where the traveller may squeeze out
A few drops of ink or salt,
On deserted promontories may think:
'No wonder. A river once turned over
In its sleep and all the cities fled.'

Now in Greece which is not yet Greece
The adversary was also strong.
Yet here the serfs have built their discontents
As spiders do their junctions, here,
This orchard, painted tables set outside
A whitewashed house,
And on a rusty nail the violin
Is hanging by one wrist, still ownerless:

Disowned by the devastator and as yet
Uncherished by its tenants in the old
Human smells of excrement and cooking:
Waiting till the spades press through to us,
To be discovered, standing in our lives,

Rhodes, death-mask of a Greek town.

1948/*1948*

FUNCHAL

At Funchal the blackish yeast
Of the winter sea I hated rubbed
And gobbled on a thousand capes,
That crumble with the traveller's confidence
In being alone, some who still tread
Decks as if they were green lawns;
But the water coiled backwards
Like a spring to press its tides
Idle and uniform as grapes in presses
Descrying a horizontal mood,
The weather slowing like a pedal,
Smelling of sick and spices,
Red leather and the spermy polish
Men in boots rub boldly on to brass.
But night is always night even here,
Beyond the introspective glare
Of the green islands on the awnings,
St. Vincent copied in the pupils,
Marrow of romance and old sea-fevers,
Seen from a sanded rail above the sharks
On this half-deck polished like a nape.

1955/1948

HIGH SIERRA

The grass they cropped converting into speed
Made green the concert of their hooves
Over the long serene sierras turning
In the axle of the sun's eye
To legs as delicate as spiders', picking out
Pathways for shadows mounted on them:
Enigma, Fosforos, and Indigo, which rumbled
Through the pursuing quarries like a wind
To where the paths fall, and we all of us
Go down with the sun, sierra by sierra, held
A moment rising in the stirrups, then abandoned
To where the black valleys from their shoes
Subtract sparks upon flints, and the long
Quivering swish of tails on flesh
Try to say 'sleep', try to say 'food' and 'home'.

1960/1948

GREEN COCONUTS: RIO

At insular café tables under awnings
Bemused benighted half-castes pause
To stretch upon a table yawning
Ten yellow claws and
Order green coconuts to drink with straws.

Milk of the green loaf-coconuts
Which soon before them amputated stand,
Broken, you think, from some great tree of breasts,
Or the green skulls of savages trepanned.

Lips that are curved to taste this albumen,
To dredge with some blue spoon among the curds
Which drying on tongue or on moustache are tasteless
As droppings of bats or birds.

Re-enacting here a theory out of Darwin
They cup their yellow mandibles to shape
Their nuts, tilt them in drinking poses,
To drain them slowly from the very nape:
Green coconuts, green
Coconuts, patrimony of the ape.

1948/1948

CHRIST IN BRAZIL

Further from him whose head of woman's hair
Grew down his slender back
Or whose soft palms were puckered where
The nails were driven in,
Rising, denounced the dust they were,
Became white lofts of witness to the sin.

Both here and on that partworn map
The legionary darned for Rome,
Further from Europe even, in Brazil
Warmed by the jungle's sap,
Finding no home from home became
Dark consul for the countries of the Will.

Here named, there honoured, nowhere understood,
Riding over Rio on his cliffs of stone
Whose small original was wood,
In gradual petrifaction of his pain,
He spreads the conscript's slow barbaric stain
Over the cities of the flesh, his widowhood.

1948/1948

THE ANECDOTES

I

IN CAIRO

Garcia, when you drew off those two
White bullfighting gloves your hairy
Fingers spread themselves apart,
And then contracted to a hand again,
Attached to an arm, leading to a heart,
And I suddenly saw the cottage scene
Where the knocking on the door is repeated
Nobody answers it: but inside the room
The fox has its head under the madman's shirt.

II

IN CAIRO
Nostos home: *algos* pain: nostalgia ...

The homing pain for such as are attached:
Odours that hit and rebuff in some garden
Behind the consul's house, the shutters drawn:
In the dark street brushed by a woman's laugh.
Ursa Major to the sailor could spell wounds,
More than the mauling of the northern bear,
At the hub of the green wheel, standing on the sea.

Home for most is what you can least bear.
Ego gigno lumen, I beget light
But darkness is also of my nature.
(For such as sail out beyond
The proper limits of their own freewill.)

III

AT RHODES

Anonymous hand, record one afternoon,
In May, some time before the fig-leaf:
Boats lying idle in the sky, a town
Thrown as on a screen of watered silk,
Lying on its side, reddish and soluble,
A sheet of glass leading down into the sea . . .

Down here an idle boy catches a cicada:
Imprisons it, laughing, in his sister's cloak
In whose warm folds the silly creature sings.

Shape of boats, body of a young girl, cicada,
Conspire and join each other here,
In twelve sad lines against the dark.

IV

AT RHODES

If space curves how much the more thought,
Returning after every conjugation
To the young point of rest it started in?

The fulness of being is not in refinement,
By the delimitation of the object, but
In roundness, the embosoming of the Real.

The egg, the cone, the rhombus: orders of reality
Which declaim coldly against the reason:
We may surround and view from every side,

We may expound, break into fields of thought,
But qualifying in this manner only spoil:
On this derogatory wheel stands Man.

Now who is greater than his greatest appetite?
Who is weaker than the least of his fears?
Who claims that he can match them perfectly,
Apprehended without to unapprehended within?

We Greeks were taught how to exhaust ideas,
Melissa, but first begin with people. There we score!
No Roman understood our sunny concupiscence,
The fast republican colour of our values.

Philosophy with us was not worked out.
We used experience up. The rest precipitated.
Soon we were still alive: but nothing else was left.

V

In Athens

At last with four peroxide whores
Like doped marigolds growing upon this balcony,
We wait for sunrise, all conscripted
From our passions by the tedium and spleen,
While the rich dews are forming
On the mind of space already thick enough
To cut with scythes on the wet marbles
Of Acropolis, intentions murdered by the cold.
I take her in my arms, a cobweb full of diamonds,
Which by some culture might be tears or pearls. . . .

One speaks Turkish, slender as an ilex,
Half asleep is boiling an egg;
A Jewess, lovely, conspiratorial,
Over a spirit-lamp by an hour-glass
Too small to have been made for timing
Anything much longer than a kiss.

VI

AT ALEXANDRIA

Wind among prisms all tonight again:
Alone again, awake again in the Sufi's house,
Cumbered by this unexpiring love,
Jammed like a cartridge in the breech
Leaving the bed with its dented pillow,
The married shoes alert upon the floor.

Is life more than the sum of its errors?
Tubs of clear flesh, egyptian women:
Favours, kohl, nigger's taste of seeds,
Pepper or lemon, breaking from one's teeth
Bifurcated as the groaning stalks of celery.

Much later comes the tapping on the panel.
The raven in the grounds:
At four thirty the smell of satin, leather:
Rain falling in the mirror above the mad
Jumbled pots of expensive scent and fard,
And the sense of some great impending scandal.

VII

AT ALEXANDRIA

Sometime we shall all come together
And it will be time to put a stop
To this little rubbing together of minimal words,
To let the Word Prime repose in its mode
As yolk in its fort of albumen reposes,
Contented by the circular propriety
Of its hammock in the formal breathing egg.

Much as in sculpture the idea
Must not of its own anecdotal grossness
Sink through the armature of the material,
The model of its earthly clothing:
But be a plumbline to its weight in space . . .

The whole resting upon the ideogram
As on a knifeblade, never really cutting,
Yet always sharp, like this very metaphor
For perpetual and *useless* suffering exposed
By conscience in the very act of writing.

VIII

IN PATMOS

Quiet room, four candles, red wine in pottery:
Our conversation burning like a fuse,
In this cone of light like some emulsion:
Aristarchus of Samos was only half a man
Believing he could make it all coherent
Without the muddled limits of a woman's arm,
Darning a ladder, warming the begging-bowl.

Quiet force of candles burning in pools of oak,
Conducted by the annals of the word
Towards poor Aristarchus. If he was only half
A man, Melissa, then I am the other half,
Not in believing with him but by failing to.

IX

IN PATMOS

'Art adorns.' Thus Galbo.
Proconsuls should be taught to leave art alone.
Before we came the men of the east
Knew it contained a capital metaphysic,
As chess once founded in astronomy
Degenerated into the game we know.

For the Western man of this Egopetal Age
Cant, rules, pains and prohibitions,
Each with its violent repulsive force.
Only in this still round, touching hands,
To live and lapse and die created,
As Socrates died penniless to leave a fortune.

X

In Britain

When they brought on the sleeping child
Bandaged on its glittering trolley
One could think no more of anecdotes:
Ugly Sappho lying under an acorn wishing,
Cyrano discountenanced by a nose like a wen,
My father's shadow telling me three times
Not to play with the scissors: None of this,
But of something inanimate about to be cut up:
A loaf with the oven scent on it exhaling
A breath of sacrifice, clouding the knife.

XI

In Britain

Instead of this or that fictitious woman
Marry a cloud and carve it in a likeness.

XII

In Rhodes

Incision of a comb in hair: lips stained
Blue as glass windows with the grapes
We picked and tasted by ourselves in Greece.
Such was the yesterday that made us
Appropriates of a place, club-members
Of an oleander-grove asleep in chairs.

XIII

In Paris

In youth the decimal days for spending:
Now in age they fall in heaps about me
Thick in concussion as the apples
Bouncing on drums to multiply the seasons
On the floors of scented granaries,
In memory, old barn, wrapped up in straw.

Literarum oblivio . . . Now the Romans
Are going to get the chance they ask for,
That hated jurist's tongue . . .
Their violence will be greater than ours.

Happily we shall not live to see it,
Melissa, nurse, augur, special self.
Once the statues lined the whole main-street
Like nightmares, returning from her house,
Night after night by rosy link-light,
A rose between my teeth, by any other name.

Now we sit in linen deck-chairs here
Looking out to sea and eating olives
From a painted jar: Flavia did this for me,
Won me these favours, this exile from myself.
The exile I had already begun, within myself
She translated like a linguist: Paris.

The King was a bore: it was not my fault he was:
I loved her because I did not know myself.
I knew her yet in the shadow cast by myself
My love was hidden. How we deceive ourselves!
Only our friends know if our wives are faithful,
They will never tell us. (Marc smiling.)

Anyway, now, this animal concupiscence
Of old age in a treaty port: still only consul.
The meteors and the wild mares
Are growing manes, my dear. Autumn is on the way.

We crouch in the wrecked shooting-galleries of progress...

And where you turn, black head of grapes, the sea
Is bluer than forget-me-nots are blue,
Where the linguist in you paraphrases sadly:
The heart must be very old to feel so young.

XIV

IN BEIRUT

After twenty years another meeting,
Those faces round, as circumspect as eggshells:
But in the candle-light fard
Depicts its own origins and ends:
Flesh murky as old horn,
Hands dry now as sea-biscuit,
Sipping the terrible beat of Time
We talk about the past as if it were not
Dead, that April when the ships pouted
From breathless harbours north of Tenedos,
And the green blood of the Delphic bushes
Put back their ears
Where the Greek wind ran, insisted, and became.

Then of poor Clea: her soul sickened in her face
Like flowers in some shadowy sick-room,
How to recall that wingless sickle of a nose,
Thinned out and famished into fever:
The liquid drops of eyes, darkened by carbon,
Brusque ways, an imperative style and voice—
Always catching her dress in doors...

Can we afford to consider ourselves more fortunate?
Lips I would have died to hear speak
Now held in complete sesame here
By a fire of blue sea-coal,
In Beirut, winter coming on.

XV

In Rhodes

From the intellect's grosser denominations
I can sort one or two, how indistinctly,
Living on as if in some unripened faculty
Quite willing to release them, let them die.

Putative mothers-in-ideas like that Electra's
Tallow orphan skin in a bed smelling faintly
Of camphor, the world, the harsh laugh of Glauca:
But both like geometrical figures now,
Then musky, carmine . . . (I am hunting for
The precise shade of pink for Acte's mouth:
Pink as the sex of a mastiff . . .)

Now as the great paunch of this earth
Allows its punctuation by seeds, some to be
Trees, some men walking as trees, so the mind
Offers its cakes of spore to time in them:
The sumptuary pleasure-givers living on
In qualities as sure as taste of hair and mouth,
White partings of the hair like highways,
Permutations of a rose, buried beneath us now,
Under the skin of thinking like a gland
Discharging its obligations in something trivial:
Say a kiss, a handclasp: say a stone tear.

They went. We did not hear them leave.
They came. We were not ready for them.
Then turning the sphere to death
Which like some great banking corporation
Threatens, forecloses, and from all
Our poses selects the one sea-change—
Naturally one must smile to see him powerless
Not in the face of these small fictions
But in the greater one they nourished
By exhaustion of the surfaces of life,
Leaving the True Way, so that suddenly
We no longer haunted the streets
Of our native city, guilty as a popular singer,
Clad in the fur of some wild animal.

XVI

In Rio

And so at last goodbye,
For time does not heed its own expenditure,
As the heart does in making old,
Infecting memory with a sigh-by-sigh,
Or the intolerable suppurating hope and wish.

It has no copy, moves in its own
Blind illumination seriously,
Traced somewhere perhaps by a yellow philosopher
Motionless over a swanpan,
Who found the door open—it always is:
Who found the fire banked: it never goes out.

We, my dear Melissa, are only typics of
This Graeco-Roman asylum, dedicated here
To an age of Bogue, where the will sticks
Like a thorn under the tongue,
Making our accent pain and not completeness.

Do not interrupt me ... Let me finish:
Madmen established in the intellect
By the domestic error of a mind that arranges,
Explains, but can never sufficiently include:
Punishes, exclaims, but never completes its arc
To enter the Round. Nor all the cabals
Of pity and endurance in the circus of art
Will change it till the mainspring will is broken.

Yet the thing can be done, as you say, simply
By sitting and waiting, the mystical leap
Is only a figure for it, it involves not daring
But the patience, being gored, not to cry out.
But perhaps even the desire itself is dying.
I should like that: to make an end of it.

It is time we did away with this kind of suffering,
It has become a pose and refuge for the lazy:
As for me I must do as I was born
And so must you: upon the smaller part of the circle
We desire fulfilment in the measure of our gift:

You kiss and make: while I withdraw and plead.

1948/*1948*

A WATER-COLOUR OF VENICE

Zarian was saying: Florence is youth,
And after it Ravenna, age,
Then Venice, second-childhood.

The pools of burning stone where time
And water, the old siege-masters,
Have run their saps beneath
A thousand saddle-bridges,
Puffed up by marble griffins drinking,

213

And all set free to float on loops
Of her canals like great intestines
Now snapped off like a berg to float,
Where now, like others, you have come alone,
To trap your sunset in a yellow glass,
And watch the silversmith at work
Chasing the famous salver of the bay . . .

Here sense dissolves, combines to print only
These bitten choirs of stone on water,
To the rumble of old cloth bells,
The cadging of confetti pigeons,
A boatman singing from his long black coffin . . .

To all that has been said before
You can add nothing, only that here,
Thick as a brushstroke sleep has laid
Its fleecy unconcern on every visage,

At the bottom of every soul a spoonful of sleep.

1955/1950

DEUS LOCI
(Forio d'Ischia)

I

All our religions founder, you
remain, small sunburnt *deus loci*
safe in your natal shrine,
landscape of the precocious southern heart,
continuously revived in passion's common
tragic and yet incorrigible spring:
in every special laughter overheard,
your specimen is everything—
accents of the little cackling god,
part animal, part insect, and part bird.

II

This dust, this royal dust, our mother
modelled by spring-belonging rain
whose soft blank drops console
a single vineyard's fever or a region
falls now in soft percussion on the earth's
old stretched and wrinkled vellum skin:
each drop could make one think
a footprint of the god, but out of season,
yet in your sudden coming know
life lives itself without recourse to reason.

III

On how many of your clement springs
the fishermen set forth, the foresters
resign their empty glasses, rise,
confront the morning star, accept
the motiveless patronage of all you are—
desire recaptured on the sea or land
in the fables of fish, or grapes held up,
a fistful of some champion wine
glowing like a stained-glass window
in a drunkard's trembling hand.

IV

All the religions of the dust can tell—
this body of damp clay that cumbered so
Adam, and those before, was given him,
material for his lamp and spoon and body
to renovate your terra cotta shrines
whose cupids unashamed
to make a fable of the common lot
curled up like watchsprings in a kiss,
or turned to *putti* for a lover's bed,
or *amorini* for a shepherd's little cot.

V

Known before the expurgation of gods
wherever nature's carelessness exposed
her children to the fear of the unknown—
in families gathered by hopeless sickness
about a dying candle, or in sailors
on tilting decks and under shrouded planets:
wherever the unknown has displaced the known
you encouraged in the fellowship of wine
of love and husbandry: and in despair
only to think of you and you were there.

VI

The saddle-nose, the hairy thighs
composed these vines, these humble vines,
so dedicated to themselves yet offering
in the black froth of grapes their increment
to pleasure or to sadness where a poor
peasant at a husky church-bell's chime
crosses himself: on some cracked pedestal
by the sighing sea sets eternally up,
item by item, his small mid-day meal,
garlic and bread, the wine-can and the cup.

VII

Image of our own dust in wine!
drinkers of that royal dust pressed out
drop by cool drop in science and in love
into a model of the absconding god's
image—human like our own. Or else in other
mixtures, of breath in kisses dropped
under the fig's dark noonday lantern, yes,
lovers like tenants of a wishing-well
whose heartbeats labour through all time has stopped.

VIII

Your panic fellowship is everywhere,
Not only in love's first great illness known,
but in the exile of objects lost
to context, broken hearts, spilt milk,
oaths disregarded, laws forgotten:
or on the seashore some old pilot's
capital in rags of sail, snapped oars,
water-jars choked with sand,
and further on, half hidden, the fatal letter
in the cold fingers of some marble hand.

IX

Deus loci your provinces extend
throughout the domains of logic,
beyond the eyes watching from dusty murals,
or the philosopher's critical impatience
to understand, to be done with life:
beyond beyond even the mind's dark spools
in a vine-wreath or an old wax cross
you can become the nurse and wife of fools,
their actions and their nakedness—
all the heart's profit or the loss.

X

So today, after many years, we meet
at this high window overlooking
the best of Italy, smiling under rain,
that rattles down the leaves like sparrow-shot,
scatters the reapers, the sunburnt girls,
rises in the sour dust of this table,
these books, unfinished letters—all
refreshed again in you O spirit of place,
Presence long since divined, delayed, and waited for,
And here met face to face.

1955/1950

EPITAPH

Stavro's dead. A truant vine
Grows out of him at either end
Like muscles through the trunk and spine
For wine was Stavro's closest friend.

Up through the barrel of the chest
To scatter on his polished dome
A vine-leaf from the poet's crown.
The pint-pot was his only home.

Out of this confusing paste
The best of us are only made,
Sleep and sloth and wine were his
Who drank and drank and never paid.

Beauty vomit truth and waste
Somehow joined to give him grace
Who clasped the sky's blue demijohn
Drunk, in a drowning man's embrace.

Silenus of these olive-groves
He broached a wine-dark universe
And tasted on the crater's brim
Mother lover hearth and nurse.

The vulgar grape his earthly task:
Wine was a cradle, muse and guide,
Till body like some leather flask
Matured a laughing sun inside.

His bounty was life's usufruct:
Such lips to lay at nature's breast
With earth below and sky above,
Till tapsters lay us all to rest.

Stained tablecloths for epitaphs!
Set us full glasses nose to nose!
Good drunkards, pledge him with your laughs
Before the city's taverns close.

1968/*1950*

EDUCATION OF A CLOUD

You saw them, Sabina? Did you see them?
Yet the education of this little cloud
Full of neglect, allowed remissly so to lie
Unbrushed in some forgotten corner
Of a Monday-afternoon-in-April sky . . .

The rest abandoned it in passing by,
The swollen red-eyed country-mourners,
Unbarbered, marching on some Friday-the-thirteenth.
They knew it was not of the savage
Winter company, this tuffet for a tired cherub,

But a dear belonging of the vernal age,
Say spring, provinces of the nightingale,
Say love, the ministry of all distresses,
Say youth, Sabina, let us call it youth—

All the white capes of fancy seen afar!

1955/*1950*

THE SIRENS

Trembling they appear, the Siren isles,
Bequeathing lavender and molten rose,

Reflecting in the white caves of our sails
Melodious capes of fancy and of terror,

Where now the singers surface at the prow,
Begin the famous, pitiless, wounded singing ...

Ulysses watching, like many a hero since,
Thinks: 'Voyages and privations!

The loutish sea which swallows up our loves,
Lying windless under a sky of lilac,

Far from our home, the longed-for landfall ...
By God! They choose their time, the Sirens.'

Every poet and hero has to face them,
The glittering temptresses of his distraction,

The penalties which seek him for a hostage.
Homer and Milton: both were punished in their gift.

1955/1951

CHANEL

Scent like a river-pilot led me there:
Bedroom darkness spreading like a moss,
The polished wells of floors in blackness
Gave no reflections of the personage,
Or the half-open door, but whispered on:

'Skin be supple, hair be smooth,
Lips and character attend
In mnemonic solitude.
Kisses leave no fingerprints.'
'Answer.' But no answer came.
'Beauty hunted leaves no clues.'

Yet as if rising from a still,
Perfume whispered at the sill,
All those discarded husks of thought
Hanging untenanted like gowns,
Rinds of which the fruit had gone ...

Still the long chapter led me on.
Still the clock beside the bed
Heart-beat after heart-beat shed.

1955/1951

CRADLE SONG
Erce . . . Erce . . . Erce
Primigravida

curled like a hoop in sleep
unearthly of manufacture,
tissue of blossom and clay
bone the extract of air
fountain of nature.

softly knitted by kisses,
added to stitch by stitch,
by sleep of the dying heart,
by water and wool and air,
gather a fabric rich.

earth contracted to earth
in ten toes: the cardinals.
in ten fingers: the bishops.
ears by two, eyes by two,
watch the mirror watching you,

and now hush

the nightwalkers bringing peace,
seven the badges of grace
five the straw caps of talent,
one the scarf of desire, go
mimic your mother's lovely face.

1955/1951

CLOUDS OF GLORY

The baby emperor,
reigning on tuffet, throne or pot
in his minority knows hardly what
    he is, or is not,
      sagely he confers
his card of humours like a vane,
veering by fair to jungle foul
    so shapes his course
through variable back to fine again.

    Then
fingers dangle over him: beanstalks.
chins like balconies impend:
kisses like blank thunder bang
    above the little mandarin,
or like a precious ointment prest
from tubes are different kisses
    to the suffrage of a grin.

He can outface
a hundred generations with a yawn
    this Faustus of the pram,
spreadeagled like a starfish, or
    some uncooked prawn
with pink and toothless mandible
    advance the proposition:
      'I
cry, therefore I am.'

the baby emperor
O lastly see
in exile on his favourite St. Helena,
corner of a lost playground gazing
    into a dark well,
manufacturing images of a lost past,
expense of spirit in a waste of longing,
    sea-nymphs hourly
    ring his knell.

small famulus of Time!
born to the legation of our dark unknowing
    the seed was not of your
sowing, nor did you make these tall
    untoppled walls
to sit here like a prisoner remembering
    only as a poem now
    the past, the white breasts
that once leaned over you like waterfalls.

1955/1951

RIVER WATER

The forest wears its coats
of oil-paint as lightly can
what only brush-strokes built,
feather and leaf and spray,
married by choice and plan.

Curve of the Danube's wrist
leans from its mossy bed,
takes the bias of earth with it
the camber of earth and sky,
divides with a ruler of lead.

Soft as an ant's patrol
fingers to fingers warm,
to relive in a favourite's touch,
warm as the oven-loaf,
to finger and wrist and arm.

We know that the dead forget:
the living reside in touch,
sweet consonance of a kiss,
or a letter from distant home,
says little and yet so much.

So much yet never enough
in the concert of night and day,
but revisit us like the dead
kisses that rise to our lips
confused in the river's spray.

Dead kisses revisit the living
in guises our bodies abet,
for mouth or elbow or thigh:
for the living must always remember
what the dead can never forget.

1955/1951

SARAJEVO

Bosnia. November. And the mountain roads
Earthbound but matching perfectly these long
And passionate self-communings counter-march,
Balanced on scarps of trap, ramble or blunder
Over traverses of cloud: and here they move,
Mule-teams like insects harnessed by a bell
Upon the leaf-edge of a winter sky,

And down at last into this lap of stone
Between four cataracts of rock: a town
Peopled by sleepy eagles, whispering only
Of the sunburnt herdsman's hopeless ploy:
A sterile earth quickened by shards of rock
Where nothing grows, not even in his sleep,

Where minarets have twisted up like sugar
And a river, curdled with blond ice, drives on
Tinkling among the mule-teams and the mountaineers,
Under the bridges and the wooden trellises
Which tame the air and promise us a peace
Harmless with nightingales. None are singing now.

No history much? Perhaps. Only this ominous
Dark beauty flowering under veils,
Trapped in the spectrum of a dying style:
A village like an instinct left to rust,
Composed around the echo of a pistol-shot.

1955/1951

A BOWL OF ROSES

'Spring' says your Alexandrian poet
'Means time of the remission of the rose'

Now here at this tattered old café,
By the sea-wall, where so many like us
Have felt the revengeful power of life,
Are roses trapped in blue tin bowls.
I think of you somewhere among them—
Other roses—outworn by our literature,
Made tenants of calf-love or else
The poet's portion, a black black rose
Coughed into the helpless lap of love,
Or fallen from a lapel—a night-club rose.

It would take more than this loving imagination
To claim them for you out of time,
To make them dense and fecund so that
Snow would never pocket them, nor would
They travel under glass to great sanatoria
And like a sibling of the sickness thrust
Flushed faces up beside a dead man's plate.

No, you should have picked one from a poem
Being written softly with a brush—
The deathless ideogram for love we writers hunt.
Now alas the writing and the roses, Melissa,
Are nearly over: who will next remember
Their spring remission in kept promises,

Or even the true ground of their invention
In some dry heart or empty inkwell?

1955/1953

LESBOS

The Pleiades are sinking calm as paint,
And earth's huge camber follows out,
Turning in sleep, the oceanic curve,

Defined in concave like a human eye
Or cheek pressed warm on the dark's cheek,
Like dancers to a music they deserve.

This balcony, a moon-anointed shelf
Above a silent garden holds my bed.
I slept. But the dispiriting autumn moon,

In her slow expurgation of the sky
Needs company: is brooding on the dead,
And so am I now, so am I.

1955/1953

LETTERS IN DARKNESS
(Belgrade)

19 February 1952

So many mockers of the doctrine
Turn away, try not to hear
The antinomian butchers
In the grape-vine of ideas.
It is we who observe who suffer,
We who confide who lie ...

They are pulling and snapping
The disordered vine-limbs, Dionysus,
The body of our body once divine,
Replacing the coveted order of desire
With all the lumber love can leave,
A star entombed in flesh, desirelessness,
In some ghostly bedroom rented for a night.

22 February 1952

Connive, Connive,
For the great wheel is turning
Under the politics of the hive.
Connive, for everywhere
Hermits and patron-saints
On the great star-wheel crucified
Pinned out lie burning, burning,
And life is being delivered to the half-alive.

24 February 1952

Old cock-pheasants when you hit one
Lumber and burst upon the ground,
The body's plump contraption splits
Their lagging rainbow into bits.
So marriage can, by ripeness bound,
From over-ripeness qualify
To sick detachment in the mind—
Dreams bursting at the seams to die
By colder coitus in the mind of God,
Stitches ripped up which used to hold
The modern heart from growing cold.

Now logic founders, speech begins.
Symbols sketch a swaying bridge
Between the states at peace or war,
Athens or Sparta fighting for
What foolish head or fond heart wins.

Much later will the lover coax
Out of the bestiary of his heart
The little hairy sexer, Pan,
The turning-point—pure laughter,
To make the reckoning round and full
If Jill comes tumbling after.
He lies in his love in shadowless content
As tongue in mouth, as poems in a skull.

27 February 1952

Jupiter, so lucky when he lay
Trampling among the roses: bodies
Of young girls . . . a cage of sighs
Beside a drifting river-picture
Was all the poet wished in youth;
But later saw the glistening dewlap
Of the man-bull, heard the cries,
The squat consorts of the passion
Twisted like figs into the legs
Of washerwomen screeching on the Liffey,
Soaping the flaccid thighs and dugs,
Remagnetized again by thoughts of old
Familiar, incoherent, measureless
Contempts the grabbing flesh must
Always hold, like thefts from human logic,
And savour till the gums and spices fade.

3 January 1953

Dear, behind the choking estuaries
Of sleep or waking, in the acts
Which dream themselves and make,
Swollen under luminol, responsibilities
Which no one else can take,
I watch the faultless measure of your dying
Into an unknown misused animal
Held by the ropes and drugs; the puny
Recipe society proposes when machines
Break down. Love was our machine.

And through each false connection I
So clearly pierce to reach the God
Infecting this machine, not ours but by
Compulsion of the city and the times;
A God forgetting slowly how to feel:
A broken sex which, lying to itself,
Could never hope to heal.
It was so simple to observe the liars,
The one impaled, and lying like a log,
The other at some fountain-nipple drinking
His art from the whole world, helplessly
Disbanding reason like a thirsty dog.

6 January 1953

Madness confides its own theology,
An ape-world bleak in its custom:
Not arbitrary, for even the delusive
Lies concert inside their dissonance:
And are apes less human than
Humans are to each other? Answer.

In clinic beds we reach to where
All cultures intersect, inverted now
By the hungry heart and jumbled out
In friends or sculpture or kissing-stuff,
Measured against the chattering
Of gross primary desires, a code of needs
Where Marxist poems are born and die perhaps.

The white screens they have set up
Like the mind's censor under Babel
Are trying to keep from the white coats
All possible foreknowledge of the enigma.
But the infected face of loneliness
Smiles back wherever mirrors droop and bleed.

9 January 1953

Imagine we are the living who inhabit
Freezing offices in a winter town,
Who daily founder deeper in
Our self-disdain being mirrored in
Each others' complicated ways of dying.

Here neither brick nor glass can warm
The sanitary dust of central heating,
And the damp air like a poultice wets
The fears of living which thought begets.

Here we feed, as prisoners feed, spiders
Important to the reason as Bruce's was;
Huge sprawling emotions kept in bottles
Below the civil surface of the mind,
That snap and sway upon the webs
Of tearless resignation bought with sleep.

Some few have what I have:
Silent gold pressure of eyes
Belonging to one deeply hurt, deeply aware.
Truly though we never speak
The past has marked us each
In different lives contending for each other:
We bear like ancient marble well-heads
Marks of the ropes they lowered in us,

Telling of the concerns of time,
The knife of feeling in the art of love.

12 January 1953

So at last we come to the writer's
Middle years, the hardest yet to bear,
All will agree: for it is now
He condenses, prunes and tries to order
The experiences which gorged upon his youth.

Every wrinkle now earned is gifted,
Every grey hair tolls. He matches now
Old kisses to new, and in the bodies
Of younger learners throws off his sperm

Like lumber just to ease the weight
Of sighing for their youth, his abandoned own;
And in the coital slumber poaches
From lips and tongues the pollen
Of youth, to dust the licence of his art.

You cannot guess how he has been waiting
For these years, these ripe and terrible
Years of the *agon*; with the athlete's
Calm foreknowledge of a deathly ripeness,

Facing perhaps a public death by blows,
Or a massive sprain in the centre of his mind,
The whole world; his champion fever glows
With all the dark misgivings of the bout.

But now even fear cannot despoil the body
And will, trained for the even contest,
Fed by the promise of his country's laurels.

So, having dispossessed himself, and being
Now for the first time prepared to die
He feels at last trained for the second life.

1955/1954

ON MIRRORS

You gone, the mirrors all reverted,
Lay banging in the empty house,
Redoubled their efforts to impede
Waterlogged images of faces pleading.

So Fortunatus had a mirror which
Imperilled his reason when it broke;
The sleepers in their dormitory of glass
Stirred once and sighed but never woke.

Time amputated so will bleed no more
But flow like refuse now in clocks
On clinic walls, in libraries and barracks,
Not made to spend but kill and nothing more.

Yet mirrors abandoned drink like ponds:
(Once they resumed the childhood of love)
And overflowing, spreading, swallowing
Like water light, show one averted face,

As in the capsule of the human eye
Seen at infinity, the outer end of time,
A man and woman lying sun-bemused
In a blue vineyard by the Latin sea,

Steeped in each other's minds and breathing there
Like wicks inhaling deep in golden oil.

1955/1954

The notion of emptiness engenders compassion.

MILA REPA

ORPHEUS

Orpheus, beloved famulus,
Know to us in a dark congeries
Of intimations from the dead:
Encamping among our verses—
Harp-beats of a sea-bird's wings—
Do you contend in us, though now
A memory only, the smashed lyre
Washed up entangled in your hair,
But sounding still as here,
O monarch of all initiates and
The dancer's only perfect peer?

In the fecund silences of the
Painter, or the poet's wrestling
With choice you steer like
A great albatross, spread white
On the earth-margins the sailing
Snow-wings in the world's afterlight:
Mentor of all these paper ships
Cockled from fancy on a tide
Made navigable only by your skill
Which in some few approves
A paper recreation of lost loves.

1955/1955

MNEIAE

Soft as puffs of smoke combining,
Mneiae—remembrance of past lives:

The shallow pigmentation of eternity
Upon the pouch of time and place existing.

I, the watcher, smoking at a table,
And I, my selves, observed by human choice,

234

A disinherited portion of the whole:
With you the sibling of my self-desire,

The carnal and the temporal voice,
The singing bird upon the spire:

And love, the grammar of that war
Which time's the only ointment for,

Which time's the only ointment for.

1955/1955

NIKI

Love on a leave-of-absence came,
Unmoored the silence like a barge,
Set free to float on lagging webs
The swan-black wise unhindered night.

(Bitter and pathless were the ways
Of sleep to which such beauty led.)

1955/1955

THE DYING FALL

The islands rebuffed by water.
Estuaries of putty and gold.
A smokeless arc of Latin sky.
One star, less than a week old.

Memory now, I lead her haltered.
Stab of the opiate in the arm
When the sea wears bronze scales and
Hushes in the ambush of a calm.

The old dialogue always rebegins
Between us: but now the spring
Ripens, neither will be attending,
For rosy as feet of pigeons pressed

In clay, the kisses we possessed,
Or thought we did: so borrowing, lending,
Stacked fortunes in our love's society—
Each in the perfect circle of a sigh was ending.

1955/1955

POEM

Find time hanging, cut it down
All the universe you own.

Masterless and still untamed
Poet, lead the race you've shamed.

Lover, cut the rational knot
That made your thinking rule-of-thumb

And barefoot on the plum-dark hills
Go Wander in Elysium.

1960/1955

AT STRATI'S

Remember please, time has no joints,
Pours over the great sills of thought,
Not clogging nor resisting but
Yawning to inherit the year's quarters;
Weaving you up the unbroken series
Of corn, ammonites and men
In a single unlaboured continuum,
And not in slices called by day and night,
And not in objects called by place and thing.

You say I do not write, but the taverns
Have no clocks, and I conscripted
By loneliness observe how other drinkers
Sit at Strati's embalmed in reverie:
Forms raise green cones of wine,
And loaded heads recline on loaded arms,
Under a sky pronounced by cypresses,
Packed up, all of us, like loaves
Human and plant, memory and wish.

The very calendar props an empty inkwell.

1955/1955

THE TREE OF IDLENESS

I shall die one day I suppose
In this old Turkish house I inhabit:
A ragged banana-leaf outside and here
On the sill in a jam-jar a rock-rose.

Perhaps a single pining mandolin
Throbs where cicadas have quarried
To the heart of all misgiving and there
Scratches on silence like a pet locked in.

Will I be more or less dead
Than the village in memory's dispersing
Springs, or in some cloud of witness see,
Looking back, the selfsame road ahead?

By the moist clay of a woman's wanting,
After the heart has stopped its fearful
Gnawing, will I descry between
This life and that another sort of haunting?

Author's Note

The title of this poem is taken from the name of the tree
which stands outside Bellapaix Abbey in Cyprus, and which
confers the gift of pure idleness on all who sit under it.

No: the card-players in tabs of shade
Will play on: the aerial springs
Hiss: in bed lying quiet under kisses
Without signature, with all my debts unpaid

I shall recall nights of squinting rain,
Like pig-iron on the hills: bruised
Landscapes of drumming cloud and everywhere
The lack of someone spreading like a stain.

Or where brown fingers in the darkness move,
Before the early shepherds have awoken,
Tap out on sleeping lips with these same
Worn typewriter keys a poem imploring

Silence of lips and minds which have not spoken.

1955/1955

BITTER LEMONS

In an island of bitter lemons
Where the moon's cool fevers burn
From the dark globes of the fruit,

And the dry grass underfoot
Tortures memory and revises
Habits half a lifetime dead

Better leave the rest unsaid,
Beauty, darkness, vehemence
Let the old sea-nurses keep

Their memorials of sleep
And the Greek sea's curly head
Keep its calms like tears unshed

Keep its calms like tears unshed.

1960/1955

NEAR KYRENIA

The old Levant which made us once
So massive a nurse and a protector
Is quiet now under the moon. In waterglass
Four noons have swallowed her,
Black as a coalface to the Turkish coast.

Your village sleeps your
Little house is tucked away and locked.

I do not know any longer what to make
Of my feelings; for example, how our bodies
Entangled in water softly floated out
Beyond the limits of freewill, wet fingers
Touching. . . . No longer to be intimidated
By this empty beach, frail horned stars,
A victim of memory who could not say
How deft, how weightless are the kisses now
Which wake this unknown, the night sea,
Unlimbered here among its silver bars.

1980/*1955*

EPISODE[1]

I should set about memorising this little room,
The errors of taste which make it every other,
Like and unlike, this ugly rented bed
Now transfigured as a woman is transfigured
By love, disfigured, related and yet unrelated
To science, to the motiveless appeals of happiness.

I should set about memorising this room
It will be a long time empty and airless;
Thoughts will hang about it like mangy cats,
The mirror, vacant and idiotic as an actress
Reflect darkness, cavity of an old tooth,
A house shut up, a garden left untended.

This is probably the very moment to store it all,
Earlobes tasting of salt, a dying language
Of perfume, and the heart of someone
Hanging open on its hinges like a gate;
Rice-powder on a sleeve and two dead pillows
The telephone shook and shook but could not wake.

1956/*1955*

¹ Originally published as 'Nicosia'.

THE MEETING

I have brought my life to this point,
Down long staircases of wanhope
To this dead house, the heart, by
Dusty parallels, by pastures of desire,
By folly out of loneliness begotten, and
Nothing I learned has been forgotten.
Yet all this time you have been climbing
The same black beanstalks of the mind,
Through meadows of unshed tears,
Quite near me though unseen,
Depicted only by a shaking branch,
A voice weeping in a cloud
Or a commotion among the birds
In every silence there has been.

I have brought my life to this point
Where the paths in darkness cross.
Now wait for the one annealing word,
Belonging as spring rain to grass—
But how if she should pass and lose
The soft collision of these mortal worlds
Called by our names? Was it for this
The climbers set out for the heart of time
Never to know the unknown face
Or like a ghost of music to exchange
Only the bitter keepsake of a smile?

1980/*1955*

JOHN DONNE

From the dark viands of the church
His food in tortured verse he bore
Impersonating with each kiss
All that he feared of love and more,

For each must earn his thorny crown
And each his poisoned kiss,
Whoever quarries pain will find
By that remove or this

The sacrament the lovers took
In wine-dark verse suborned his book,

In every sensual measure heard
The chuckles of the daemon Word.
He saw the dark blood in the cup
Which one day drank his being up.

1960/1955

BALLAD OF PSYCHOANALYSIS
Extracts from a Case-Book

MONDAY

She dreams she is chased by a black buck-nigger
But a fall in the coal-face blocks out the dream,
Something as long and lank as a lanyard,
Slow as a glacier, cold as cold cream—
Something inside her starts to scream . . .

TUESDAY

Dreams she is chased by a man in a nightshirt,
Lawrence of Arabia dressed in a sheet:
Then locked by the crew of a Liberty Ship
With rows and rows and rows of refrigerated meat
While the voices keep repeating 'Eat'.

WEDNESDAY

Dreams she is handcuffed to a dancing-partner
And dragged round a roller-skating rink.
She swallows the ring on her wedding-finger
Falls through the ice but doesn't seem to sink
Though her party clothes begin to shrink.

THURSDAY

Dreams she is queen of a mountain of cork,
Too hot to sit on, too cold to wear,
Naked, she pricks with a toasting-fork
A statue of Venus reclining there
With a notice saying: No charge for wear and tear.

FRIDAY

She dreams she's a dog-team tugging poor Scott,
Sheer to the confines of the Pole:
Suddenly the Arctic becomes a-burning hot,
And when they arrive it's just an empty hole,
A geyser whistling in a mountain of coal.

SATURDAY

Dreams she's the queen of a city-culture
Lovely as Helen but doomed to spoil:
Under her thighs roll the capital rivers,
The Rhine and the Volga flowing like oil.
Hamlet offers her a buttoned foil.

SUNDAY

What has she got that we haven't got?
Isn't she happy and lovely too?
She dreams that her husband a bank-director
Locked in the Monkey-House at the Zoo—
Here's the clinical picture but what can we do?

1956/1955

AT THE LONG BAR

Bowed like a foetus at the long bar sit,
You common artist whose uncommon ends
Deflower the secret contours of a mind
And all around you pitying find
Like severed veins your earthly friends . . .

(*The sickness of the oyster is the pearl*)

Dead bottles all around infect
Stale air the exploding corks bewitch—
O member of this outlawed sect,
Only the intolerable itch,
Skirt-fever, keeps the anthropoid erect.

Husband or wife or child condemn
This chain-gang which we all inherit:
Or those bleak ladders to despair
Miscalled high place and merit.
Dear, if these knotted words could wake
The dead boy and the buried girl . . .

(*The sickness of the oyster is the pearl*)

1956/1955

STYLE

Something like the sea,
Unlaboured momentum of water
But going somewhere,
Building and subsiding,
The busy one, the loveless.

Or the wind that slits
Forests from end to end,
Inspiriting vast audiences,
Ovations of leafy hands
Accepting, accepting.

243

But neither is yet
Fine enough for the line I hunt.
The dry bony blade of the
Sword-grass might suit me
Better: an assassin of polish.

Such a bite of perfect temper
As unwary fingers provoke,
Not to be felt till later,
Turning away, to notice the thread
Of blood from its unfelt stroke.

1955/1955

THASOS
To My Godson
Rupert Burrows

Indifferent history! In such a place
Can we choose what really matters most?
Three hundred oars munched up the gulf.
A tyrant fell. The wise men turned their beds
To face the East—this was war. Or else
Eating and excreting raised to the rank of arts:
Sporting the broad purple—this was peace,
For demagogues exhausted by sensations.
From covens of delight they brought
The silver lampreys served on deathless chargers
By cooks of polity and matchless tact.
Only their poets differed in being free
From the historic consciousness and its
Defeats: wise servants of the magnet and
The sieve, against this human backdrop told
The truth in oracles and never asked themselves
In what or why they never could believe.

1955/1955

A PORTRAIT OF THEODORA

I recall her by a freckle of gold
In the pupil of one eye, an odd
Strawberry-gold: and after many years
Of forgetting that musical body—
Arms too long, wrists too slender—
Remember only the unstable wishes
Disquieting the flesh. I will not
Deny her pomp was laughable, urban:
Behind it one could hear the sad
Provincial laughter rotted by insomnia.

None of these meetings are planned,
I guess, or willed by the exemplars
Of a city's love—a city founded in
The name of love: to me is always
Brown face, white teeth, cheap summer frock
In green and white stripes and then
Forever a strawberry eye. I recalled no more
For years. The eye was lying in wait.

Then in another city from the same
Twice-used air and sheets, in the midst
Of a parting: the same dark bedroom,
Arctic chamber-pot and cruel iron bed,
I saw the street-lamp unpick Theodora
Like an old sweater, unwrinkle eyes and mouth,
Unbandaging her youth to let me see
The wounds I had not understood before.

How could I have ignored such wounds?
The bloody sweepings of a loving smile
Strewed like Osiris among the dunes?
Now only my experience recognizes her
Too late, among the other great survivors
Of the city's rage, and places her among
The champions of love—among the true elect!

1955/1955

ASPHODELS: CHALCIDICE

'No one will ever pick them, I think,
The ugly off-white clusters: all the grace
Lies in the name of death named.
Are they a true certificate for death?'
  'I wonder'

'You might say that once the sages,
Death being identified, forgave it language:
Called it "asphodel", as who should say
The synonym for scentless, colourless,
  Solitary,

Rock-loving . . .' 'Memory is all of these.'
'Yes, they asserted the discipline of memory,
Which admits of no relapse in its
Consignment, does not keep forever.'
  'Nor does death.'

'You mean our dying?' 'No, but when one is
Alone, neither happy nor unhappy, in
The deepest ache of reason where this love
Becomes a malefactor, clinging so,
  You surely know—'

'Death's stock will stand no panic,
Be beautiful in jars or on a coffin,
Exonerate the flesh when it has turned
Or mock the enigma with an epitaph
  It never earned.'

'These quite precisely guard ironic truth,
And you may work your way through every
Modulation of the rose, to fill your jars
With pretty writing-stuff: but for death—'
  'Truly, always give us

These comfortless, convincing, even, yes,
A little mocking, Grecian asphodels.'

1955/1955

246

FREEDOM

O Freedom which to every man entire
Presents imagined longings to his fire,
To swans the water, bees the honey-cell,
To bats the dark, to lovers loving well,
Only to the wise may you
Restricting and confining be,
All who half-delivered from themselves
Suffer your conspiracy,
Freedom, Freedom, prison of the free.

1956/1956

NEAR PAPHOS

Her sea limps up here twice a day
And sigh by leaden sigh deposes
Crude granite hefts and sponges
Sucked smooth as foreheads or as noses;
No footprints dove the labouring sand,
For terrene clays bake smooth
But coarse as a gipsy's hand.

A rose in an abandoned well,
The sexless babble of a spring,
A carob's torn and rosy flesh,
A vulture sprawling on a cliff
Will tell the traveller nothing.

The double axe, the double sex,
The noble mystery of the doves,
Before men sorted out their loves
By race and gender chose
One from these dying groves.

This much the sea limps in to touch
With old confining foam-born hand
While lovers seeking nothing much
Or hunting the many through the one
May taste in its reproachful roar
The ancient relish of her sun.

1966/1956

THE OCTAGON ROOM
(1955)

Veronese grey! Here in the Octagon Room
Our light ruffles and decodes
Greys of cigar-ash or river clay
Into the textual plumage of a mind—
Paulo, all his Muses held
Quietly in emulsion up against
A pane of cockney sky.

It is not only the authority
Of godly sensual forms which pity
And overwhelm us—this grey copied
From eyes I no more see,
Recording every shade of pain, yes,
All it takes to give smiles
The deathly candour of a dying art,
Or worth to words exchanged in darkness:
Is it only the dead who have such eyes?

No, really,
I think it is the feudal calm
Of sensuality enjoyed without aversion
Or regret . . . (incident of the ring
Lost in the grass: her laughter).

I should have been happy
In these rainy streets, a captive still
Like all these glittering hostages
We carried out of Italy, canvases
Riding the cracking winds in great London
Parks: happy or unhappy, who can tell you?

Only Veronese grey walks backwards
In the past across my mind
To where tugs still howl and mumble
On the father river,
And the grey feet passing, quiver
On pavements greyer than his greys ...

Less wounding perhaps because the belongers
Loved here, died here, and took their art
Like love, with a pinch of salt, yes
Their pain clutched in the speechless
Deathless calm of Method. Gods!

1960/*1956*

EVA BRAUN'S DREAM

First come the Infantry in scented bodices,
Deployed, and after them the Birdwomen,
(The Ladies Air Arm) clad in shirts of male,
And riding gravid chargers shod with spurs.
In shrill capitulation like some endless wife.

After them in rumbling families
Symbolic engines only found in Jung,
Bombs polished on the lathe like eggs,
Grey mammary tanks, forceps and hooks with eyes,
Unbuttoned panzers, huge uncircumcised artillery,
Grave in procession rustle past the stand.

'One age, one land, one leader and one sex.'

1980/*1957*

THE COTTAGER

Here is a man who says: Let there be light.
Let who is dressed in hair walk upright,
The house give black smoke, the children
Be silenced by fire and apples. Let
A sedative evening bring steaming cattle
The domestic kettle, contagion of sleep,
Deeper purer surer even than Eden.
Twin tides speak making of two three
By fission by fusion, a logarithmic sea.

What was bitter in the apple is eaten deep,
Rust sleeps in the steel, canker will keep.
Let one plus one quicken and be two,
Keep silence that silence keep you.

1960/1960

NIGHT EXPRESS

Night falls. The dark expresses
Roll back their iron scissors to commence
Precision of the wheels' elision
From whose dark serial jabber sparks
Swing swaying through the mournful capitals

And in these lighted cages sleep
With open eyes the passengers
Each committed to his private folly,
On hinges of wanhope the long
Sleeping shelves of men and women,
A library of maggots dreaming, rolls.

Some retiring to their sleeping past;
On clicking pillows feel the flickering peep
Of lighted memories, keys slipped in grooves
Parted like lips receiving or resisting kisses.
Pillars of smoke expend futurity.

This is how it is for me, for you
It must be different lying awake to hear
At a garden's end the terrible club-foot
Crashing among iron spars, the female shrieks,
Love-song of steel and the consenting night.

To feel the mocking janitor, sleep,
Shake now and wake to lean there
On a soft elbow seeing where we race
A whiplash curving outwards to the stars,
A glowing coal to light the lamps of space.

1960/*1960*

MYTHOLOGY

Miss Willow, secretly known as 'tit' . . .
Plotkin who slipped on new ice
And wounded the stinks master
The winter when the ponds froze over . . .

Square roots of the symbol Abraham
Cut off below the burning bush,
Or in the botany classes heads
Drying between covers like rare ferns,
Stamen and pistil, we were young then.

Later with tunes like 'Hips and Whores'
The song-book summed us up,
Mixing reality with circumstance,
With Hotchkiss cock of the walk
Top button undone, and braided cap,
He was the way and the life.

What dismays is not time
Assuaging every thirst with a surprise,
Bitterness hidden in desiring bodies,
Unfolded strictly, governed by the germ.

Plotkin cooked like a pie in iron lungs:
Glass rods the doctors dipped in burning nitrates
Dripped scalding on in private hospitals
And poor 'tit' Willow who had been
Young, pretty and perhaps contemptuous
Dreaming of love, was carried to Spain in a cage.

1960/1960

CAVAFY

I like to see so much the old man's loves,
Egregious if you like and often shabby
Protruding from the ass's skin of verse,
For better or for worse,
The bones of poems cultured by a thirst—
Dilapidated taverns, dark eyes washed
Now in the wry and loving brilliance
Of such barbaric memories
As held them when the dyes of passion ran.
No cant about the sottishness of man!

The forest of dark eyes he mused upon,
Out of ikons, waking beside his own
In stuffy brothels, on stained mattresses,
Watched by the melting vision of the flesh;
Eros the tutor of our callowness
Deployed like ants across his ageing flesh
The crises of great art, the riders
Of love, their bloody lariats whistling,
The cries locked in the quickened breath,
The love-feast of a sort of love-in-death.

And here I find him great. Never
To attempt a masterpiece of size—
You must leave life for that. No
But always to preserve the adventive
Minute, never to destroy the truth,
Admit the coarse manipulations of the lie.
If only the brown fingers franking his love
Could once be fixed in art, the immortal
Episode be recorded—*there* he would awake
On a fine day to shed his acts like scabs,
The trespasses on life and living slake

In the taste, not of his death but of his dying:
And like the rest of us he died still trying.

1964/1960

BALLAD OF KRETSCHMER'S TYPES[1]

(*pyknics are short, fat and hairy,*
leptosomes thin and tall)

The schizophrene, the cyclothyme
Swerve from the droll to the sublime,
Coming of epileptoid stock
They tell the time without a clock.

The pyknic is the prince of these
And glorifies his mental status
Not by his acts on mind's trapeze
But purely by divine afflatus.

Oblivious to the critic's canon
The rational booby's false décor
He swigs away the Absolute
And then demands some more.

[1] Lines 3–6 of this poem first appeared in a letter from the editors of *The Booster* which was published in the *New English Weekly*, XII: 4 (4 November 1937).

Pity the lanky leptosome
Myoptic tenebrous and glum
Whose little pigs must stay at home
Unless they move by rule of thumb.

Salute the podgling pyknic then
That gross and glabrous prince of men,
Contriver of the poet's code
And hero of the Comic Mode.

And Lord, condemn the leptosome
To Golgotha his natural home
The pyknic who's half saint half brute
O waft him on Thy parachute,
And may his footsteps ever roam
Where alcohol is Absolute.

1960/*1960*

BALLAD OF THE OEDIPUS COMPLEX

From Travancore to Tripoli
I trailed the great Imago,
Wherever Freud has followed me
I felt Mama and Pa go.

(The engine loves the driver
And the driver loves his mate,
The mattress strokes the pillow
And the pencil pokes the slate)

I tried to strangle it one day
While sitting in the Lido
But it got up and tickled me
And now I'm all Libido.

My friends spoke to the Censor
And the censor warned the Id
But though they tried to hush things up
They neither of them did.

(The barman loves his potion
And the admiral his barge,
The frogman loves the ocean
And the soldier his discharge.)

(The critic loves urbanity
The plumber loves his tool.
The preacher all humanity
The poet loves the fool.)

If seven psychoanalysts
On seven different days
Condemned my coloured garters
Or my neo-Grecian stays,

I'd catch a magic constable
And lock him behind bars
To be a warning to all men
Who have mamas and pas.

1960/*1960*

APHRODITE

Not from some silent sea she rose
In her great valve of nacre
But from such a one—O sea
Scourged with iron cables! O sea,
Boiling with salt froths to curds,
Carded like wool on the moon's spindles,
Time-scarred, bitter, simmering prophet.
On some such night of storm and labour
Was hoisted trembling into our history—
Wide with panic the great eyes staring . . .

Of man's own wish this speaking loveliness,
On man's own wish this deathless petrifact.

1964/1961

ELEUSIS

With dusk rides up the god-elated night,
Perfume of goatskin and footsore stone
Where plants expire in chaff and husk
On marble threshing-floors of bone.

Here in the gallery where the initiates strained
To lick the sacred ribbon from the soil,
Still wet from the libation's stains of
Honey, grain and this year's olive-oil.

Well: to sit down, to anonymise a bit
By some unleavened altar which preserves
An echo of truth for the precocious will,
Of some disinherited science of the nerves.

'How long will the full Unlearning take?
How long the unacting and unthinking run?
When does the obelisk the sleeper wake
Repaired and newly minted like a sun?'

'The issues change, alas the problems never.
The capital question cuts to the very bone.
Drink here your draught of the eternal fever,
Sit down unthinking on the Unwishing stone.'

1966/1961

A PERSIAN LADY

Some diplomatic mission—no such thing as 'fate'—
Brought her to the city that ripening spring.
She was much pointed out—a Lady-in-Waiting—
To some Persian noble; well, and here she was
Merry and indolent amidst fashionable abundance.
By day under a saffron parasol on royal beaches,
By night in a queer crocketed tent with tassels.

He noted the perfected darkness of her beauty,
The mind recoiling as from a branding-iron:
The sea advancing and retiring at her lacquered toes;
How would one say 'to enflame' in her tongue,
He wondered, knowing it applied to female beauty?
When their eyes met he felt dis-figured
It would have been simple—three paces apart!

Disloyal time! They let the seminal instant go,
The code unbroken, the collision of ripening wishes
Abandoned to hiss on in the great syllabaries of memory.
Next day he deliberately left the musical city
To join a boring water-party on the lake.
Telling himself 'Say what you like about it,
I have been spared very much in this business.'

He meant, I think, that never should he now
Know the slow disgracing of her mind, the slow
Spiral of her beauty's deterioration, flagging desires,
The stagnant fury of the temporal yoke,
Grey temple, long slide into fat.

On the other hand neither would she build him sons
Or be a subject for verses—the famished in-bred poetry
Which was the fashion of his time and ours.
She would exist, pure, symmetrical and intact
Like the sterile hyphen which divides and joins
In a biography the year of birth and death.

1964/1961

It will be some time before the Pursewarden papers
and manuscripts are definitively sorted and suitably
edited; but a few of his *boutades* have turned up in the
papers of his friends. Here are two examples of what
someone called his "incorrigibilia"; he himself
referred to them as Authorised Versions. The first,
which was sung to the melody of *Deutschland,
Deutschland Uber Alles*, in a low nasal monotone,
generally while he was shaving, went as follows:

> Take me back where sex is furtive
> And the midnight copper roams;
> Where instead of comfy brothels
> We have Lady Maud's At Homes.
> Pass me up that White Man's Burden
> Fardels of Democracy;
> Three faint cheers for early closing,
> Hip-Hip-Hip Hypocrisy!
> Sweet Philistia of my childhood
> Where our valiant churchmen pant:
> 'Highest standard of unliving,
> Longest five-day week of Cant.'
> Avert A.I.! Shun Vivisection!
> Join the RSPCA,
> Lead an anti-litter faction!
> Leave your leavings in a tray!
> Cable grandma I'll be ready,
> Waiting on the bloody dock;
> With a hansom for my luggage—
> Will the French release my cock?
> Take me back in An Appliance,
> For I doubt if I can walk;
> Back to art dressed in a jockstrap,
> Back to a Third Programme Talk.
> Roll me back down Piccadilly
> Where our National Emblem stands,
> Watching coppers copping tartlets,
> Eros! wring thy ringless hands!

Ineffectual intellectual
Chewing of the Labour rag,
Take me back where every Cause
Is round the corner, in the bag.
Buy me then my steamer ticket
For the land for which I burn . . .
Yet, on second thoughts, best make it
The usual weekday cheap return!

1980/*1962*

FRANKIE AND JOHNNY
New Style

Livin' in a functional greenhouse
In tastefully painted tones,
Squattin' on chairs of tubular steel
And dicin' with the baby's bones.
    Chorus: He was her man, etc.

Goldfish swimming in a circle,
Swimming round and round like thoughts,
While a frigidaire keeps the bottle cold
And the drinks in their glass retorts.
    Chorus: *Ibid.*

Help us to bear all our follies
In a forest of sanitary bricks,
Where no bed-bug lives in the closet
And no death-watch beetle ticks.
    Chorus: *Ibid.*

With faces blanker than porcelain
In a forest of termite steel
Where the saxophones keep repeating
'The People shall not feel.'
    Chorus: *Ibid.*

Where the psyche fades like a violet
Overlooked in a dry box-wall;
We're rehearsing the Second Coming
Unaware of the Second Fall.
    Chorus: *Ibid.*

Riffle a book in the library,
Yawn at the clocks in the sky,
Rove the city streets with a briefcase,
Feeling your life go by.
    Chorus: *Ibid.*

Once the saints were good box-office
And the times seemed full of sap,
But things haven't been right since Eden.
Come here and sit in my lap.
    Chorus: *Ibid.*

It's the end of a city culture
And an end of the age of Sex,
Soon we'll multiply by fission
By courtesy of World Shell-Mex.
    Chorus: *Ibid.*

A kiss to the deathless Helen
An embrace to the Prodigal Son,
For the nerves are dying in their bodies
Horribly, one by one.
    Chorus: *Ibid.*

The taste buds die like mushrooms
And the sex buds die like spore
And this ain't no time to wake them
  Cause there ain't no Time no more.
    Chorus: *Ibid.*

There ain't no *n*-dimensions
To make a place for love
And there ain't no Space to fit it in
Below or up above.
    Chorus: *Ibid.*

Frankie and Johnny were lovers
But the Lord waxed mighty wroth
When he saw them trying to die together,
A-knitting their own winding-cloth.
    Chorus: *Ibid.*

For their race was the race of Adam,
Their mother was the golden Eve,
But they died in the XXth Century
Leaving nothing to believe.
    Chorus: *Ibid.*

1980/*1962*

BYZANCE

Her dust has pawned kings of gold,
Bodies the winter entered and tubed
In cerements of damp their fallen stars,
Invader of the minds their lichen covered,
And between the stones moss,
And between the bones fingernails and hair.

Only the objects of their past estate remain,
Dispersing now like limbs in different museums.
The crowns and trumpets tarnish easily,
The tangles of ribbon rot like heads of hair
In cupboards where they kept the holy chrism.
Only the eye in an ikon here or there
Amends and ponders and reflects neglects:
Dead monarchs toughened to a stare.

1966/*1963*

ODE TO A LUKEWARM EYEBROW

'Mr Durrell and Miss Compton-Burnett meet with such praise in France as to raise many a lukewarm English eyebrow ...'

'There is something in the English temper that loves a shortage, be it of words ...'

The Times Literary Supplement

And dost thou then, Roderick, once more raising
In Blackfriars that traditionally O but so lukewarm
Eyebrow, which doubtless thou spellest highbrow, chide me,
And from the frugal and funless fund of thy native repository
Of culture, lay thyself once more open, O literary mooncalf,
To a creative's friendly but well-aimed suppository?

Nay, Rod, who from thy bleak and apricot anonymity
Dost in prose bald and breathless exhale an ineffable
Condescension, spattering on poor art thy spinsterish appraisals
Surely thy muse misleads thee, or lies under some shadow cursed,
Forever to gnaw, nibble, gnash termite-wise at thy betters,
With thy English Eyebrow lukewarm, thy lips and sphincters pursed?

Has she not told thee, fog-bound Thames-bedevilled fabulator
That the rewards of laziness will be a conferred mereness, a dark
Sterility, the pedant's parasitic portion? That somehow thou
Must struggle to snap the gyve and unequivocally quit
The cold steamed cod of thy monochrome prosing or else
Be dubbed forever a *pince-fesse* of English Lit.?

1968/1963

OLIVES

The grave one is patron of a special sea,
Their symbol, food and common tool in one,
Yet chthonic as ever the ancients realised,
Noting your tips in trimmings kindled quick,
Your mauled roots roared with confused ardours,
Holding in heat, like great sorrows contained
By silence; dead branch or alive grew pelt
Refused the rain and harboured the ample oil
For lamps to light the human eye.

So the poets confused your attributes,
Said you were The Other but also the domestic useful,
And as the afflatus thrives on special discontents,
Little remedial trespasses of the heart, say,
Which grows it up: poor heart, starved pet of the mind:
They supposed your serenity compassed the human span,
Momentous, deathless, a freedom from the chain,
And every one wished they were like you,
Who live or dead brought solace,
The gold spunk of your berries making children fat.
Nothing in you being lame or fraudulent
You discountenanced all who saw you.

No need to add how turning downwind
You pierce again today the glands of memory,
Or how in summer calms you still stand still
In etchings of a tree-defining place.

1966/1963

SCAFFOLDINGS: PLAKA

For how long now have we not nibbled
At the immediate past in this fashion, words,
Regretting our ignoble faculty of failing,
Slipping between whose fingers?
Melting between whose lips?
The disabused ruins of history's many
Many costumes we discarded.

The little shop has been pulled down
Where we bought stamps, tobacco, Easter ribbons.
A sort of little face now uprooted which
Once determined a whole order of joy,
Ruled over a pulse-rate, made so imperative
And magical the re-reading of a forgotten epic.

How everything in nature diminished
Or increased when it simply spoke!
We did not spot the scaffolding of bone
Until the last winter, the immense despondency
Once more gained full control, the immense despondency.

Old walls wrinkle into dust, windows
Poked out to render sightless
A city loyal to those handsome minds,
Her squares and parks designed for someone's loving.
The masons' picks have touched with their derision,
Unspare the whitewash of the old disorders,
Say what you like it's gone.

One blow can shatter the heroic vision.

1964/1963

STONE HONEY

Reading him is to refresh all nature,
Where, newly elaborated, reality attends.
The primal innocence in things confronting
His eye as thoughtful, innocence as unstudied . . .
One could almost say holy in the scientific sense.
So while renewing nature he relives for us
The simple things our inattention staled,
Noting sagely how water can curl like hair,
Its undisciplined recoil moving mountains
Or drumming out geysers in the earth's crust,
Or the reflex stroke which buries ancient cities.

But water was only one of the things Leonardo
Was keen on, liked to sit down and draw.
It would not stay still; and sitting there beside
The plate of olives, the comb of stone honey,
Which seemed so eternal in the scale of values,
So philosophically immortal, he was touched
By the sense of time's fragility, the semen of fate.
The adventitious seconds, days or seasons,
Though time stood still some drowsy afternoon,
Became for him dense, gravid with their futurity.
Life was pitiless after all, advancing and recoiling
Like the seas of the mind. The only purchase was
This, deliberately to make the time to note:
'The earth is budged from its position by the
Merest weight of a little bird alighting on it.'

1964/1963

CONGENIES

The horizon like some keystone between soil and air
Halves out all earth in quiet distribution,
In tones of dust or biscuit, particularly kind to
Loaves of the sunburnt soil the plough turned back,
Is merciful to marls in their haphazard colours,
Blood, rust, liver, tobacco, whatnot . . .
So far so good; but then comes the king-vine.

Winter slew so many but the old face it out,
Dynasties of sturdy cruciform manikins, their butt
The secateur snopped back, in circumcision,
Or spreadeagled helpless on a garden wall
And left to crucify into the small green
Pilot-leaf of flame, distrustful, lame, confiding,
The horns of snails; mind you, all of this
Before the wine's dark missile is foreseen.

And the human version matches—the stock thick.
Thighs roll to the whistle and snatch of scythes.
Bonemeal grows necks of rock and teeth like dice.
Their natural tutelary worship is the vine.
In it you can read the bloody caucus of the past,
Dour fuse of ageless feuds which smouldered out
Among these tumbled Roman walls and towers,
Either on the thorn-starred circle of the nights
Or here by day, this immensely quiet valley

Alive to the clicking of the pruners' toil.

1966/*1963*

PICCADILLY

At the hub of Empire little Eros stands
Warming his testicles in chilly hands;
They dare not take him down before
They pass the anti-masturbation law.
But when at last the nation's purity
Is one day locked in firm security,
They'll shift the Roman exile for to be
The patron saint of our psychiatry.

1980/*1963*

STRIP-TEASE

Soft toys that make to seem girls
In cool whitewash with two coral
Valves of lip printing each others' grease. . . .
A clockwork Cupid's bow. Increase!
Their cherry-ripe hullo brims the open purse
Of eyes washed white by the marmoreal light;
So swaying as if on pyres they go
About the buried business of the night,
Cold witches of the elementary tease
Balanced on the horn of a supposed desire. . . .
Trees shed their leaves like some of these.

1980/*1963*

IN THE MARGIN

From recollection's fund
One ikon still can move,
Grey eyes, whose graphic doubt
Smile to the last remove.
Light candles and pour out
The slim wine in the glass,
Then softly frame your lips
To blow the darkness out,
In some forgotten room
In some forgiven town
Co-evals of a wish
Made half the darkness bloom.
O timepiece shedding time
Misprisoned by the dark,
Now running like a noose
Or spilling like a gland;
At leafpace gliding on
Or catching like a spark.
Foreknowledge of the end
Calm as the night's serene
Erasure of the light,

Two pupils of the sense
Knowing not where nor whence
Our history bleeds on.
It will not heed this wreath;
Two spendthrifts of the death
The dark bed held beneath.

1966/1964

POEMANDRES

The hand is crabbed, the manuscript much defaced,
Fly-spotted and faint even in good light.
But it is clear that in search of an absolute
Precision, he found all faces, all brows placid.
Yet beneath the enigma gnawed him like an acid ...
Men and women squirted into semblances,
Their hair growing up unpruned, foliage of eagles.

He wished to touch the angelic man,
To conquer the mystical spouse, his syzygy.
A vision of the soul flashed across him
With the great harpoon buried in her!
And by the great wound set free the whole
Wheat-ear and the epoptic mystery.

The black back-bone of death,
The gold back-bone of life,
Between them spheres of self-delusion,
War to the very knife.
The poor lame scholar cried out:

'O ineffable chrism! O horn or flask!'
The laughter rolled about, thunder in gloves.

Steadily he traced back all the copies,
The undermeanings and deposits of the actual love.
My God! The great engine of the sky.
My God! The black monitors of the Cabiri,
The chirping and squeaking of the souls like bats,
The endless plumbline of his sighs—

'*Cri d'une âme qui fait éclater*
Son enveloppe charnelle. Le mal
Est plus grave que vous ne pensez'

All critics quote it as excessive now.

'He beholding the form like to himself
Existing in her, in her Very Water,
Loved it and willed to live it;
And with the will came the Act and so at last
In the due season of the fact
He vivified naked Form devoid of Reason.'

But down there in the obvious world Laïs
Is still somehow part of the canon of loss.
The cool persuasion of the smile exists,
Her style, though a mere sheath for love.
Yet she is still giving men apples printed
With the bite of her white teeth.

1964/1964

PORTFOLIO

Late seventeenth, a timepiece rusted by dew,
Candles, a folio of sketches where rotting
I almost found you a precarious likeness—
The expert relish of the charcoal stare!
The copies, the deposits, why the very
Undermeaning and intermeaning of your mind,
Everything was there.

Your age too, its preoccupations like ours . . .
'The cause of death is love though death is all'
Or else: 'Freedom resides in choice yet choice
Is only a fatal imprisonment among the opposites.'
Who told you you were free? What can it mean?
Come, drink! The simple kodak of the hangman's brain
Outstares us as it once outstared your world.
After all, we were not forced to write,
Who bade us heed the inward monitor?

And poetry, you once said, can be a deliverance
And true in many sorts of different sense,
Explicit or else like that awkward stare,
The perfect form of public reticence.

1966/1964

PRIX BLONDEL

Ah! French poet, confrere, who remaineth so
Obstinately *maudit*,
Inhabiting for preference some deplorable
Taudis: who between spells of aristocratic
Lassitude explores the cosmic laws
Conjugating *amo et odi*.

Sometimes you are ever so mildly *assouvi*
By some rebarbative abstract movie,
But for the most part it is *le néant*
Which bemuseth or the *faux néant*
Not to mention the *fainéant*:
With what careful disdain you avoid *le béant*,
Staying within arm's reach of *le puant*
Never to affront *le géant* . . .
Yea, *tonitruant* you revolve in *le fuyant*,
So countering the critic's cold rebuke
By getting and staying awfully *chnouk*.

You carry your reader's head on the tallest pike,
Spit on kind hearts and coronets alike.

1980/1965

SUMMER

The little gold cigale
Is summer's second god, the lovers know it,
His parched reverberating voice
Deepens the gold thirst of the noons
And follows the black sun's long
Fig-ripening and vine-mellowing fall
So leisurely from heaven's golden car
Day by successive day to end it all . . .

And where the Latin heat has stretched
The skin of valleys will his voice
Rubbing and scraping at the lover's ear
Oracles of past suns recall,
Prodigals of leisure and brown skins,
Wine mixed with kisses and the old
Dreamless summer sleeps they once enjoyed
In Adam's Eden long before the Fall.

1968/1965

DELPHI

Beseech the great horned toad
To turn that jewelled head,
If beckonings won't prevail
Or voices from the dead,
Try memory's seditious brew
And turn he must to answer you.

Honey-gold the Great Bear's eye,
The spiral of a tripod's smoke,
Turn he must to answer you
In time's true-false moving quiet
All that memory dares evoke
Under a catafalque of stars
Hushed the marbles, choked the vase.

Once upon the Python spoke,
Now he lacks interpreters,
Withering in his laurelled fires
All the bitter rock inters,
From within those jewelled eyes
Tells you only what you know,
Know, but dare not realise.

1966/1965

SALAMIS

A treatise of the subtle Body,
Dark van of winter-pledging stars,
Spearheads of the advancing deep
In waters whose commotions keep
The tracery of ships' lace spars.
Another island: another small eternity,
Many tonight must smell the thunder
Look up uneasily from yellowing books:
Is the work of art really a work of nature,
To mobilise the sense of wonder,
Revise all time's nomenclature?

On the dark piers to paraphrase,
A blue rust dusted to tones of soots,
Plum dark the countenances move in mist
And the seaman's iron-shod boots
On the wet quays loiter and list,
While some lost tug hoots and hoots.

A night of leavetakings and summaries,
Inventory of the capes unwinding
In their old smoke and cursing spray
In scarves of smoking suds—
Never to leave, perhaps, never to go away,
And yet past the heart's reminding
See the soft underthrust of water sway
The spending loin come combing out

Ringlets washed back from a dead sea-king's
Face, a helm of gold, a mask
In the autumnal water's writhing.
To remain and realise were the hardest task.

1966/1965

TROY

By maunding and imposture Helen came,
Eater of the white fig, the sugar-bread;
Some beauty, yes, but not more than her tribe
Lathe-made for stock embraces on a bed.
I am astonished when they talk of her,
The shattered cities, bone from human bone
Torn; defaced altars and the burning hearths.
For such as she deaf impulse worked in men:
They dug up graves and ripped down scions of stone,
In act and wish unseparated then.
The test for cultures this insipid drone!
Yes, for a doll the hero, wild-eyed freak
Howled at his mother's grave, yet stopped to dry
One tear of Helen on the sarcastic cheek.

1966/1965

IO

In the museums you can find her,
Io, the contemporary street-walker all alive
In bronze and leather, spear in hand,
Her hair packed in some slender helm
Like a tall golden hive—
A fresco of a parody of arms.
Or else on vases rushing to overwhelm
Invaders of the olive or the attic farms:
Reviving warriors, helmets full of water,
Or kneeling to swarthy foreigners,
A hostage, someone's youngest daughter.
All the repulsion and the joy in one.

Well, all afternoon I've reflected on Athens,
The slim statue asleep over there,
Without unduly stressing the classical pallor
Or the emphatic disabused air
Street-girls have asleep; no,
All that will keep, all that will keep.
Soon we must be exiled to different corners
Of the sky; but the inward whiteness harms not
With dark keeping, harms not. Yet perhaps
I should sneak out and leave her here asleep?
Draw tight those arms like silver toils
The Parcae weave as their supreme award
And between deep drawn breaths release
The flying bolt of the unuttered word.

1966/1965

ONE GREY GREEK STONE

Capes hereabouts and promontories hold
Boats grazing a cyclopean eyeball,
No less astounding
Snow-tusk or toffee-round hill
In shaggy presences of rock abounding
Charm the sick disputing will.

Old dusty gems of bays go flop:
Water polishes on a sleeve to buff,
Trembles upon an eyelash into stars.
How strange our breathing does not stop.
One sovereign absence should be quite enough?

Tell me, the codes of open flowers,
Lick up the glance to pocket a whole mind.
Nothing precipitates, is left behind,
The island is all eyes. Shout!
The silence ponders, notes, and codifies.
We discover only what we set out to find.

I am at a loss to explain how writing
Turns this way this year, turns and tends—
But the line breaks off as voices do, and ends.

Image coiled in image, eye in eye,
Copying each other like guesses where the water
Only dares swallow up and magnify,
So precise the quiet spools
Gather, forgive, heap up, and lie.

Under such stones to sleep would be
The deepest luxury of the deliberate soul,
By day's revivals or the plumblue fall
Of darkness bending like a hoop the whole—
Desires beyond the white capes of recall.

1966/1965

LEECHES

Yellow bottles in a barber's door
Turn slowly as if driven by them
The softly squirming colourless mass;
Here they tell the weather by leeches.
Auxiliaries of science too, how on a thigh

Or temporal vein will settle with a sigh
As babes to breast, painless and yet perverse,
Their thirst brings health to the sick,
Impervious to all things but common salt
The ordinary cattle love to lick:
One pinch of that and the creatures die.

Bent like old harpoons
The seamen stoop to bowls, each old
Patched wineskin of the belly sags,
Capricious and indifferent fortune's tolls,
But the old one there who always brags

Will turn to yellow bottles for his lore,
Consult to see though clouds in coma lie
Black on the harbour where men sleep
If he dare snatch his passage from the deep.

1966/1965

GEISHAS

All airs and graces, their prevailing wind
Blows through the tapestry to stiffen
The fading girls, complexions of tea-roses,
With pets upon provincial laps
And hair combed back against the grain
In innocent professional poses
Sit centred, watching time elapse.
Scented abundance of black hair built back
In studied rolls of merchandise to loom
Over strangers' visitations: ladies of pleasure.
Their musical instruments are laid aside,
O lethargy of educated leisure
That palls and yawns between these silken walls.
But one, luckier or younger, stands apart
On a far bridge to enjoy a private wish,
Casting the aquiline fishing-rod of gold
Angles for other kinds of fish.

1980/1965

THE IKONS

They have taken another road,
Dionysus and all his cockledom,
The ogres in dry river beds
Hair flying, breast-bone full of eyes.
A madman walks alone in the dark wood
Swinging a lantern; nobodies march,
Lute-player, card-sharper, politician,
Until here lastly the condign
Majestic stance of something else
Apparelled for death: Byzantium.

The eyes won't change, no, but the
Going forward or going back
Can be read off as on a clock-face.
Here the population of clocks multiplied,
They bore the suffocating fruits of chime, hours.
All day long the belfries reminded
All night the prayers besieged.
A cross rose, wish-bone of the defeated,
The chicken-souled, the guilty.
It has got worse since, of course,
And can hardly get any better now.

A café is the last Museum and best,
To observe a great man in the middle
Of a collapse; but parts work still,
The crutches are incidental, adding variety.
Some injudicious pleasures will remain,
The sexual phosphorescence of youth is gone,
But here on naptha-scented evenings still
He sits before the tulip of old wine,
In a red fez, by some sunken garden,
Watching for shooting-stars.

1966/1966

APTEROS

Sky star-engraved, the Pleiads up,
Autumn's old ikonography
In falling fruit and turning sea,
The whole spins in a drinking-cup.
Incised the crater of heaven burns
Recovering all she gave,
Into the cooling ground returns
Fruit, star and promiscuous wave,
To die by the universal variable
And scribble on a stone our scope,
The phosphorescence of desire
To a season of wanhope.

277

Kiss of white caryatids which lean
With broken boxers' noses here
On armatures of lead,
Year after summer year incline
To appear and re-appear.

How much will time exempt in us
How much replace?
Shapes of the carnal void,
Cracked smile of marble mouth,
Starred emblem of a stone embrace.

1966/1966

KEEPSAKE

To increase your hold
Relax your grip,
Exploit the slip twixt
Cup and lip.

Enjoy and bid and let it grow,
Superior sense of vertigo,
The adepts' sixth infernal sense
Spells passionate indifference,
So by the racing pulse express
A discipline of laziness.

To increase your scope
Relax your hold
Not wish nor hope
One second old
The key to open all the locks
Of this insidious paradox,
Not wish nor hope one second old
So all that glitters may be gold.

1966/1966

CAPE DRASTI

Who told you you were it,
Acrobat without arms,
Ringmaster of the choice whiplash,
Opening and shutting drawers
In long apathies or pedantic calms,
Or barking all night at cliffs
Too high to remember how to climb?

Skippers have other names for you,
Who mark you only by fathom,
But to me a blue specie somehow,
In the nostril of a westerly,
Or T-bone under night spars
Out of some slangy mood disperses,
Carves out a beach in cripples.

Come March and you'll sharpen minds,
Ropes all chewn out, sheets purged,
Or splitting down the middle race
To bang boats together like heads.
No, lion-paw, ape of every mood,
Steeplejack of the tilted breakers,
How nice land feels to watch you go by on.

1966/1966

NORTH WEST

The dying business began hereabouts,
A pewter plain, a shrubless frugality,
An anarch sea, cliffs, nothing.
It promised a local action merely
But the death-rot somehow spread from
Limb to limb and mind to mind,
Became endemic. The body politic
Was touched, began to suppurate once more.
An empire began to have dizzy spells,
One fever to cast out another
One man to cast down another.

Who can apportion a historic fault?
A few hundred years of average misery,
A thousand more of abstract villainy,
The precious culture pilfered into dust.

They spoke of starting again at the beginning
But by then few had looked upon it fresh,
And the frenzied young were building away
From it, towards some tributary death.
A little contempt goes a long way,
Smashed well-head with gorgons
Clothed now with self-renewing moss.

1966/1966

THE INITIATION

Spoonful of wine, candle-stump and eyes.
The cuckold-mixture as before;
Nothing time so approves
In each superb disguise,
The patents of the wish,
Sweet but deluding law,
The infinities which must discern
A fever's point of no return.

Or a child's voice which calls
Behind tall garden walls,
Calls, and falls silent in despair,
He or she will never be there,
Where images still swarm
And pour from the broken hives
Never to recover the obedient smiles
Nor mend disfigured lives.

Here at this candid hour
By one unfaltering gleam
Remembering it as it glows
The fever's auguries
Till the dismantled dream
Where all the ancient loyalties foreclose.

The road leads softly down
On avenues of darkling recognition,
Compass or sextant none
Towards death's suave audition.

So, harking back to it, spoonful
Candle-stump and eyes one sees
In their majority,
With razors whispering on the lard
What fruit the barbers shave
To the last dimple of the self-regard.

1966/*1966*

ACROPOLIS

the soft *quem quam* will be Scops the Owl
   conjugation of nouns, a line of enquiry,
powdery stubble of the socratic prison
   laurels crack like parchments in the wind.
who walks here in the violet dust at night
   by the tower of the winds and water-clocks?
   tapers smoke upon open coffins
surely the shattered pitchers must one day
   revive in the gush of marble breathing up?
   call again softly, and again.
the fresh spring empties like a vein
   no children spit on their reflected faces
but from the blazing *souk* below the passive smells
   bread urine cooking printing-ink
will tell you what the sullen races think
   and among the tombs gnawing of mandolines
confounding sleep with carnage where
   strangers still arrive like sleepy gods
   dismount at nightfall at desolate inns.

1966/*1966*

PERSUASIONS

We aliens are too greedy. They took their time,
Being sure there was abundance of such
Blueness, waters of mint in sheaves,
Demotic and reasonable the sky through leaves.
Easy does it, they said; it did much the same,
Echoed the confidence of infinite extension:
Nothing specially prudent or benign
About Greek space or form or line,
Yet beyond it lay the promise of heirs—
The future like the past was theirs.

Man sat a boat like a gull,
Gull sat a rock like a star,
All fishermen's lecheries entangled were,
Sharing the diversionary water-dream,
The hunter's pious stare,
Till finally the silence was supreme
And neither any more was really there.

Only . . . oar hankered for the blue,
Prow ached for it, rope had a mind to stretch,
Anchor to plummet and to delve,
So a harmony of reciprocal functions grew
Between the none-existent two, a truce
While the same horizon softly insisted:
'The perfect circle is incapable of further development.'

1966/*1966*

MOONLIGHT

I cannot read Pliny without terror.
It seems that in trees the sap
Is moon-governed, rising and falling
In absolute surrender, and if trees
Then the menstrual pattern reconverts
Some rhythms into human sap
For the night's silver thermometer.
Easy to knock off branches in your sleep,
Overturn and sever the whole trunk,
But how to stop the perpetual bleeding?
I cannot tell, but so much is clear,
Freewill is simply another carnal proverb
Of worthless minds. A man standing,
Leaning at a gate waiting, a frugal décor,
Either in some northern city of steel vegetation
Or in the ungovernable brilliance
Of an island, at the same gate the same man
Waiting, can be seen less as animal
Than mineral, a besotted cistern
For wine or blood, ebbing and flowing,
Waxing and waning in the ungovernable fury
Of something's phosphorescence. Yet he waits,
He simply waits and smokes and goes on waiting,
You know why, you know when, you know for whom.

1966/1966

BLOOD-COUNT

A falling mulberry stained this page
As it might have been under the golden barrel
Of a microscope the eosin-stained précis
Of a war fought in the long blue canals
Of the human heart, red corps against the white:
Dominion of one or other love disproving.
Meanwhile upon the outer rind there is
No sickness in the heart of time,
The fruit breathes on the tree and gestures,
The bark fresh, the leafage of hands dewy
Drives the beautiful wand of your flesh
Upwards into another spring, sap rising.

1966/*1966*

KASYAPA

When one smile grazed the surface
Nobody breathed and nobody spoke,
As ringed as a tree's old age
Or stone-splashed circles in water
Widening out to infinity the joke—
Neither he nor they nor the mage.

In their silence one can recognise
The illnesses it was invented to heal.
Yes, pattern of brush or pen have merit
But the other thing does not feel
And leaves nothing to inherit,
The historian's dusty archives etc.
All the rhetoric of the unreal.

So the peculiar smile broke cover
Sharp as the Pleiads of a new unknowing
To lap at the confines of our reason still,
The purposeless coming and going,
The never quite never quite still.

Nor does it matter much, given the fact
The date the season and the hour
That I have forgotten not the smile
Kasyapa, but the name of the flower.

1966/1966

VIDOURLE

River the Roman legionary noosed:
Seven piers whose sharpened fangs
Slide from stone gums to soothe and comb
Where the lustrous nervous water hangs.
A stagnant town: a someone's home-from-home.
If the bored consular ghost should reappear
He would re-pose the question with a sigh,
Find it unanswered still: 'What under heaven
Could a Roman find to amuse him here?'
It won't: he's gone on furlough unregretted,
Now powdered with drowsy lilies, hobbled,
Dusted by old Orion the glib waterfloor
A planet-cobbled darkness re-inters
The history the consul found a bore.

Pour sky in water, softly mix and wait,
While birds whistle and sprain and curve . . .
They must have faltered here at the very gate
Of Gaul, seduced by such provender, such rich turf
Bewitched, and made their sense of duty swerve.
No less now under awnings half asleep
Pale functionaries of a similar sort of creed
All afternoon a river-watching keep,
Two civil servants loitering over aniseed.

1966/1966

PAULLUS TO CORNELIA[1]

I

Cornelia, dry your cheek, poor shade,
This last and most exact of visions,
Old wedding-rings our fires won't eat
Ash under grey cypresses,
Old half-forgotten implausible decisions
By going leaving you incomplete.

                And now your message: yes,
                Our house is very still,
                And at the third watch always
                I conceive your five fingers
                Softly placed upon a sill,

What to convey? I saw how gluttonous
Candles smack their meek fat lips,
Oaken pyres, the small skull broken open,
Lick out the ears with a befriending kiss.
Who spoke? Who heard? What was confided?
No, you simply woke that morning and decided
To refund your private meaning into This.

Water entering water forever keeps
Her identical flavour: so one death into Death,
The abstract portions of a simple whole,
Soon the sweet seasons claim control.
It would be squandering you to tell
With what precision we were given
A form for all our looking-for in loving,

The looking-glass, the spell,
An embrace becomes didactic and less moving
Although the autumns harden and I live,
Still learning, eye to eye, mind mind, lip lip,
Thus have you taken all I could not give.

[1] See the eleventh elegy of Propertius.

From cellars full of dark air
An introspection costing life
Reducing death's dimension,
Cuts through feeling like a knife.

Yet even more deeply sounded,
With more rapid pulse those fevers,
By broken seamarks, in old granaries,
Among ferns, stones, olive-trees,
Costumes of old deceivers,
Where once you so abounded
I feel our grave latin code insist
And what you are and were become confounded.
So close at hand as never to be missed.

II

You were that search for the Sovereign Form
Which each of us owns, and each
Must find and bury: all the disciplines
We only summarise in simple dying,
It is all there, we know it, within reach,
Nor is there ever any hurry,
For those who get beyond the maze of speech
To where such vision waits, all knots untying.

That Form perhaps like the dew-lined 'form'
Of some solitary hare in frosty grass
On the unfrequented mountainsides
Of the mind's inmost narrative mind:
Yes, only there you know the search has ended,
Cornelia, and she's rediscovered,
Image of silence and all deaths befriended.

1966/*1966*

PRESS INTERVIEW

Capacities in doubt and lovers failing?
We feel time freshen but we keep on sailing.

No, sir, I do not cannibalise my fellow-man
In writing of him. I just fict.
Unfashionable if you wish, or even unreal
So to evict the owner from his acts
In propria persona; spit out the bones
When once the bloody platter's licked.

Of course things experienced or overheard
Swarm up the wall and knock;
But we disperse them as they flock
And redistribute, word by silly word.

But when Totals turn up and insist
We give them way; and only then you see,
However chimerical or choice or few,
One cannot copy to unearth the new.

1966/*1966*

CONFEDERATE

At long last the wind has decided for itself,
Skies arch and glass panes shudder inwards,
My shutter croaks and now you tell me
It is time for those last few words. Very well.
Epoch of a whitewashed moon with
Frost in the bulb and the quailing local blood.
Very well; for not in this season will kisses
Dig any deeper into the mind to seek
The mislaid words we have been seeking,
Delegates of that place which once
The whole of suffering seemed to occupy—
O nothing really infernal, a simple darkness.
But because I came both grew abruptly
Aware of all the surrounding armies
So many faces torn from the same world,
Whole lives lost by mere inattention.

1973/1967

OWED TO AMERICA

I

America   America
I see your giant image stir
O land of milk and bunny
Where the blue Algonquin flows
Where the scrapers scrape the ceiling
With that dizzy topless feeling
And everything that simply *has* to, goes!

II

Land of Doubleday and Dutton
Huge club sandwiches of mutton
More zip-fastener than button
Where the blue Algonquin flows
Home of musical and mayhem
Robert Frost and Billy Graham
Where you drain their brains but pay 'em
Then with dry Martinis slay 'em
Everyone that drinks 'em knows.

III

America   America
Terra un peu hysterica
For me as yet incognita
I see your giant image stir
Here no waffle lacks for honey
Avenues paved with easy money
Land of helpless idealism
Clerical evangelism
Land of prune and sometimes prism
Every kind of crazy ism
Where the blue Algonquin flows.

IV

America   America
So full of esoterica
One day I'll pierce the veils that hide
The spirit of the great divide
The sweet ambition which devours
You, super duper power of powers—
But for the nonce I send you flowers.

V

If there was a cake you'd take it
If I had one heart you'd break it
Where the blue Algonquin flows
Looking forward, looking back
There seems nothing that you lack
America   America
Pray accept this cordial greeting
On a visit far too fleeting
Rest assured I'll soon be back.

1980/*1968*

THE OUTER LIMITS

The pure form, then, must be the silence?
I'd tear out a leaf of it and spread it,
The second skin of music, yes,
And with a drypoint then etch in quick
Everything that won't talk back, like
Frost or rain or the budget of spring:
Even some profligate look or profitable
Embrace—here to imprison it,
So full of a gay informal logic,
A real reality realising itself,
No pressures but candid as a death,
A full foreknowledge of the breathing game
Taut as a bent bow the one simple life
Too soon over, too soon cold; memory
Will combine for you voice, odour, smile.

1973/*1968*

SOLANGE

Author's Note

This poem was originally written at the same time as
'Elegy on the Closing of the French Brothels' (*c.* 1938), but
I wasn't happy with it and the draft was left behind in a
notebook until 1967, when I retouched it and lengthened it
by about half.

I

Solange Bequille b. 1915 supposedly
Far from Paris towards April sometime,
Familiar of the familiar XIV arrondissement
> four steps up
> four steps down
> two three four *five*
> where the sewers discharge
> by the turret of an urinal
> six seven eight
> steel ducts voiding
> in shade and out of the wind . . .
Relatively impossible despite so much practice
To word-parody the tantamount step, but easier
Copy for the lens a powder-blue raincoat, beret,
Cicada brooch, belted and bolted waist of wasp,
Dumb insolent regimental shoes, sheeny rings,
The whole of it amberstuck through twenty winters,
Carried round the globe in damp suitcases,
Some pedlar's pack of visionary ware like
Her rings of a vulgar water reflecting
> black testicles of buoys
> tugging at the Seine
> lovers in leaden coffins
> pelting the dead with crusts
> the prohibitions of loneliness
> being twenty-two with a war
> hanging over them, its belly hard,
> noting the orgasm of Hegel
> defining all death as 'the

collapse into immediacy'.
Ah, dangerous salients of youth,
loving in a crucial month.

II

Over the bridges the meandering scholars
Deambulating flowed over the Pons Asinorum
Of the five arts between the capable white
Wide-flowing thighs of their seventh muse,
A sharpshooter by a steel turret
Waiting to smelt down whole faculties,
Captives of youthful salt with their elaborate tensions,
They passed and passed but always hesitated,
Leaving their satchels when they could not pay,
The score was kept on a matchboard wall.
A hundred a quick one, five the whole night,
Whole doctorates granted in prime embraces.
The arts of the capital being matured and focused.
Five for the collective wisdom of this great city!

> baisers O noirs essaims
> desires grown fair of dark
> the cross-roads of smiling eyes
> complexities of season, spring
> or winter's black water
> bridges of funereal soot
> working with pink tongue or tooth
> towards some mystical emphasis,
> a life without sanctions
> in the forever, so long ago,
> so far away from all this
> contemporary whimperdom
>   Solange
> sole angel of the seekers,
> their prop medal and recourse
> faces crisper than oak-leaves
> your burial service covered all
> the coward and the brave
> the perfectly solid fact as
> symbol of humanity's education

less a woman with legs than
something, say that oven into which
Descartes locked himself in order
to enunciate the first principle
of his system; the oven Planck
consulted after all the
spectroscope's thrilling finery
to deduce the notion of quanta.
Always the same oven, never any bread,
the XXth century loaf is an equation
                    Solange
be like mirrors accumulating nothing.

III

The change from C major to A flat
Is always associated with summary thefts,
Certain women powdered by suns,
Street-lamps' fresh breath in cradles,
As simply as birds reacting to rain
We recover small fragments of the unknowable
To render back to nature her darkest intents
In allegorical bandages of old hotels
Receiving into their no-womb the anti-heroes,
Tang of the metro and rotting dustbins
Needles seeking the iron vein
Astrology's damp syringe
                    a woman of good intent
                    distributing the river winds,
                    drawing with scarlet fingernail
                    on foggy panes high above Paris,
                    one glassed-in balcony
                    with tubs for plants' green hives
                    so apt for tall trees' dews
                    days robbed and nights replaced
                    whatever the single vision traced
                    four steps up
                    four steps down
                    wherever the emphasis was placed
                    whoever the woman's image finds
                    dyed into living minds

By the dead butts of infernal cinemas
Or at the Medrano lulled by some old
Circus animal's tarnished roars,
See the heads discharged by guns in baskets falling
Smelling of new bread or blood. The muscles
Now hanging in Museums, the thoracic cage shaken
By typical sobs, the eyes of congers' spawn,
Then the plumage of soft shrieks in dark streets,
The running feet, silence, and something lying
In Paris on such April nights when stars
Crunch underfoot the Luxembourg's cool gravels,
Night poised like a lion's paw
Where her prowl crosses some angle of the abstract town.
    four steps up
    four steps down
    where the sewers discharge
    by the urinal's turret
    stairs too narrow for the coffin,
    minds too narrow for recognitions,
    hearts too severe for introspection,
    different categories of the same
    insolent vision marrying
    four steps up
    confederates of the darkness
    soon they must all die or
    go away, soon you will be left
    alone, writing wholly for yourself,
    struggling with the idea of a city
    a whore of the city's inward meaning,
    animal intents all bruising
    the wingpoint of other myths
    outmoded or outvoted gods
    the muffled censors of the time
    ripening in the latest ages
    beyond the scope of liveried men
    past the intentions of the wise
    towards a death promoted by the sages.

IV

Even then was he somehow able to undress his dolls' thoughts to sleep beside the sleeper, lay figures of the dreams which uncoiled among the mnemonic centres of the mind which thinks without knowing that it thinks, slips, punctures process with ideas. Faut-il enfin dépasser le point de tangence qui sépare l'art et la science, tout en les traitant comme les religions primitives en faillite? Oui mais comment? Even then, even then; but his snores might not awake the tiny amorous snores as of the congress of guinea-pigs in vivisectionists' cages, unaware of being watched, syringe in hand. Et le chaos même, dandy ou nègre? Faut-il éprouver la plénitude charnelle d'un acte spontané? In the cheap edition of 'Causality' she had given Leibniz a moustache and printed a lipstick kiss to hide the crucial figure, adding in the margin the proverbial merde. If only she could have delivered him from the vices of introspection, the verses in p'tit nègre, the torn paper tablecloths with their thorny sketches; but alas vers libre is like le ver solitaire. The head shows and the atlas of the stare; it can be broken off by the forceps, but there will always be more packed in the gut. Beware.

> the communes raise their walls
> around the dreamer's bed,
> cold crusts of cults devoured
> the science-mocking magics spread
> like viruses distributed
> by the redeemers' dreams
> on altars sourly smoke
> the witnesses disperse
> among the smoke of thought
> to share the ignoble joke
> some medieval urinals
> mingle the proferred wine
> to pour from snouts of stone
> the griffins far below
> on the river's quays
> famous star-waterways incline
> turn water into wine,
> the simple torturers go
> when night undresses all the trees
> unsleeping gargoyles tell you so.

Born of torpid country-folk versed in cumbrous ways and too hap-
hazard to chime with this spawn of factories with anvils and poisonous
oxygen, this decomposing fabric of stone, the sepia cards of churches
begging for disablement pensions; but kindly stubborn intractable
stock, she imported into the deadly estate of the town frail rural vir-
tues, rotted in a primeval humus. Gone this Solange or that, but the
mould remained unbroken revolving through worlds of dissimulation,
spheres, hatcheries of unique sensation, seen through the pinshead of a
tiny mind. Turning slightly towards the sun as winter flowers may do,
the bonfires and speeches and the eternal inquests within the frontiers
of the self, still the fated questions yawned as they do for all of us. And
what then of Pascal, the man she loved: sullen, morose and leaden when
not in the air flying from ring to ring with an acrobat's fury, the
webbed feet, sympelmous toes, O rabid specialist in a bird's beauty.
They exchanged wordless days, and doses, the sempiternal clap. In full
flight over the city he took her like a ring, swung over the edge of the
abyss. I studied their famous loves to reimburse myself. Once I saw the
expression on his face which must have settled her fate—in mid-air
swinging in an orgasm of fear and stress, but shriven too; this look had
impaled her mind. Then he went, without saying goodbye, perhaps on
tour, but never to return I believe; perhaps much later to dangle from
some whore's rafter or at the end of a silken parachute illustrating some
mysterious law. But his undertow haunted her body for a season, celeb-
rated in absinthe and funereal silences; many profited from this exper-
ience, many coupled through her with the wiry loins and loafing smile.

> statues on cubes of frost
> equestrian pigments of the snow
> somewhere the carrefour was crossed
> munching footsteps trail and slow
> stealthy gravels underfoot
> sectioned by the tawny bars
> street lamps fiction up the dusk
> world unending of past wars
> when will the exemplars come
> four steps up
> four steps down
> where the sewers discharge
> by the urinal's turret.

VI

The dreams of Solange confused no issues, solved no problems, for on the auto-screen among our faces appeared always and most often others like Papillon the tramp, a childhood scarecrow built of thorns. He turned the passive albums of her sleep with long fingers, one of them a steel hook. Papillon represented a confederacy of buried impulses which could resurrect among the tangled sheet, a world of obscure resentments, fine and brutal as lace, the wedding-cake lying under its elaborate pastry. His ancient visions sited in that crocodile-mask fired her. And such dreams as he recounted revived among her own—Paris as some huge penis sliced up and served around a whole restaurant by masked waiters. And the lovers murmuring 'I love you so much I could eat you'. She takes up knife and fork and begins to eat. The screams might awake her, bathed in sweat, to hear the real face of Marc the underwriter saying something like: 'All our ills come from incautious dreaming.' There were so many people in the world, how to count them all? Perhaps causality was a way of uniting god with laughter? Solange avec son œil luisant et avide, holding a handbag full of unposted cards.

Add to the faces the Japanese student whose halting English was full of felicities only one could notice; as when 'Lord Byron committed incense with his sister, and afterwards took refuse in the church'. He too for a season cast a spell. Then one day he recited a poem which met with her disfavour.

> She was eighteen but already god-avowed,
> She sought out the old philosopher
> Expressly to couple with him, so to be
> Bathed in the spray of his sperm
> The pneuma of his inner idea.
> Pleasure and instruction were hers,
> She corrected her course by his visions.
> But of all this a child was born,
> But in him, not in her, as a poem
> With as many legs as a spider
> In a web the size of a world.

Then Deutre, the latest of our company
Who believed all knowledge to be founded
Deep in the orgasm, rising into emphasis
As individual consciousness, the know-thyself,
Bit by bit, with checks and halts, but always
By successive amnesias dragged into conception,
A school of pneuma for the inward eye
Reflecting rays which pass in deliberate tangence
To the ordinary waking sense, focuses the heart.
Patiently must Solange pan for male gold
White legs spread like geometer's compasses
Over her native city. The milk-teeth fall at last.
Gradually the fangs develop, breathing changes,
And out of the tapestry of monkey grimaces
Born of no diagrams no act of will
But simple subservience to a natural law, He comes,
He emerges, He is there. Who? I do not know.
Deutre presumably in the guise of Rilke's angel
Or Balzac's double mirrored androgyne.
Deutre makes up his lips at dusk,
His sputum is tinged with venous blood.
Nevertheless a purity of intent is established
Simple as on its axis spins an earth.
It was his pleasure to recite
With an emphasis worthy of the Vedas
Passages from the Analysis Situs: as
               la géometrie à *n* dimensions
               a un objet réel, personne n'en
               doute aujourd'hui. Les Etres
               de l'hyperespace sont susceptibles
               de définitions précises comme ceux
               de l'espace ordinaire, et si nous
               ne pouvons les réprésenter nous
               pouvons les concevoir et les étudier.

The third eye belongs to spatial consciousness
He seems to say; there is a way of growing.
It was he who persuaded me at Christmas to go away.
Far southwards to submit myself to other towns
To landscapes more infernal and less purifying.
He persuaded Solange to lend me the money and she
Was glad to repay what the acrobat had spent,
But she saw no point in it, 'Who can live outside
Paris, among barbarians, and to what end?
Besides all these places are full of bugs
And you can see them on the cinema without moving
For just a few francs, within reach of a café.
But if go you must I will see you off.'

Remoter than Aldebaran, Deutre smiled.
Only many years later was I able
To repay him with such words as:
'Throughout the living world as we know it
The genetic code is based on four letters,
The Pythagorean Quarternary, as you might say.'
He did not even smile, for he was dying.
Man's achievement of a bipedal gait has freed
His hands for tools, weapons and the embrace.

> the days will be lengthening
> into centuries, Solange
> and neither witness will be there,
> seek no comparisons among
> dolls' houses of the rational mind
> coevals don't compare
> a gesture broken off by dusk
> heartless as boredom is or hope
> blood seeks the soil it has to soak
> in the fulfilment of a scope
> fibres of consciousness will grow
> lavish as any coffin load
> and every touching entity
> the puritan grave will swallow up
> the silences will atrophy.

So we came, riding through the soft lithograph
Of Paris in the rain, the spires
Empting their light, the mercury falling,
Streets draining into the sewers,
The yokel clockface of the Gare de Lyon
On a warehouse wall the word 'Imputrescible'
Then slowly night: but suddenly
The station was full of special trains,
Long hospital trains with red crosses
Drawn blinds, uniformed nurses, doctors.
Dimly as fish in tanks moved pyjama-clad figures
Severed from the world, one would have said
Fresh from catastrophe, a great battlefield.
'O well the war has come' she said with resignation.
But it was only the annual pilgrimage to Lourdes,
The crippled the lame the insane the halt
All heading southwards towards the hopeless miracle.
Each one felt himself the outside chance,
Thousands of sick outsiders.
A barrel organ played a rotting waltz.
The Government was determined to root out gambling.
My path was not this one; but it equally needed
A sense of goodbye. Firm handclasp of hard little paw,
The clasp of faithful business associates, and
'When you come back, you know where to find me.'

> four steps up
> four steps down
> the station ramp eludes
> the mangy town
> the temporary visa
> with the scarlet stamp
> flowers of soda
> shower the quays
> engines piss hot spume
> giants in labour
> drip and sweat like these
> slam the carriage door
> only this and nothing more.

I write these lines towards dusk
On the other side of the world,
A country with stranger inhabitants,
Chestnut candles, fevers, and white water.
Such small perplexities as vex the mind,
Solange, became for writers precious to growth,
But the fluttering sails disarm them,
Wet petals sticking to a sky born nude.
The magnitudes, insights, fears and proofs
Were your unconscious gift. They still weigh
With the weight of Paris forever hanging
White throat wearing icy gems,
A parody of stars as yet undiscovered.
Here they tell me I have come to terms.
But supposing I had chosen to march on you
Instead of on such a star—what then?
Instead of this incubus of infinite duration,
I mean to say, whose single glance
Brings loving to its knees?
Yes, wherever the ant-hills empty
Swarm the fecund associations, crossing
And recrossing the sky-pathways of sleep.
We labour only to be relatively
Sincere as ants perhaps are sincere.
Yet always the absolute vision must keep
The healthy lodestar of its stake in love.
You'll see somewhere always the crystal body
Transparent, held high against the light
Blaze like a diamond in the deep.
How can a love of life be ever indiscreet
For even in that far dispersing city today
Ants must turn over in their sleep.

1980/ 1969

THE RECKONING
For Miriam Cendrars

Later some of these heroic worshippers
May live out one thrift in a world of options,
The crown of thorns, the bridal wreath of love,
Desires in all their motions.
'As below, darling, so above.'
In one thought focus and resume
The thousand contradictions,
And still with a sigh these warring fictions.

Timeless as water into language flowing,
Molten as snow on new burns,
The limbo of half-knowing
Where the gagged conscience twists and turns,
Will plant the flag of their unknowing.

It is not peace we seek but meaning.

To convince at last that all is possible,
That the feeble human finite must belong
Within the starred circumference of wonder,
And waking alone at night so suddenly
Realise how careful one must be with hate—
For you become what you hate too much,
As when you love too much you fraction
By insolence the fine delight . . .

It is not meaning that we need but sight.

1973/*1971*

NOBODY

You and who else?
Who else? Why Nobody.
I shall be weeks or months away now
Where the diving roads divide,
A solitude with little dignity,
Where forests lie, where rivers pine,
In a great hemisphere of loveless sky:
And your letters will cross mine.

Somewhere perhaps in a cobweb of skyscrapers
Between Fifth and Sixth musing I'll go,
Matching some footprints in young snow,
Within the loving ambush of some heart,
So close and yet so very far apart . . .
I don't know, I just don't know.

Two beings watching the skyscrapers fade,
Rose in the falling sleet or
Phantom green, licking themselves
Like great cats at their toilet,
Licking their paws clean.
I shall hesitate and falter, that much I know.

Moreover, do you suppose, you too
When you reach India at last, as you will,
I'll be back before two empty coffee cups
And your empty chair in our shabby bistro;
You'll have nothing to tell me either, no,
Not the tenth part of a sigh to exchange.
Everything will be just so.
I'll be back alone again
Confined in memory, but nothing to report,
Watching the traffic pass and
Dreaming of footprints in the New York snow.

1973/1971

RAIN, RAIN, GO TO SPAIN

That noise will be the rain again,
Hush-falling absolver of together—
Companionable enough, though, here abroad:
The log fire, some conclusive music, loneliness.
I can visualise somebody at the door
But make no name or shape for such an image,
Just a locus for small thefts
As might love us both awake tomorrow,
An echo off the lead and ownerless.
But this hissing rain won't improve anything.
The roads will be washed out. Thinking falters.

My book-lined walls so scholarly,
So rosy, glassed in by the rain.
I finger the sex of many an uncut book.
Now spring is coming you will get home
Later and later in another climate.
You vanished so abruptly it took me by surprise.
I heard to relearn everything again
As if blinded by a life of tiny braille.

Then a whole year with just one card,
From Madrid. 'It is raining here and
Greco is so sombre. I have decided
At last to love nobody but myself.'
I repeat it in an amused way
Sometimes very late at night.
In an amazed way as anyone might
Looking up from a classic into all the
Marvellous rain-polished darkness.

As if suddenly you had gone
Beyond the twelfth desire:
You and memory both become
Contemporary to all this inner music.
Time to sift out our silences, then:
Time to repair the failing fire.

1973/1971

APHROS MEANING SPUME

Aphros Aphrodite the sperm-born one
Could not collect her longings, she had only one,
Soft as a lettuce to the sound,
A captive of one light and longing
Driven underground.

Sadness is only a human body
Seeking the arbitration of heaven,
In the wrong places, under the rose,
In the unleavened leaven.

Tell what wistful kisses travel
Over the skin-heaven of the mind
To where an *amor fati* waits
With fangs drawn back, to bleed
Whoever she can find.

But vines lay no eggs, honey,
And even apostles come to their senses
Sooner or later you may find.
The three Themes of this witchcraft
Are roses, faeces and vampires.
May they bring you a level mind.

1973/1971

A WINTER OF VAMPIRES

From a winter of vampires he selects one,
Takes her to a dark house, undresses her:
It is not at all how the story-books say
But another kind of reversed success.
A transaction where the words themselves
Begin to bleed first and everything else follows.

The dissolution of the egg
In the mind of the lady suggests new
Paths to follow, less improbable victories,
Just as illusory as the old, I fear.
Well, but when the embraces go astray,
When you finger the quick recipes
Of every known suggestion, why,
The whole prosperity of the flesh may be in question.

1973/1971

FAUSTUS

As for him, he'll die one day for sure.
But you, you'll turn into a word.
How pathless the waters of language!
Now others will speak this word aloud,
Others constrain you with this noun.
There are purchases in the mind
For such a word, at once vulnerable
Yet strong to take root. Wait and see.

It might be something a dead Greek
Felt about sirens or a Pythia,
One sole sound in the huge glossary
Of whispers, the code of love. . . .

Then, after, with death forfeited,
To melt upon the silence of the tongue,
A Margaret or a second Helen,
Half-dreaded hauntress of the waking dream.

1980/1971

PISTOL WEATHER

About loving, and such kindred matters
You could be beguiling enough;
Delicacy, constancy and depth—
We examined every artificial prison,
And all with the necessary sincerity, yes.

Some languages have little euphemisms
Which modify suddenly one's notions,
Alter one's whole way of adoring:
Such as your character for 'death',
Which reads simply 'A stepping forever
Into a whiteness without remission.'
With no separation-anxiety I presume?

Surely to love is to coincide a little?
And after I contracted your own mightier
Loneliness, I became really ill myself.
But grateful for the thorny knowledge of you;
And thank you for the choice of time and place.

I would perhaps have asked you away
To my house by the sea, to revive us both,
In absolute solitude and dispassionately,
But all the time I kept seeing the severed head,
Lying there, eyes open, in your lap.

1973/*1971*

LAKE MUSIC

Deep waters hereabouts.
We could quit caring.
Deep waters darling
We could stop feeling,
You could stop sharing
But neither knife nor gun
From the pockets of mischance pointing;
How slowly we all sink down
This lustful anointing
Ankles first and thighs.
The beautiful grenades
Breasts up to lips and eyes
The vertebrae of believing
And the deep water moving
We could abandon supposing
We could quit knowing
Where we have come from
Where we are going.

1973/*1971*

STOIC

I, a slave, chained to an oar of poem,
Inhabiting this faraway province where
Nothing happens. I wouldn't want it to.
I have expressly deprived myself of much:
Conversation, sweets of friendship, love . . .
The public women of the town don't appeal.
I wouldn't want them to. There are no others,
At least for an old, smelly, covetous bookman.
So many things might have fed this avocation,
But what's the point? It's too late.

About the matter of death I am convinced,
Also that peace is unattainable and destiny
Impermeable to reason. I am lucky to have
No grave illness, I suppose, no wounds
To ache all winter. I do not drink or smoke.
From all these factors I select one, the silence
Which is that jewel of divine futility,
Refusal to bow, the unvarnished grain
Of the mind's impudence: you see it so well
On the faces of self-reliant dead.

1973/1971

?

Waters rebribing a new moon are all
Dissenting mirrors ending in themselves.

Go away, leave me alone.

Someone still everywhere nearby
So full of fervent need the mouth
The jewelry of smiling: a confession,
Tidemarks of old intentions' dying fall,
Surely that is all now, that is all?

People don't want the experience
Any more: they want an explanation,
How you go about it, when and why.

But all you can say is: Look, it's manifest
And nobody's to blame: it has no name.

Spades touch a buried city,
Calm bodies suffocated by ashes
It happened so quickly there was no time,
Their minds were overrun
The sentry stiffened over a jammed gun,
And waters bribing a new moon are all
The flesh's memories beyond recall.

The voice may have come from a cloud
But more likely the garden's wet planes
A bird or a woman calling in the mist
Asking if anything remains, and if so

Which witch? Which witch? Witch!
I am the only one who knows.

1973/1971

SIXTIES

The year his heart wore out—
It was not you nor you
Distributing the weight
Of benefits of doubt.
A surgeon season came
And singled loving out.
A power-cut in a vein
To abruptly caption stone,
And echoing in the mind
Some mindless telephone.

Prophets of discontent,
Impenetrable shades
It was not you nor you
Nor something left unsaid
To elaborate the night,
But a corn-sifting wind
Was never far behind.
Be steadfast where you are
Now, in the sibyllic mind,
His one companionable star.

It was not you nor you
The year his heart wore out
But cryptic as a breath
One crystal changed its hue;
Thus words in music drown,
Comparisons are few,
Nor will we ever know,
Tellurian loveliness,
Which way the fearless waters flow
That softly fathom you.

1973/1971

AVIS

How elapsing our women
Bought with lullaby money
To fill with moon-fluids,
To goad quench and drench with
Quicksilver of druids
Each nonpareil wench.

How spicy their blood is
How tiny their hands
They were netted like quail
In faraway lands.

Come, pretty little ogre
With the fang in your lip
Lest time in its turnings
Should give us the slip.

1973/1971

ONE PLACE

Commission silence for a line or two,
These walls, these trees—time out of mind
Are temples to perfection lightly spent,
Sunbribed and apt in their shadowy stresses,
Where the planes hang heads, lies
Something the mind caresses;
And then—hardly noticed at noon
Bells bowling, the sistrum bonged
From steeples half asleep in bugle water.
(This part to be whispered only.)

To go or stay is really not the question;
Nor even to go forever, one can't allow here
Death as a page its full relapse.
In such a nook it would always be perhaps,
Dying with no strings attached—who could do that?

1973/1971

REVENANTS

Supposing once the dead were to combine
Against us with a disciplined hysteria.
Particular ghosts might then trouble
With professional horrors like
Corpses in evening dress,
Photoglyphs from some ancient calendar
Pictographs of lost time.
The smile frail as a toy night-light
Beside a sleeping infant's bed.
The pallor would be unfeigned,
The child smile in its sleep.

To see them always in memory
Descending a spiral staircase slowly
With that peculiar fond regard

Or else out in silent gardens
Under stone walls, a snapped fountain,
Wild violets there uncaring
Wild cyclamen uncurling
In silence, in loaf-leisure.

Or a last specialised picture
Flickering on the retina perhaps
The suave magnificence of a late
Moon, trying not to insist too much.
Emotions are just pampered mirrors,
Thriftless provinces, penurious settlers.
How to involve all nature in every breath?

1973/*1971*

THE LAND

The rapt moonwalkers or mere students
Of the world-envelope are piercing
Into the earth's crust to punctuate
Soils and waters with cherished trees
Or cobble with vines, they know it;
Yet have never elaborated a philosophy
Of finite time. I wonder why? Those
Who watch late over the lambs, whom sleep
Deserts because there's thunder in the air.
Just before dawn the whole of nature
Growls in a darkness of impatience.
The season-watchers just march on
Inventing pruning-hooks, winnowing fans
Or odd manual extensions like the spade
Inside the uniform flow of the equinoxes
Not puzzled any more, having forgotten
How brief and how precarious life was,
But finding it chiefly true yet various,
With no uncritical submission to the Gods.

1973/*1971*

JOSS

Perfume of old bones,
Indian bones distilled
In these slender batons;
A whiff of brown saints,
An Indian childhood. Joss.

More mysterious than the opaque
Knuckles of frankincense
The orthodox keep to swamp
Their Easter ikons with today.

The images repeat repent repent (*da capo*)
A second childhood, born again in Greece.
O the benign power, the providing power
Is here too with its reassurance honey.
After the heartbreak of the long voyage,
Same lexicon, stars over the water.

Hello there! Demon of sadness,
You with the coat of many colours,
The necklace of cannibals' teeth.
You with the extravagant arch
To your instep, a woman walking alone
In the reign of her forgiveness
In the rain.

Moi, qui ai toujours guetté le sublime
Me voici de nouveau dans le pétrin,
Hunting the seven keys to human stress,
The search always one minute old,
A single word to transcend all others,
A single name buried excalibur in a stone.

1973/*1971*

315

AVIGNON

Come, meet me in some dead café—
A puff of cognac or a sip of smoke
Will grant a more prolific light,
Say there is nothing to revoke.

A veteran with no arm will press
A phantom sorrow in his sleeve;
The aching stump may well insist
On memories it can't relieve.

Late cats, the city's thumbscrews twist.
Night falls in its profuse derision,
Brings candle-power to younger lives,
Cancels in me the primal vision.

Come, random with me in the rain,
In ghastly harness like a dream,
In rainwashed streets of saddened dark
Where nothing moves that does not seem.

1973/1971

INCOGNITO

Outside us smoulder the great
World issues about which nothing
Can be done, at least by us two;
Inside, the smaller area of a life
Entrusted to us, as yet unendowed
Even by a plan for worship. Well,
If thrift should make her worldly
Remind her that time is boundless,
And for call-girls like business-men, money.

Redeem pleasure, then, with a proximate
Love—the other problems, like the ruins
Of man's estate, death of all goodness,
Lie entombed with me here in this
Oldfashioned but convincing death-bed.

Her darkness, her eye are both typical
Of a region long since plunged into
Historic ruin; yet disinherited, she doesn't care
Being perfect both as person and as thing.

All winter now I shall lie suffocating
Under the débris of this thought.

1973/1971

SWIMMERS

Huit heurs . . . honte heurs . . . supper will be cold.
Sex no substitute for
Science no worship for . . .
At night seeing lights and crouching
Figures round the swimming pool, rapt.
They were fishing for her pearls,
Her necklace had broken while she swam.
'Darling, I bust my pearls.'

But all the time I was away
In sweet and headlong Greece I tried
To write you only the syntax failed,
Each noun became a nascent verb
And all verbs dormant adjectives,
Everything sleeping among the scattered pearls.

Corpses with the marvellous
Property of withoutness
Reign in the whole abundance of the breath.
Each mood has its breathing, so does death.
Soft they sleep and corpsely wise
Scattered the pearls that were their eyes.
Newly mated man and wine
In each other's deaths combine.
Somebody meets everything
While poems in their cages sing.

1973/1971

BLUE

Your ship will be leaving Penang
For Lisbon on the fourteenth,
When I have started pointedly
Living with somebody else.
Yet I can successfully imagine a
Star-crossed circumference of water
Providing a destiny for travellers—
Thoughts neither to pilfer nor squander
During the postcard-troubled nights.

How stable the feeling of being lost grows!
The ocean of memory is ample too,
It wheels about as you crawl over the surface
Of the globe, having cabled away a stormy wish.
Our judgement, our control were beyond all praise.
So prescient were we, it must prove something.

Madam, I presume upon somewhere to continue
Existing round you, say the Indian Ocean
Where life might be fuller of
Such rich machinery that you mightn't flinch;
And how marvellous to be followed
Round the world by a feeling of utter
Sufficiency, tinged a little, I don't doubt,
With self-righteousness, a calming emotion!

I too have been much diminished by wanting;
Now limit my vision to a sufficient loveliness,
To abdicate? But it was never our case,
Though somewhere I feel creep in
The word you said you hated most: 'Nevertheless'.
Well, say it under whatever hostile stars you roam,
Embrace the blue vertigo of the old wish.
And if it gets too much for me
I can always do the other thing, remember?

1973/1971

MISTRAL

At four the dawn mistral usually
A sleep-walking giant sways and crackles
The house, a vessel big with sail.
One head full of poems, cruiser of light,
Cracks open the pomegranate to reveal
The lining of all today's perhapses.

Far away in her carnal fealty sleeps
La Môme in her tiny *chambre de bonne.*
'*Le vent se lève . . . Il faut tenter de vivre.*'

I have grave thoughts about nothingness,
Hold no copyright in Jesus like that girl.
An autopsy would fuse the wires of pleading.
It is simply not possible to thank life.
The universe seems a huge hug without arms.
In foul rapture dawn breaks on grey olives.
Poetry among other afflictions
Is the purest selfishness.

I am making her a small scarlet jazz
For the cellar where they dance
To a wheezy accordion, with a one-eyed man.
Written to a cheeky begging voice.

> *Moi je suis*
> *Annie Verneuil*
> *Dit Annie La Môme*
> *Parfois je fais la vie*
> *Parfois je chome*
> *Premier Prix de Saloperie*
> *De Paris à Rome*
> *Annie La Môme*
> *Fléau du flic le soir*
> *Sur La Place Vendôme,*
> *Annie Verneuil*
> *Annie La Môme*

Freedom is choice: choice bondage.
Where will I next be when the mistral
Rises in sullen trumpets on the hills of bone?

1973/*1971*

ENVOI

Be silent, old frog.
Let God compound the issue as he must,
And dog eat dog
Unto the final desecration of man's dust.
The just will be devoured by the unjust.

1973/*1971*

LAST HEARD OF

The big rivers are through with me, I guess;
Can't walk by Thames any more
But the inexpressible sadness settles
Like soft soot on dusk, becoming one whole thing,
Matchless as twilight and as featureless.
Yes, the big rivers are through with me, I guess;
Nor the mind-propelling, youth-devouring ones
Like Nile or Seine, or black Brahmaputra
Where I was born and never went back again
To stars printed in shining tar.
Yes, the big rivers, except the one of sorrows
Which winds to forts of calm where dust rebukes
The vagaries of minds in silent poses.
I have been washed up here or there,
A somewhere soon becoming an empty everywhere.
My memory of memories goes far astray,
Was it today, or was it yesterday?
I am thinking of things I would rather avoid
Alone in furnished rooms
Listening for those nymphs I've always waited for,
So silent, sitting upright, looking so unowned
And working my destiny on their marble looms.

1973/*1971*

SEFERIS

Time quietly compiling us like sheaves
Turns round one day, beckons the special few,
With one bird singing somewhere in the leaves,
Someone like K. or somebody like you,
Free-falling target for the envious thrust,
So tilting into darkness go we must.

Thus the fading writer signing off
Sees in the vast perspectives of dispersal
His words float off like tiny seeds,
Wind-borne or bird-distributed notes,
To the very end of loves without rehearsal,
The stinging image riper than his deeds.

Yours must have set out like ancient
Colonists, from Delos or from Rhodes,
To dare the sun-gods, found great entrepôts,
Naples or Rio, far from man's known abodes,
To confer the quaint Grecian script on other men;
A new Greek fire ignited by your pen.

How marvellous to have done it and then left
It in the lost property office of the loving mind,
The secret whisper those who listen find.
You show us all the way the great ones went,
In silences becalmed, so well they knew
That even to die is somehow to invent.

1973/1972

VEGA

A thirst for green, because too long deprived
Of water in the stone garrigues, is natural,
Accumulates and then at last gets sated
By this lake which parodies a new life
With a boat outside the window, breathing:
Negative of a greater thirst no doubt,
Lying on slopes of water just multiplying
In green verdure, distributed at night
All on a dark floor, the sincere flavour of stars . . .

This we called Vega, a sly map-reference
Coded in telegrams the censored name to
'Vega next tenth of May. Okay?'
'Okay.' 'Okay.' You came.

The little train which joined then severed us
Clears Domodossola at night, doodles a way,
Tingling a single elementary bell,
Powdered with sequins of new snow,
To shamble at midnight into Stresa's blue.
One passenger only, a woman. You.

The fixed star of the ancients was another Vega,
A candle burning high in the alps of heaven,
Shielded by rosy fingers on some sill
Above some darkly sifted lake. They also knew
This silence trying to perfect itself in words.

Ah! The beautiful sail so unerringly on towards death
Once they experience the pith of this peerless calm.

1973/1972

POEM FOR KATHARINE FALLEY BENNETT'S
BIRTHDAY

Katharine, Queen Eleanor's shadow hovers over you
And your birthdays must take a little from her history:
Be like her, both wise and gay
And keep the little touch of tragedy
Like swords of the soul.

1980/1972

VAUMORT
For 'Buttons'

Seemingly upended in the sky,
Cloudless as minds asleep
One careless cemetery buzzes on and on
As if her tombstones were all hives
Overturned by the impatient dead—
We imagined they had stored up
The honey of their immortality
In the soft commotion the black bees make.

Below us, far away, the road to Paris.
You pour some wine upon a tomb.
The bees drink with us, the dead approve.

It is weeks ago now and we are back
In our burnt and dusty Languedoc,
Yet often in the noon-silences
I hear the Vaumort bees, taste the young wine,
Catch a smile hidden in sighs.

In the long grass you found a ring, remember?
A child's toy ring. Yes, I know that whenever
I want to be perfectly alone
With the memory of you, of that whole day
It's to Vaumort that I'll be turning.

1980/1972

SPRING SONG

My lovely left-handed lover
Will be riding down from Geneva
On the afternoon Catalan bound for Barcelona.
I'll catch her all honeygold at Nîmes
And embrace her on behalf of the city council,
On behalf of Apollinaire, on behalf of Lou.
Ah, Lou, Lou, she is somewhat like you.
My lovely slowcoach, come, I'll teach you.
The Geneva train is faster than a river.
I am no laborious and insipid drone,
But an Irish poet, and thus perfectible.
Together we will submit
To the mesmerism of objects
Painted or hewn—and without too much cheating.
And all this nonsense about women's liberation
Will fade into the fifty-fifty of kisses shared.
Let us be enemies of intellectual cosiness.
Every embrace is an empirical exchange of vitamins.
Your last postcard from the dark lake read:
   'Se réaliser? Oui. Mais comment?
   Darling, I am buying a clockwork mouse
To show my independence from men.
     Signed: A REAL WOMAN.'
Perhaps now do you see why?

1980/1972

HEY, MISTER, THERE'S A BULGE IN YOUR COMPUTER

How loud the perfume of common gin
How morose the pigment that covers a lipid
How soft the equal gauze of quits
How purple the pits of amazing berries
How snuff the cough of the rough shark

Your sake, my sake, his sake, her sake
Everyone is entitled to one sake.

1980/1972

ON THE SUCHNESS OF THE OLD BOY

Such was the sagacious Suchness of the Sage
That all of a sudden in his old age
He was uplifted bodily by
A wonderful Umptiousness.
He became Umptious in the highest degree.

A heraldic uproariousness of mind possessed him
And he said: *If so things are, why let them be.*
Enough of the doctors of high degree
Whose rhetoric is the purest road-haulage,
Damn the deep freeze, bugger the cold storage
Of minds as cold as a lavatory seat.
I will just squat here in my umptious extravagance
Until all the extremes agree to meet.

It was another way of saying
That he had discovered the heraldic law
Namely, that while someone somewhere
Weeps and tears his hair with his claws
In some other spot someone is laughing:
And both from the same damn cause.

Look not for reason anywhere; but keep
Revelation for those who least care.
Be umptious if you can, it's everywhere.
Be umptious asleep, awake, dressed or undressed.
The scrumptiousness of Umptiousness can not be overstressed.

Is your gaiety fully enigmatic,
Or are you at odds with some bedwetting ghost?
A mouse gnawing at a coffin is not static.
Why do the many never reach the Most?

To decode even the narrow and finite
Stuff of life is to tumble upon answers.
If only space had edges it would bite.
If time flowed more it would melt into dancers.

The best philosopher of the cryptic mode
Is at best a primrose in the carnal mind.
He only discovers what he set out to find.
There is no sense in all your deadlock.
Consider the bees, they are all born out of wedlock.

Enough of this huge fornication rosary,
Wearisome are the great commonplaces.
They have no aptitude for death, agree,
The million upon million non-Umptious faces.

In the days of all our Yore
Folklore was the only Yolklore
Imprinting was the natural sire
Of earth air water fire.
Now to our vapid visual age
We present our whitewashed cage,
The present burns in iron symmetry
With love built in like a geometry.

If cleanliness is next to Godliness
Umptiousness is a sort of Sumptuousness,
Umption the ultimate fruit
Of holy Gumption.
It is not a question of being conscious
Or washing your little white hands like Pontius.

So spake the Sage, disbursing Suchness
Like a fine sow, a more than Muchness.
To have broad canopy with zip and twang
Is the mark of the sage in his cosmic charabanc.

Pain may be relieved so often
By its own intensification.
How well we know those elephant neuroses
Lead to the girls who always dish out doses.
Live the life of a stowaway in this world,
All places, languages or nations,
Old couples clinging together like tired gloves
Images of disaster in a renewal of patience.

Everywhere revisited is only
Half of the real story, for death is free.
The naked runners braked by the soft sea,
A naked silence going on a spree.
Spread it like butter over he and she.

Whole winters long my ape and I
Winnowed and mused, discussed as best we could,
The fake images, the true-to-what effect
To distil the great elixir of the elect,
Sorting the perfect from the merely good.
And when at last it died, without presumption,
I wept, but gave it the extreme Umption.

This is my choice now, music and tobacco,
As happy on my hilltop I review
The vistas of a world it never knew,
To which my Umption is the only clue.
Always at midnight when I hear the chimes,
I tell myself while pouring out a drink,
Things are less complicated than you think.
Dreams, therefore crimes, honey,
Dreams, therefore crimes.

1973/*1972*

THE OPHITE
For Saph

First draw the formal circle O
Of the whole oblong mind, as in the snake
Where mouth and anus meet to complete it.
　　　The onus
　　　The harness
Of the heartwhole whose cool apples conspire
Against the serpent like all perverse fruit;
Which identify with sin but remain innocent.
　　　The tree of good and oval
　　　Soft branch of all renewal
Where the sincere milk of the whole word
First set the gnostic grimly dreaming
To furnish an alphabet of pure dissent,
　　　　　Dark night of the Whole
　　　　　Convincing to the finite mole.
Warp and woof like magnets coming together
In silence thumbless as a pendulum.
It could be accident. Believe what you prefer.
No advice worth giving is worth taking.

1973/*1973*

ALPHABETA

Some withering papers lie,
The bloody spoor of some great
Animal anxiety of a poem he wounded
And followed up in fear, holding his breath.
The blood was everywhere, the yellowing inks
Of old manuscripts reproached.
In stark terror that loaded pen was ready,
With the safety catch turned off,
Only the target lacked,
Crouching somewhere in its own blood.
Some hideous animal without a name.
To be called man, but with such a rotten aim!

1973/*1973*

A FAREWELL

Colours have no memory, friend,
And can therefore prophesy,
Turn whiter than tea-roses can
With whom to exchange addresses
In far away cities for a good-luck goodbye.

Time slips her moorings soon, and the
Surf-gathering boom of candles can retrace
To the whisper of canvas on the sky
A tiller's lug, jerked like some big dog,
The muscle-softening farewell embrace.

Survivals and calamities supported
In thoughts now, no more in words,
Out there on the flailing waters of everness,
The flora of tumultuous oceans around me,
And for company archaic folding birds.

I will seek out now
All the arts of silence and of anger
For many such Aprils have come and gone.
The lines of your palm are always changing
As you move from the unknown to the known.

So often the bountiful hemlock beckoned me,
I guess it would undeceive,
Ransacked the secret childhood of the race,
To pinpoint the groups of fearfulness
And pardon the terrors it could not reprieve.

The dangerous years approach, friend.
You will be lucky to come through whole.
This speck of lead, a word, fired into the mind
Will in its queer way change it
While never seeking to argue or console.

One thing about death—it isn't far to fall,
Its brightness disfigures every silence,
Its reflections splashed about like in spoons
Gives a reassurance to the dusty kiss of stars,
The cold procession of worn-out harvest moons.

1973/*1973*

MANDRAKE ROOT

Vagina Dentata I love you so,
You are wide as my dreams are long,
Like the kipling hiss of the cobra,
Or the screams of Fay Wray in King Kong.

Vestal of fire lethargic
Whose seminal doctrines extract
The rivets from Caliban's backbone
To leave him less fiction than fact.

Aphrodite Urania we need you
To lighten the people's path,
By the marvellous insights of Crippen
Or the Brides in the Bath.

O precious pudendum of seeming,
We come from the Gullible Isles,
Where the cannibal complexes frolic
And the Mona Lisa smiles.

1973/*1973*

APESONG

Hatch me a gorilla's egg
And catch me in the offing,
Buckle me to a wedding ring
And make me die of laughing.

Rock me in the XVI psalm
And fill my bowels with honey,
Up in the trees I'll find a mate,
If not for love, then money.

1973/*1973*

WANT TO LIVE DON'T YOU?

Somewhere in all this grace and favour green
Autumnal in the public gardens,
Sunk on benches between all ages
Under the braying foliage mimeographed
Like the Lord's Prayer for a computer
In this fate-forgiven corner of reflection
The genetic twilight of a race evolves:
Dreaming in codes, you only think you think.
Sweet rainwashed cobbles of old towns
A moving spur on sundials recording.

The roll of drums buried in the soil,
Somewhere a pair of fine eyes looking out
Under a magnificent forehead, but so full
Of an immense and complicated mistrust
Of human ways: very reasonable indeed
I should say, very reasonable indeed.
Our glances lie unfermented among statues.
A hunchback pokes a dead swan with a stick
While children buzz and cannot fathom.

Then, tied as if to a buoy far out at sea
An emancipated municipal orchestra makes
Some shallow confidences to the prams.
This very spot where the writings of solitaries
Limp off take passage for foreign lands,
Falter to an end, there being nothing left
With which to compare them,
Never looking back. Well then, goodbye.

1973/1973

THE GREY PENITENTS

Far away once, in Avignon, the Grey Penitents
Set up their chapter on a drear canal
For podgy minds to bleed with happiness
Upon the waters of a supposed redemption
Under the orders of twelve concise pigs,
Revealed their goodness like smooth-feathered men.
They tried like later you and me
To find one beauty without sophistry.

   Alas!
I lit a candle for you once
But it was slow to the last match;
The tiny wick, like loving, wouldn't catch.

Nature's lay penitent, I taught thee to fuck;
But winter came and we were out of luck.
'When the pupil is ready the master always appears,
But sometimes after 9 lifetimes of a thousand years.'

Pale students of the Quite Alone
Whose dreams cut to the very bone
Add or subtract the kisses of the mind,
They will not catch, the engine will not fire,
A vestal love no destiny could bind.

Now on the far side of Europe
We suddenly meet far from that faltering candle,
Not guilty like the penitents of laic misdemeanours,
Wishing never to have been born, all that stuff.
And knowing quite well that even without you
I can easily go on breathing.
But why you come back I cannot fathom.
It reminds me of something I once achieved
To love someone at the speed of thought.

Walking the loops of the companionable Liffey
It came to me to think that over these actual
Waters no shadows lie between there and here,
Thou and I, you and myself, the far and the near.
Nor is the remedial therapy of an embrace the answer.
Dark plaintiff of the courtly love how wisely
Your reason has subdued the heart's long pace:
And tomorrow we'll be gone to leave no trace.

Perhaps the primal illness which is loneliness
Can't be countered by a stupid candle
Burning however rosy in the flesh
Of a writer's concise and loving wish.

Would you have supposed, with night
Coming on over the thorn-curdled hills
And the snowy dales, that after this long
Discouragement about you I got kind of severed
Even from poetry, and for so many years?
How foolish to make no distinction between the two of you;

The penitents must have documented so much
That ordinary lovers spurn, but to their cost.
A farthing dip is all it costs to formulate
A wish that burns a dogged lifetime through.

1973/*1973*

DUBLIN

Sweet sorrow, were you always there?
I did not recognise
At first the grave tilt of the head,
Or the meek dark eyes.

To share my deepest joy with you
I sought you—but you seemed to hide
Far in the mindless canyons of your love
Which lay for you, like me, near suicide.

That rainbow over Joyce's tower
Was another rare deceit,
Raising once more those vaulting hopes
You soon proved counterfeit.

1973/*1973*

SAGES

The old men said: to wet the soul with wine or urine
Then stretch it like choice kid over a drumhead,
Tapping on the cartridge of words one might
Encapsulate the truth of something latent
In time, in destiny, in natural lore,
A caricature of simple intuitions. Giving back.
The old men said: you might arrive at last
To pierce behind the mask, for evermore
Match passion and clarity—that hopeless task.

1973/*1973*

BY THE SEA

Thumb quantum
Thumb quantum
The fingerdrum drubs, the fingerdrum taps,
We rise into the navy sky
The islands booming with skulls.
With her a feast of white figs,
Cold water crystal on sand beaches,
A late moonrise seeming impromptu.
One could happily die here, perhaps one has,
Too little said about these matters.

One almond-eyed medusa nods
Her fine blond Circassian hair
Twisted up in the shape of an acorn.
With eyes pistachio green to grey,
Like an enamel medal of ancient Greece,
But verifiable and kind to touch.

1973/*1973*

CICADA

Transparent sheath of the dead cicada,
The eyes stay open like a dead Jap,
Financially no spongy parts to putrefy
Simply snap off the scaly integument of mica.
You could make a tiny violin of such a body,
Lanterns for elves, varnish into brooches
And wear by lamplight this transparent stare of noon,
In gold or some such precious allegorical metal,
Which spells out the dead wine which follows soon.

1973/*1973*

THE MUSES

Time spillers, pain killers, all such pretty women,
Whose tribal name so nearly rhymes with semen.

In dull male dough they infiltrate their leaven,
Which, though the spawn of hell, tastes like pure heaven.

Time wasters, food tasters, bachelor haters,
They hunt with the science of the great predators.

In their mad dreams of one-and-onliness
They feel the self-murder of Kant's loneliness.

Critics of Pure Reason they don't reck,
The quivering kiss, the bullet in the neck.

1973/*1973*

CERTAIN LANDFALLS

That last summer quite definitely the dead
Began to outnumber the living in his village.
He would always remember the month exactly,
Hopes capsized and grey hairs abounding.
And so the dead with all their precious talk
Stacked up inside them, loaves of whole wit,
Long roes of gossip or pomegranate seeds
Of poetry peeping out of wounds, decamped.
Gone the vainglory of beautiful
Skin and regular teeth when the sun brought out
The wine's brown perfume on the rocks
Of old blood mellowed in Adam's evils.

In this small walled garden, apricots falling,
He stirred about in the embers of his time
Under a sky the colour of elephant hide.
He now knew she did not like his house
Nor his style of life buried in the hills,
With monotony, the artist's only aliment.
Silences bruised by the echoes of dead talk,
Foliage of voices, fists of forgotten applause.
No, she did not like the place at all.

Cold will be the wind now, dark the storms,
Ending of a visionary delight. Why to care?
His art would marry the image it deserved,
As a sculptor's hand breaking the soft clay
Of old desires; mind you, the very same hand
That broke the dark bread to model hunger,
A presage of the faultless child in him.

1980/1974

A PATCH OF DUST

In all this summer dust O Vincent
You passed through my loyal mind,
And I saw the candlepower of stored light,
Like water in the humps of camels or in
Canopies of fire smouldering in volcanoes
Like ancient prostitutes or doges.
Memory giving the ikon of love a morbid kiss!

It doesn't matter; in the silent night
Fragrant with the death of so many friends, poets,
The major darkness comes and art beckons
With its quiet seething of the writer's mind.

Your great canvas humming like a top.
But the terror for me is that you didn't realise
That love, even in inferior versions, is a kind
Of merciful self-repair. O Vincent you were blind.
Like some great effluent performer
Discharging whole rivers into hungry seas.
I do not mean the other kind of love,
Born in newspapers like always exchanging
Greasy false teeth. Not of that kind.

In these shining canvases I commend
A fatal diagnosis of light, more light;
Famous last words to reach the inessential.
They seem to assume that death is unnecessary
And in discreet images make ethical strife stationary,
Signposting always desires at bay.
Goodness! It is canny in its way.

Because the irritation of light leads onwards
Towards blindness which is truth, an unknowing,
And the constraints of unlucky companionship
Hinder like a foolish marriage. One must act.
It is no good explaining things with unction,
You will never get beyond their primal function.

But you directly saw the splendour of the
Dying light redeemed. Have mercy on us!
You went mad, they say, the companionship
Of angels grew too loud to bear. You felt
That what was done was quite beyond repair.
So madness, why not? An irrational respect
For tin or pincushions, a whole architecture.
The girl you loved was grave yet debonair
Like the French whore I live with I suppose.
And dying of self-importance is the usual thing;
The creed of loneliness is all that's left,
And art, the jack o'lantern to console and punish.
All this I saw in a patch of dust at St Remy
During the fatal year of 1974.

1980/1974

POSTMARK

So back to a Paris grubby as a bowel
Where mated to some second-hand man
In foreign loves recycled by the moon
You'll be some night the countess of somewhat;
A cocktail face beheaded by the smile.
Wanted as orchids may be in a season
Then left as cool as the perfumed marbles of Rome.

In some default of reason you may hurt
For tunes the small particulars recall.
The globe is mighty but not limitless
And fame will prevent him from being ever loved,
While age will stare you out of ownership.

Allowance made for all self-pitying muses
Stare from the wide shipwreck of your bed
And stealthily awake, your version make,
Count down the stars towards the death of time.

1980/1974

IN DEEP GRASS

A reptile of ancient stars winking,
The rectangles of lost casements
But in which country now, remember.
Such simple conceptions can capsize.
It would cost heavy postage to signal.
Yet the magnitude of the sky,
The Pleiades arise in frozen spray,
The magnitude of the night sky,
The magnitude is never: it's simply all here.

So lying alone, thinking, in deep grass
It doesn't matter much if the mind is
Howling at the moon, or the old
Jackal of a fading earth: expressing sorrow.

Lonely product of a ninepenny womb,
Full of a fierce psychic reticence
One gladiator of the simple sense
Carving out poetry for his tomb.

Listen, the cloud-stampede goes south
In the lumber of a sunset red,
The skeleton keys of fireflies soon
Will prick the ancient dark again—
Deforming logic which was once
Harmonious but now out of tune.

You make me feel all loose at the roots;
Then comes illness, the most acute form
Of mental laziness to hide oneself in;
The very precious icy feeling for
One person, issue of matter, breathing,
And wearing a final skin, will trade
Everything for it always, even reason.

1980/*1974*

Index of First Lines

345

347

348

349